AN UNEXPECTED MATCH

SHELLEY SHEPARD GRAY

HEARTWARMING

If you purchased this book without a cover you should be aware that this book is stolen property. It was reported as "unsold and destroyed" to the publisher, and neither the author nor the publisher has received any payment for this "stripped book."

Recycling programs for this product may not exist in your area.

ISBN-13: 978-1-335-46042-4

An Unexpected Match

For questions and comments about the quality of this book, please contact us at CustomerService@Harlequin.com.

Harlequin Enterprises ULC
22 Adelaide St. West, 41st Floor
Toronto, Ontario M5H 4E3, Canada
www.Harlequin.com

HarperCollins Publishers
Macken House, 39/40 Mayor Street Upper,
Dublin 1, D01 C9W8, Ireland
www.HarperCollins.com

Printed in U.S.A.

"Just before we headed back to the shelter you tensed."

"Yes," she replied, glad that he'd gotten her started. "You see, I thought I saw someone across the way."

"You said that. It was no big deal. There were a lot of people around."

"There were, but this man? Well, I knew him. I mean, I thought I did." She closed her eyes in shame, hating that she was a grown woman but was reacting like the insecure child she'd used to be.

Hunt was quiet on the other line. She could hear him breathing, letting her know that he was listening but wasn't going to press her to hurry up. As if he was on her timeline. Following her lead.

Few things had ever felt so reassuring.

And it gave her the confidence she needed to say the words. No, to give him the explanation he deserved.

Dear Reader,

Thank you for picking up *An Unexpected Match*! I thoroughly enjoyed writing a story about a pretty, awkward dental office receptionist and a somewhat grumpy, older army captain turned handyman. Both characters made me laugh more than once.

I have a funny writing habit. I not only record each day's word count and page numbers, but I also write down the date and where I am (if I'm not at home in my office). When I was looking over some notes for this book, I realized that I had written five pages when I was in Houston on my brother's wedding day! Yep, after being certain that he'd never marry again, my brother met a widow and had his own unexpected match! Both the bride and groom were in their sixties and looked so very happy.

I'm sad to say goodbye to this series, but I'm grateful to have had the opportunity to write these three books. Not only did they feature a hero and heroine falling in love, but each character in the books wanted to be a little bit better. They all made me want to be a little bit better, too!

I hope you enjoy it, as well.

Shelley

New York Times and *USA TODAY* bestselling author **Shelley Shepard Gray** has published over a hundred novels for a variety of publishers. She currently writes Amish and inspirational romances for Revell, Kensington and Harlequin. With over two million books in print, and translated into more than a dozen languages, her novels have been HOLT Medallion winners and Inspirational Readers' Choice and Carol Award finalists.

Shelley has been featured in the *The Philadelphia Inquirer*, *The Washington Post*, *TIME*, *Woman's World*, *First for Women* and *USA TODAY*.

She currently lives in northern Ohio, walks her dogs, bakes too much and writes full time.

Books by Shelley Shepard Gray

Harlequin Heartwarming

The Sargeant's Christmas Gift

A Matchmaker Knows Best Romance

Their Surprise Reunion
Christmas Promises

Inspirational Cold Case Collection

Widow's Secrets
Amish Jane Doe
Amish Fugitive

Visit the Author Profile page
at Harlequin.com for more titles.

For all the readers who love Harlequin Heartwarming romances as much as I do.

Acknowledgments

There are some places I hate to say goodbye to, and my matchmaking world set in Medina, Ohio, is one of them. Thank you to Medina County Public Library for your support, for the many readers who gave this series a try and, of course, for a group of volunteers in New Brunswick, Canada, for inspiring me in so many ways.

Of course, I'm so grateful for my editor, Johanna Raisanen, executive editor, Kathleen Scheibling, and everyone else in the Heartwarming team who continually make my books better. They're not only great to work with but they're wonderful people, too.

Finally, a big thanks to Jean Volk, a longtime reader who's turned into a good friend, street team organizer and FB "Buggy Bunch" moderator. Jean, thank you for somehow managing to keep everything moving smoothly. It's because of you that I'm still able to do what I do best—which is make things up.

CHAPTER ONE

HE WAS EARLY. Kinsey Zaleski glanced at the clock, weighed the time against the pile of dental appointment reminder cards she'd been determined to address for Dr. Martin, and debated what course of action would give her the least amount of problems.

She was really good at doing that.

She'd learned back in foster care that keeping her head down and avoiding trouble was the easiest route to go. Good kids who didn't make waves got nicer foster parents. The green, naive fosters. The do-gooders. The ones who had good food. The problem kids who were harder to place got the stinky homes.

Of course, she'd never called them that. She used to call them sucky homes just like everyone else. Occasionally, she'd add a four-letter word into the mix for shock value. Larry and Claudia Martin, her last set of fosters, had encouraged her to cuss less and smile more.

Now that she worked for Dr. Martin, Kinsey hardly ever cussed at all. She also smiled and did her best to keep things in the office organized and hassle free. If she planned everything to the best of her ability, she didn't get any surprises. And she loved living a calm life, both at the office and at home.

Which was why she was debating whether to finish her last task of the day and leave the reception desk neat and orderly like usual…or head out now and avoid all but the most minimal of communication with Hunt Vargo.

"You're still here."

Kinsey looked up. There he was. Six feet of muscle and gorgeousness all wrapped up in permanent bad mood. She'd spent too long debating about what to do. *Shoot!*

She pasted a smile on her face. "Hey, Hunt. How are you?"

Reaching into his pocket, Hunt clicked a button on his phone. And then pulled out one of his earbuds. It took him two seconds, but somehow he made it look as if doing such a thing was really inconvenient. "You're usually gone by this time on Fridays."

That was it. No hello, no greeting. Not even a hint of a smile. As usual, the handyman who Dr. Martin had hired to freshen up the thirty-year-old office space was in a mood. Currently, he was acting like she was gum stuck to the bottom of his shoe.

And as usual, it grated on her last nerve.

Hunt didn't need to know that, though. Looking at the clock on the wall, Kinsey attempted a fake chuckle. "Yeah, I guess I am here later than usual. I should be out of here within thirty minutes, though." Give or take.

He pursed his lips. "Yeah, all right. I was going to paint the baseboards in here, but I guess I can go to one of the examining rooms first."

Ugh. Hunt sounded like she was making him drive across town during five-o'clock traffic. His attitude, combined with the fact that she felt kind of bad that she was throwing him off his routine, twisted up her insides. Made her want to both apologize and roll her eyes.

So, Kinsey decided to do something she hadn't done in quite a while. Not since she'd promised herself she'd stop doing it when she'd turned twenty-six a couple of months ago.

She kind of picked a fight.

She tilted up her head in order to look him in the eye. "Just to let you know, Hunt, you're here earlier than usual. Like, forty minutes early. Plus, I'm here working, not filing my nails. So, it's pretty rude of you to act like I'm putting you out."

His blond eyebrows, barely visible against his permanent tan, rose. "Are you telling me how to act?"

She shivered. Pretended his deep voice combined with that military bearing didn't tug on her insides and hold on tight. Hoping she looked calmer than she felt, Kinsey wheeled back her chair and crossed her legs. "No, I'm just pointing out that it would be nice if you didn't glare at me like I was in your way." All the time.

Hunt's mouth pressed into a thin line just as his gaze darted down at her legs. For a few seconds, a new tension filled the air. Surprise.

She swallowed.

He noticed.

Then, before she could get ahold of herself and say something that would put the two of them back on neutral ground, Hunt turned around.

"I'll go paint somewhere else," he muttered. He put his earbud back in, fiddled with his phone, and walked away.

Efficiently blocking her out.

Kinsey felt her cheeks heat. Bit her bottom lip when she realized that her black knit skirt had ridden up an inch or so. She was barely showing her knees, but she supposed she didn't have great-looking knees. He'd likely been turned off.

In the space of ten minutes, she'd practically thrown away every single lesson Mrs. Martin had tried to teach her about acting like a lady. Or at least a nice person who wasn't carrying around a chip on her shoulder.

She'd picked a fight with the guy who was not only doing his best to transform this office into something modern and fresh but was an army veteran to boot. And Dr. and Mrs. Martin's next-door neighbor.

But instead of being gracious, she'd acted like a spoiled-brat receptionist. Like that girl in the house in Westlake, where Kinsey had lived for a couple of months. The pretty girl who had her own room and her own family and wasn't all that crazy about having to share a bathroom with a shy, skinny foster kid who cursed a blue streak when she didn't think anyone was around.

Boy, she hoped Dr. Martin didn't find out she'd acted like that.

She needed to leave.

With shaking hands, she gathered up the postcards, secured them with a rubber band, and placed them in the top right-hand drawer of her desk. Threw out her empty can of root beer that she had every day at two o'clock. Shut down the computer, locked the file cabinets. Returned the calendar, container of office pens, and office phone to their correct positions on the desk. When she was satisfied everything was in order, she retrieved her purse, double-checked that she had her cell phone, and finally slipped on her fitted jean jacket over the white T-shirt she'd chosen to wear with that black skirt and black flats.

And then she took a deep breath, pretended she wasn't squirming in shame, and walked out the front door of the dental office.

When the door shut behind her with a thwack,

Kinsey pulled out her keys and locked the dead bolt. Hunt would leave out the back door and set the alarm when he finished working.

All day long, Kinsey had planned on doing a little bit of shopping in Medina's downtown square. Or walk down two blocks to the big Root Candle Factory and see what was on sale. Since it was the middle of June, the weather was perfect, and she'd been excited to decorate her apartment with a couple of cute place mats and candles.

But now she wasn't in the mood. When she spied a woman walking in the front door of Loaves of Love, the town's food pantry and community kitchen, Kinsey knew what she needed to do. Instead of volunteering there on Saturday morning, she'd stop by this afternoon. With any luck, Edna, the manager of the organization, would be working the front desk and allow her to bake some bread.

She could chat with the other volunteers, concentrate on kneading two loaves of bread, and get her head back to where it was supposed to be. On something good and positive.

Not someone tall, blond, and surly.

Feeling much better already, Kinsey walked to the crosswalk and pressed the button. Smiled at the elderly lady in her Buick who'd stopped at the red light. Sure, she wasn't perfect, but she was still trying to be.

Just like Margaret, another of her social workers, used to say, trying was half the battle.

By the time she'd reached the front door of Loaves of Love, she'd almost forgotten Hunt Vargo.

Who had stood in the shadows near the dental office's front window to make sure she'd made it safely across the street.

CHAPTER TWO

SOME WOULD SAY that his audience wasn't the most sympathetic, but Hunt reckoned that was because they didn't know any better. The pit bull he was sitting with in one of the "get to know you" rooms at the animal shelter were completely focused on his every word.

They didn't seem to be scared of him either, which was a big difference from a certain brown-eyed brunette he couldn't seem to stop thinking about.

"So that's the deal, Clyde," he said as he continued to gently run his hand down the center of the dog's back. "Once again that gal acted as if my very presence was ruining her day."

Clyde tapped his leg with a paw. His signal for Hunt to continue petting him.

Hunt decided it was also his signal to explain himself. "Look, I know Larry and Claudia are amazing people. They always have been. But I'm really starting to wonder if the problem isn't my surliness but Kinsey's attitude." Liking how that sounded, he rubbed Clyde's head. "Yeah. That's what she needs. An attitude adjustment." Looking down at the dog's scarred face, he murmured, "What do you think, buddy?"

The dog closed his eyes as he fell asleep.

"I don't blame you, buddy. I do drone on about her way too much, don't I?"

Leaning his head back against the wall, Hunt tried to pinpoint just what he didn't like about her. He couldn't think of a single thing.

"That's because you don't hate the woman. You like her, you dumb nut," he muttered to himself. "That's the problem. Even though you aren't in the market for a new relationship, there's some part of you that feels differently and wants to get to know her better." And, maybe, get close enough to figure out if that vanilla-peppermint scent that he couldn't ignore was either from her lotion or shampoo.

He hoped it was lotion. Then, when he wrapped his arms around her and held her close, that scent would still linger on her skin.

"She'll probably push you away for doing that," he mumbled. "No woman wants a guy sniffing her neck. That's weird."

"Hey, Hunt. Ready for the next one?"

"Sure." He stood up and fastened the lead back on Clyde while he was stretching. After giving his hand a swipe with a sloppy, wet tongue, Clyde allowed Ron to lead him out of the room. As Hunt watched the four-year-old dog walk out, he reminded himself that it was sunny outside. That meant Ron would take Clyde for a fifteen-minute walk before returning him to his cage.

Where the dog would sleep and wait for someone to visit him again.

Hunt had long ago tried to come to peace with the fact that he couldn't adopt a dog. Dogs, especially shelter dogs, needed stability and companionship. Hunt could give them those two things, but he also had a number of problems that prevented him from being a pet owner. The first was the most obvious. His knee was constantly letting him know that it was intact only because of a certain major's skill in the desert.

Half the time it locked up so tight, he didn't want to move. The other times that knee sent out a dull ache through the rest of his body. If he did too much, the dull ache became sharp lasers, practically zapping the rest of the nerves in his leg and lower back into submission.

If all that wasn't enough, he sported a crisscross pattern of ugly red scars on his chest, arms, and belly. Those were compliments of the shrapnel that had embedded in his body instead of blowing up his knee.

All that meant he was nobody's idea of good looking. Especially not a pretty woman who could have any man she wanted. Shoot, after getting set up by a friend of his sister's and learning real quick that she hadn't thought he should've been overseas to begin with, Hunt had stopped trying to date. He couldn't change who he was inside, and he didn't care enough about his scars to go through any plastic surgery. He was what he was.

He knew dogs didn't care about such things, though.

But he still had nightmares about once a week. No matter how much time went by, Hunt couldn't erase the moment when their convoy hit the IED and thousands of metal shards flew at them. Too many of his buddies hadn't made it out.

No way was a dog—especially a dog who'd already been through trauma—going to be able to deal with that.

"Here you are!" Queenie said in a bright voice. "This is Belle. Belle, this is Hunt."

"You brought me a pug?"

"Nothing wrong with pugs, Hunt," Queenie proclaimed as she unhooked the lead and gave the little blonde furball a scratch on the head.

"I didn't say there was. I'm just surprised. You guys usually give me bigger dogs."

"As a matter of fact, I was talking to Noah about that in the back. We decided that even big guys like you could take a turn with Belle."

"Thanks for bringing her in. Do you want me to walk her after our time in here?"

"Nope. She already had a walk today. Plus we got a carful of high school students at midday. They cleaned cages, washed water bowls, and walked almost everyone. We decided to just give you a couple of dogs to sit with."

"That works for me."

Darting a glance at his knee, Queenie nodded. "I figured as much."

When the door closed again, Hunt got out a couple of soft squeaky toys and arranged the assortment in front of him.

"Here, Belle. Want to squeak some toys for a bit?"

Her dark eyes met his. Seemed to take his measure before finally approaching with a very matronly waddle.

In no time, Belle had sniffed all three, picked out a lamb, and carried it in her mouth as she climbed onto his lap. Then, in a fairly impressive move, she balanced all four paws on his thighs, did a twirl, and then curled into a ball. Seconds later, Belle was sawing logs and he had time on his hands.

Reminding himself that so many of the animals in the shelter missed a human touch, he carefully rubbed Belle's wrinkled forehead and rested his head back against the wall.

And finally attempted to think of things other than the desert or Kinsey.

CHAPTER THREE

It was June. Flowers were blooming, the farmers market was back every Saturday, and she hadn't even needed to put on a sweater for her walk that morning.

Edna knew she should be feeling content and happy.

After all, she had lots of blessings in life to be thankful for. Everything at Loaves of Love was running like clockwork. They'd begun to receive so many volunteers that Edna had started limiting the number of times a person could work in the kitchen every month. At first she wasn't too keen on that idea. After all, not only had she started her organization in order to provide food and companionship to folks experiencing food scarcity, but it was to connect residents in a meaningful way.

Her husband, Wayne, had carefully reminded her that growth wasn't a a bad thing. All it took was a little more juggling.

But as she sat at the reception desk and listened to snippets of conversation between the volunteers baking bread floating through the doors, she realized that she was a little bored.

Maybe she needed to plan a vacation? She and Wayne hadn't taken more than a couple of days off since their honeymoon.

Two years ago.

"Who would've ever seen that happening?" she murmured to herself.

Reconnecting with one of her first husband's old work buddies had been serendipitous, and that was a fact. Wayne was a great companion and always made her smile. He also made her feel special. Sometimes, when she caught him looking at her, there was a light in his eyes. As if he liked what he saw, and he saw only her.

Her cheeks heated. Goodness. She was acting like a silly schoolgirl. Feeling flustered, Edna sighed. If no one showed up soon, she was going to have to go take a walk or something. She was far too restless.

As if he'd been reading her mind, the front door of Loaves of Love opened and in walked Hunt Vargo. "Hi, Hunt!" she exclaimed. Just a little too loudly.

Hunt, who was wheeling a toolbox behind him, stopped short. "Hey, Edna. Is everything all right?"

"Everything's fine." Standing up, she walked around to the front of the reception desk. "I'm just happy to see you. Things have been a little slow here."

Hunt lifted his head. Scanned the filled kitchen behind her. "Yeah, it looks pretty quiet."

"Ha, ha. I know. There's actually a lot going on." She shrugged. "Maybe it's just, ah…spring fever."

"Or summer," he murmured.

"Indeed. So, what are you planning to work on today?" When she'd first approached Hunt about doing a number of odd jobs around the old building, she'd asked if he could space out the projects over several months. Not only would that allow her to pay for them more easily, but it wouldn't cause a great deal of chaos for either the food bank or the volunteers.

"I thought I'd tackle your office today. You're still wanting a built-in desk and shelves, right?"

"Yes. How long will it take you?"

"Two or three days. Give or take." Looking away, he added, "I also happened to notice that the storage closet in the hall needs to be cleaned out and organized."

"It does, but there's no need for you to worry about that." She was so embarrassed. She'd been sitting in that chair feeling restless when she could have been using her time to tackle that space.

"I'd like to do that as a favor. No charge."

"I couldn't ask you to do that."

"You aren't asking." Looking at her directly, he explained, "I'm not one for large groups of people. As much as I'd enjoy a loaf of fresh bread as anyone else, the thought of working in there..." He shrugged. "Let's just say that ain't going to happen."

"I understand. Of course I'd love your help with that closet. Honestly, if you worked on that first, I could let you know what needs to be kept and what needs to be sorted."

"You could do that, if you'd like. But I could probably figure it out."

"Whatever you wish, Hunt."

"I'll work on the closet tomorrow. I brought in the kit we ordered for the desk. I'm going to get started. Is your office unlocked?"

"I'll walk down with you to do that."

"Thanks."

After peeking inside the kitchen to ask one of the volunteers to keep an eye on the reception area, she walked down the hall by Hunt's side. "How are things going with you otherwise?"

"Otherwise?" He raised an eyebrow.

"You know. Things besides work."

"Things are fine."

She inwardly sighed. Sure, it wasn't any of her business, but she couldn't help but feel that Hunt needed a helping hand in life. Here he was, a decorated veteran, hardworking, and handsome. And he even made time out of his week to sit with shelter dogs and take them for walks every now and then, too.

He also offered to do nice things like volunteer at the food pantry. She didn't know too many thirty-five-year-old men who did so many nice things.

Come to think of it, she didn't know of too many men or women of any age like that. Hunt was special.

She needed to know more about him. Maybe he had a lady friend and she wasn't aware of it? Clearing her throat, she said, "You know what? It occurred to me that I don't know much about you."

His footsteps slowed. "I thought we covered all of that when you first hired me to work here."

"Oh, we did. I know you were in the army and you grew up next door to Dr. Martin. But, ah, I don't know much else."

Hunt stopped. Looked at her curiously. "What do you need to know?"

"I don't need to know anything. I mean, I don't need to know anything about you that's real private…or classified," she added quickly, thinking maybe a term like that might make more sense to a military man.

His eyebrows rose. "Classified?"

"You know. A secret." She was making a cake of herself, and it was no one's fault but her own! "I sound ridiculous, don't I? I'm just curious about your girlfriend."

"My girlfriend?"

"Yes. Um, maybe she'd like to volunteer here

sometime? It's a great way to meet new people." And for Edna to see what kind of woman he liked.

Pure wariness entered his eyes as he started walking down the hall again.

She increased her stride, doing her best to keep at his side. She could practically feel the unease wafting off of him. Not like he was spooked, but like she was a pesky butterfly and he didn't want it anywhere near his face. Who could blame him? "Listen, if you'd rather not talk about her, just let me know."

"Okay. I'd rather not talk about this, especially since I'm not dating anyone."

"No?" Pulling forth all her acting skills, she made a little tsking noise. "I'm surprised."

"I'm not."

"Really? A handsome, nice guy like you? Well, don't worry. I bet you'll meet the right woman soon."

"I'm in no hurry for that," he said quickly. "I'm good."

"You might be good. But you know what? When I met Wayne I realized that I had only been living halfway. He opened my eyes. We're really happy together. Everyone needs someone special in their life. Don't you agree?"

"I don't disagree, but relationships are not for me."

He made it sound like happiness wasn't for him.

That was completely wrong. "Hmm. Perhaps we should try one of those dating apps."

"We?"

"You know." She waved a hand. "Just in case you had trouble with your profile and all."

"I'm not going to do a dating app."

"Oh. Well, then. Maybe..."

"I really need to get to work. I have other jobs in addition to this one." He pointed to her door. "If you could unlock it, ma'am?"

"Oh. Yes. Of course." She did as he asked.

He twisted the knob, walked into her office, and turned on the light. "Thank you. I'll let you know if I need anything."

She'd been effectively dismissed. Peeking inside, she saw her office was the way she and Wayne had left it two days ago. He'd come up to help her clear away the area so Hunt could get right to work. Against a wall was the desk kit that had been delivered the week before. Everything was in order.

There wasn't a single reason for her to be loitering around, getting in his way. "Thanks again. If you need anything, please let me know."

"I'll be fine."

"You know, a bottle of water." She winked. "Or a loaf of bread to take home..."

"I don't need either."

"Understood. I guess I better head on back to the front."

"I imagine so."

He was standing still, his hands loosely clasped behind his back. She could just imagine him doing that for one of his officers back in the day. Giving them the respect they expected…but maybe with a part of him wishing that he could be completely honest and share just what was on his mind.

She smiled. "See you later, Hunt."

For a split second, his lips almost curved into the barest trace of a smile. Almost.

It was enough for her to decide that she hadn't completely embarrassed them both.

Turning around, Edna headed back down the hall. Decided to go inside the kitchen and offer a helping hand if someone needed one. It would be the perfect opportunity to look around and see if there were any women who might be a good match for Hunt.

It was obvious that he needed a little help in the romance department. She would be happy to do just that.

CHAPTER FOUR

KINSEY SHOULD'VE KNOWN something strange was going on when Edna greeted her with a bright smile as she walked through the front door of Loaves of Love. Not only did the owner and manager of the organization seem especially chatty, but Edna had even volunteered to escort Kinsey to one of the workstations in the back of the room.

That had never happened since the first time she'd come to volunteer.

Shrugging off the vague feeling that she was about to be set up, Kinsey said, "Thanks for walking me back here."

"I have time. Everything seems to be working like clockwork around here this afternoon."

Kinsey could've been wrong, but Edna didn't seem to be treating that as if it was a good thing. "It's my lucky day."

"Mine, too," she replied in a light tone. "So… how are you, dear?" Edna asked as they wove in between filled tables of volunteers.

"I'm fine—thank you."

"Anything new?"

Kinsey noticed that Edna had ignored the two women who'd called out a greeting, and she kept studying her. It not only wasn't like her, it didn't make sense. Kinsey couldn't think of a single thing that she'd done recently to garner such attention from Edna. Wondering if she had a piece of lettuce stuck between her teeth, she shook her head. "I'm sorry. What did you say?"

"Nothing new with me," she finally answered as they approached an Amish couple near the ovens. "Hi," she said to them. "Is it okay if I work here with you?"

"Of course," the woman said.

But instead of moving away, Edna edged a little closer to Kinsey. "Nothing new at work?"

"Nope. I mean, nothing to speak of."

"Oh? I'm sure things must be very exciting, working in a dental office like you do."

"I'm only the receptionist there, Edna. It's a good job and I like it fine, but it's not very exciting."

"Don't say 'only.' I bet you're a very important reason that everything runs like clockwork."

Kinsey tried that on for size. Honestly, Dr. Martin was kind and had been very patient when she'd had so many questions for him to answer. But he was not the type of man to heap on praise. Especially when it wasn't warranted.

Eager to stop talking about work, she said, "All in all, it's been pretty quiet. The only thing of note was when a lady almost fainted because she was so worried about getting a filling."

Edna blinked. "What?"

"Some people have a legit fear of sitting in a dental chair. That woman was one of them."

"What did you do?"

"I got her a glass of cold water and sat with her until one of the hygienists could come out."

Edna smiled. "So you saved her."

"Um, no. I just gave her water."

The Amish couple across the table didn't say a word, but Kinsey was pretty sure they were very amused.

"I see. Well, now that it's the weekend, you can put all that unpleasantness behind you." She waggled her eyebrows. "I bet you have a hot date."

Kinsey bit the inside of her lip so she wouldn't giggle. "I don't know if anyone says 'hot date' anymore."

"I suppose not. What do you girls call it?"

"Just a date." She glanced at the Amish couple for help. But other than the man looking like he was still trying not to laugh, neither said a word.

"So, do you?" Edna asked.

"Do I…?"

"Date?"

"Yes, but not lately. Sorry, no hot dates. Not even any lukewarm ones." She grinned, liking her joke.

Edna didn't so much as chuckle. Instead, she

was kind of studying Kinsey's face, like she was worried that she was coming down with something. "I'm surprised."

"I'm not. I've been pretty busy, and a lot of the guys my age seem a little immature."

Edna's eyes brightened. "You do seem mature for your age. And you have every right to be picky."

"That doesn't sound good, does it? It's not that I'm picky, it's that..." She shrugged. "Well, you know my story. I don't have a family and I haven't had one for a long time. Some of the guys I've gone out with are still living with their parents. Or they're upset because they don't have the truck they want yet. Or the boat. Or the right phone." She shook her head. "I can't relate."

"I should say not. You need someone older. A man who's not so insecure."

"Maybe. But I think when the time is right, I'll know. Besides, like I said, I'm busy now."

"Maybe I could help you make a list." Smiling, she added, "We could write down a list of attributes you find attractive."

This conversation was getting worse and worse. Kinsey had long passed feeling awkward and was now beginning to head into uncomfortable territory.

Actually, they were already there. Right in the middle of uncomfortable. "Edna, thanks for your concern, but I just came in here to relax and make some bread."

"Oh. Of course." She lowered her voice. "I'm sorry if I seemed a little too inquisitive. It's just that I've recently found love again, you know."

Relaxing again, Kinsey smiled. "I'd forgotten about that. I had a friend at CCC who was always trying to set up other couples."

"CCC?"

"Cuyahoga Community College. I went there for a year to take some business courses."

"You are a go-getter. Well, I believe you know Daniel and Laura?" She smiled at the Amish couple.

"I do now." She smiled at them.

"We'll make sure she has everything she needs, Edna. Don't worry," Daniel said.

"Oh. Yes, of course." Edna patted Kinsey on her hand as she walked away.

Kinsey hoped the older woman was all right. She'd really been acting strange.

Shaking off the worries, she turned to the pair at her table. "My name's Kinsey, by the way. It's good to meet you."

"Is this your first time here?"

"Oh, no. I think it's my seventh or eighth visit. I'm not really sure why Edna was so concerned about me today."

"We're glad you're here."

"I'll go wash up and put on an apron." She

crossed the area to the large commercial-sized stainless-steel sink against the side wall.

After putting on a hair net, gloves, and the apron, she gathered her supplies, arranged her ingredients, measuring cups, and pan exactly how she liked, then got started. Every volunteer who helped make bread made two loaves. One to give to someone visiting the food pantry and one to take home.

Like many others in the room, Kinsey had never baked homemade bread until she'd started volunteering there. Her birth mom hadn't liked to cook, and she sure hadn't been given the opportunity in any of the homes she'd been placed in before the Martins'. Claudia had been happy to teach her some kitchen basics, but she'd also confided that she didn't enjoy baking as much as making a stew or some other savory dish.

"What brings you here?" Daniel asked.

"I work in the reception area at a nearby dental practice. Making bread is a nice change from clerical tasks. What about you two?" Belatedly, she wondered if Amish folks liked to talk about themselves.

Laura smiled at her husband. "We were up here in Medina seeing my brother, Jack. He's been telling us about this place for the last year. When Jack got called in for an emergency and we lost our ride back, Daniel asked if we could come over here instead of sitting around his house. Jack introduced us to Edna, and we got to work."

"What kind of emergency did Jack have to deal with? Is he a doctor?"

"He's a veterinarian," Daniel supplied. "One of Jack's patients is a Jack Russell terrier having a litter of pups. I think the dog was having some trouble."

"Oh no! Well, I hope everything will be okay."

Laura shrugged. "I hope so, too. But it's all in the Lord's hands, ain't so?"

"Yes, I guess so." She thought about that as she turned out the mixture in the bowl, sprinkled some flour on the dough, and then started kneading.

Across from her, she noticed that Laura was dividing her bread into two sets of muffin pans. "What are you making?"

"We've each already made two loaves of bread. I asked Edna if I could maybe make some rolls now." Laura shrugged. "I figure someone might enjoy something new. After all, not everyone needs a fresh loaf of bread."

"I bet she was excited about that idea. I heard the volunteers made cinnamon bread last year for Christmas and it was a big hit."

Laura smiled at her husband. "There's always room in one's heart for something new, I think."

"I think so, too."

Laura exchanged a look with her husband, then

said, "Speaking of new things, did I overhear Edna asking you about your dating life?"

"She sure did." Kinsey couldn't resist chuckling. "To be honest, she caught me off guard."

"You looked a bit like a bug caught in a spider's web," Daniel teased.

"It felt a little like that. She got me good, too. I didn't think she was going to drop it."

"Maybe she has someone in mind for you," Laura suggested. "Wouldn't that be something?"

"It would, but I hope she doesn't."

"Why is that?"

"I don't know. I guess because I just got out on my own. I want to spend some time figuring myself out before I give my heart away."

"I canna fault you for that, but I'd be remiss if I didn't tell ya that falling in love isn't as much as giving one's heart away as it is having another to keep you going," Daniel said.

Was it really like that? How could they be so sure? How did they ever get on this topic? "I guess we'll see what happens," she said.

"I'm sure we will." Looking at the tins that were now filled with dough, Laura wiped her hands with a soft towel. "I'm going to take these over to the racks by the ovens to rise. Daniel, do you want to do the same with your last loaf?"

"Jah. I'll be right there." After Laura was out of earshot, he said, "I'm sorry if we offered you too much free advice. We meant no disrespect."

"None was taken. It was nice to meet you both."

"Hopefully, we'll see you again one day."

"I hope so." Kinsey divided her dough and continued to knead it. As always, the repetitive movements helped her relax.

Eventually, she watched the Amish couple leave, and a pair of volunteers slipped cooled loaves of bread into plastic sleeves.

After her dough rested for twenty minutes, she punched it down and arranged it in her loaf pans, then finally cleaned up the table where the three of them had been working.

Ready to head home and order Chinese from her favorite take-out place, she placed her two loaves of bread on the racks by the ovens, checked in with the volunteer, and told him how much longer the bread needed to rise before it was baked.

"You may take your loaf now," he said. "Thanks for volunteering."

"No thanks needed. I love coming in."

Just as she turned around, Edna poked her head into the work area. "Kinsey, bring out an extra loaf, would you please? I want to hand another one off."

"Sure thing." Dutifully, she turned around and walkcd back to the volunteer.

"Here you go, Kinsey," he said with a grin. "Have a good evening."

"You, too. Thanks." Nodding to a couple of people who she passed on her way out, Kinsey opened the door and headed toward the reception desk. Edna was standing next to it and talking to a man that was just out of sight. She looked more animated than usual. Pleased.

Thinking that the man must've been a good friend of hers, Kinsey decided to set the loaf of bread on the table. "The bread's on the table, Edna," she said in a soft voice. "Have a good night," she added as she turned toward the front door.

"Oh, don't go yet, Kinsey."

Surprised, she turned back around. And then realized who Edna had been talking to. Hunt Vargo. The very last person in Medina she wanted to talk to.

Flustered, she fought to school her features.

"Thank you, dear." Ever gracious, Edna picked up the bread and handed it to Hunt. "Hunt, this is Kinsey Zaleski. Have you two met, by any chance?"

"Yeah. We have."

Meeting his gaze, Kinsey knew at once that he was just as uncomfortable as she was. "Hi, Hunt."

"Kinsey."

Like always, he looked like a rough-around-the-edges G.I. Joe doll come to life. Today he was wearing faded jeans, a painted-on army-green T-shirt, and his usual scowl.

Seemingly oblivious to the tension brewing between them, Edna said, "Kinsey, Hunt was just sharing how he grew up in Medina."

"Oh?"

"Yes! Just like you. And get this…even though you two are practically strangers, you guys have something in common—Doc Martin. Isn't that something?"

"It sure is," she murmured, though a part of her was aching to point out that her childhood and his were the complete opposite of being "just like" each other. She'd lived in a variety of foster homes all over the county. He'd lived next to Dr. and Mrs. Martin, two of the nicest people in the entire world.

Of course, right on the heels of that dark thought was the knowledge that she had no real inkling of what Hunt's childhood had been like.

"I believe you both know Larry Martin."

"Yes," she said. Since Hunt, who was holding that loaf of bread like a football, said nothing, she continued. "I was finishing up work and he was doing some remodeling for Dr. Martin."

"What a small world. And now here you both are. Standing in the middle of Loaves of Love."

This conversation was getting as uncomfortable as a root canal. "Yes. What a small world."

"Hunt, careful with that loaf, dear. I'm afraid you're smooshing the middle of it."

Hunt looked down, seemed to realize he'd been

holding it in a death grip, and tossed it into the sack next to his feet. "Sorry."

"No harm done. Even smooshed, it will taste good with your supper."

"Yeah. Thanks again for all of this," Hunt said.

Kinsey was confused about what they were talking about until she took a better look at that bag. And then, like the pieces of a jigsaw puzzle, it suddenly all clicked into place.

Hunt was at Loaves of Love for food.

Here she'd been thinking all kinds of catty things about him because he hadn't wanted to talk to her at work, but he'd obviously had a lot of far more important things on his mind. Why, he'd likely been hungry.

She remembered how embarrassed she'd been when someone at one of her many schools would tease her about her hand-me-down clothes. Or worse, ask her if she really was just a foster kid. Kinsey felt a fresh wave of sympathy roll through her.

She was an awful person! She should have been so much kinder to Hunt.

"I hope you enjoy the bread," she said in a weak voice.

He narrowed his eyes. "Thanks."

She needed to get out of there, fast. "Sorry, but I have to get a couple of things done. I better be on my way."

"I'll walk you out," said Hunt.

"There's no need."

"I insist."

"Oh, let him be a gentleman, Kinsey," Edna teased. "He was an army officer, you know."

"Come on," Hunt said. After they told Edna goodbye, he held the door open for her.

Outside, the late-afternoon sun was still bright, but the air was slightly cooler than it had been when she'd walked inside.

"I didn't know you volunteered here," he said.

"I usually try to come a couple of days a month. I don't always make it, though."

"Ah." He scanned the parking lot. "Where's your vehicle?"

"It's, um, over there."

"Gonna have to be more specific."

"Fine. It's the white Honda."

"Gotcha."

Realizing that she wasn't going to be able to shake him, she mumbled, "It's nice of you to do this. Thanks."

"It's not a problem."

"Actually, I'm starting to realize that we don't know too much about each other."

"I thought the same thing."

She could've been wrong, but she was pretty sure he'd just almost smiled. "Here's my car."

"Want me to wait until you get in and start it up?"

He was serious. She had a feeling that he would have said the same thing if it was twenty degrees and snowing. He'd wait until she felt safe and settled.

Even though he was obviously going through some difficult times.

Just as he turned to walk away, Kinsey knew what she had to do. "Hunt, um, before we part, I want to apologize."

He paused mid-step. "For what?"

"I realize now that you probably have a lot on your mind. I shouldn't have been so impatient and rude the other night." Frustrated with her lame excuse, she shook her head. "What I'm trying to say is that I should have been more understanding."

"Understanding?" he repeated.

"Yes." Feeling the need to explain, she added, "Look, I know you don't know me very well, but I really am pretty nice. I don't try to make people feel less than or insignificant. I should've been more sensitive to what you might be going through." Pleased with her awkward explanation, she pulled out her keys. "I'll see you later."

He reached out. Grabbed hold of her arm. "Hey. Wait a sec." When she raised her eyebrows, he dropped his hand. "Sorry for grabbing you, but I'm really confused. Kinsey, what do you think I have on my mind?"

"Oh...you know." She sure didn't want to spell it out. Why couldn't Hunt just accept her apology and move on?

He shook his head. Stared at her intently. "Sorry,

but I don't. I'm afraid you're going to have to be clearer than that."

Now she had no idea how to respond. She hadn't thought it was possible, but she'd just managed to make things worse.

CHAPTER FIVE

HUNT HAD A container of homemade lasagna and a loaf of fresh bread in his hands. They smelled amazing, and he'd been looking forward to going home, taking a hot shower, and scarfing down both while he watched the latest Guardians game on TV.

He was going to do that, too. As soon as he figured out what in the world Kinsey was talking about. "When did I hurt your feelings?"

"When we talked in Dr. Martin's office last night." Looking pained, she averted her eyes. "But it's fine. I realize now that you probably had a lot on your mind and I was rude and impatient. I shouldn't have given you such a hard time. It was wrong of me. I hope you'll eventually be able to forgive me."

It had been a really long time since anyone had looked at him the way she was. He'd always been bigger and tougher than most. Even after he'd gotten his knee just about blasted off, the medics, doctors, and nurses had been compassionate but hadn't been staring at him with something...akin to pity? Plus, why was she apologizing for being honest? Did she think he couldn't take it? Once again, he had to search his brain to think of a time when anyone had treated him like this. He sure hadn't treated any of his men that way…like they were weak.

He didn't like it.

"What's going on?"

"Hmm?"

Hunt fought to not roll his eyes. "Look, you don't owe me any apology. Not ever."

"That's not really fair."

"It's true, though. I'm not the most social person on my best day. Worse, I've gotten kind of used to being short-tempered with pretty much everyone I come in contact with. It's a terrible habit. I should've been more patient with you. So…whatever I said to you, try and forget about it, okay?"

"Whatever you said?"

"Yeah. I honestly don't remember."

Kinsey flashed him a look of annoyance. Then, right when it seemed he was going to dress him down, she glanced at his paper sack and visibly swallowed her comment. "Okay."

"Okay? That's it?"

"Yep. Now, I better go, but I hope you have a good weekend."

Her words sounded as fake as her smile. But did he want to push her anymore? No. "Yeah. Ah, you, too," he said. "See you Monday."

Her smile tightened before she turned.

Hunt felt curiously dismayed as he watched her walk away. Not that he wanted to get into a verbal sparring match, but he'd kind of enjoyed the way she didn't put up with his surliness. A part of him respected that.

Okay. He kind of thought it was cute.

As he watched her get into her vehicle, Hunt was tempted to call out her name. Tell her they weren't done talking about…whatever they were talking about. Say something to rile her up a bit. Anything would be better than seeing her so dejected.

But that would likely just make things worse. He shook it off and strode to his truck and headed home.

Home, for him, was his childhood house. His parents had taken good care of it, and it had been paid off for years. When they'd decided to downsize and follow his sister, Kim, across the country, Hunt had bought it from them.

His dad had put up a token fight about taking his money until Hunt had reminded him that he had a good, solid savings account. He'd entered the army as a second lieutenant and had quickly been promoted to both first lieutenant and then captain. His colonel had hinted that another promotion was in his future just a couple of days before he'd been injured.

In addition, he'd earned even more money for his two deployments overseas. All that meant that he'd retired from the army with lifelong benefits and a healthy nest egg.

He also enjoyed a quiet lifestyle. He wasn't a traveler, and he'd never had extravagant tastes. Not beyond his truck, he supposed.

Walking into his kitchen, he smiled as he set Edna's lasagna on the counter, then trotted into his bathroom and took a shower.

His sister liked to tease him about his new love for hot showers. It was a rare day that he didn't take at least two. He'd never thought too much about having unlimited hot water until he'd been in the desert. There, he'd be lucky if he could get five minutes of a lukewarm trickle when it had felt as if he had a sandpaper second skin.

After showering, he poured himself a giant glass of sweet tea and sat out on the back porch. His mother's garden was in full bloom, and it was attracting every butterfly and hummingbird in the area. He'd added a couple of bird feeders, too. It was rare that he couldn't find the time to sip tea, scan apps on his phone, and listen to the birds.

An activity he would have never imagined he'd enjoy.

He'd drunk about half his tea when the phone rang. He smiled when he saw who it was. "Hey, Mom."

"Hi, Hunt. I'm so glad I caught you. Where are you?"

"Home. I'm sitting on the back porch and watching a pair of cardinals give an annoying goldfinch what for."

"How are my daylilies doing?"

He stood up and scanned the area. "They look good, Ma. Everything does."

"Ah. It's moments like this when I really wish I was back in Ohio."

He knew the feeling. "How's Dad?"

"He's good. He's playing golf today with two guys he met at the club last week. Kim and Jackson are at swim lessons."

"So you're home alone." He smiled. Everyone knew that his mother was the opposite of him. As much as he craved solitude, she enjoyed being around crowds and activities. The more the merrier.

"I am, but don't worry. I'm going to meet some ladies for a walk later."

"Good."

"Listen, as much as I enjoy catching up, I called for a reason. Dad and I are flying home at the end of the month. We're going to go to Melissa Atkinson's engagement party."

"Missy's engaged? Good for her."

"I heard she's thrilled, and so in love. Plus, the party is going to be at the country club there in Medina. You're invited, Hunt."

"I want to see you and Dad, but I doubt I'll be up for that party."

"Will you please think about it before you make up your mind? You and Missy were once so close."

They had been. He and Missy had hung out a lot together in middle school and the first couple of years in high school because they'd been in the same youth group. They'd gone to catechism classes on Sunday nights together for two years, then were confirmed together.

More than one person had tried to turn them into a couple, but both of them had stopped any talk of that. Sure, they'd had a lot in common, but not a bit of it was because there was a spark between them.

"Ma, I really am happy about Missy, but you know that I don't like big crowds or loud music anymore."

"Barb knows that, but she thought that maybe if you had a job to do there, it would make the time go by easier."

"What kind of job would that be?"

"Escorting Missy's freshman roommate."

Just as he was about to remind her that he had no idea who that was, he remembered getting together with half his senior class two years out of high school. He'd been granted leave for Thanksgiving, and Missy had brought Allison to a pub to meet everyone.

Missy had been great. The same as ever. Allison had been very unimpressed with the pub, the drinks, their town, and the company.

He couldn't imagine that she was much different now.

"That's not a job, Mom. That's asking too much."

"Come on. Allison is a nice woman."

"Sorry, but I disagree. She wasn't nice when I met her."

"I bet you got off on the wrong foot."

"Ma, she complained about the fact that she couldn't get a decent bagel in Medina. She even told the server that her food wasn't cooked well and had them remake it."

"Well…"

"Twice."

"Oh."

"Yeah, Ma. I promised myself that I would do my best to never see her again."

"That was a long time ago. Things can change. People can change."

"Not for her and me. We are not a great match."

"I'll see if I can find someone else."

"Don't."

"Won't you think about it before you say no again?"

"Ma."

"Please? Barb told me that Missy specifically asked for you to keep Allison company."

He didn't date. He didn't want to date. But if he did…it would not be some random woman he hadn't liked years ago.

On the other hand, his mother rarely asked him

for much. How could he tell her no without even pretending to give it some thought?

"I'll let you know soon."

"Does that mean you'll do it?"

"That means I'll think about it, Ma."

"Hunt, what kind of answer is that?"

"It's as good as I can give you right now."

"Fine. But let me know your answer soon."

"I will. You and Dad are going to stay here, right?"

"Yes, if that's okay?"

"Mom, it's your house. Of course it is."

"It's your house. And don't even think about giving us the main bedroom either. We'll be in the guest room."

That would be weird, but he wasn't up for arguing about it. "It will be good to spend time with you. I love you, Ma."

"You, too. Don't forget to eat."

"I won't."

After another two minutes of reminders from her and promises from him, they hung up. He went inside, popped the lasagna into the microwave, and got ready to spend the rest of his evening on the couch, watching a ball game, and trying not to think about Kinsey.

Especially not how he would much rather be set up with her than a woman like Allison.

CHAPTER SIX

It was a perfect morning. It wasn't too hot or too humid. Peaceful, too. She really wished she'd decided to take a personal day.

"Miss." *Tap, tap, tap.* "Miss? Hello?"

Kinsey slid open the glass partition that the previous receptionist had asked Dr. Martin to install. When she'd first started working, she'd been tempted to ask Doc to remove it.

Now she realized that it had been installed for a very good reason. Sometimes a person needed a little bit of space.

Reminding herself that the patients had every right to ask questions, Kinsey pasted on a pleasant expression. "Yes, Mrs. Freedland?"

"I'm still waiting."

"Yes, ma'am. I realize that. But I'm afraid that you came thirty minutes early for your appointment. The hygienist is with another patient."

"So I just have to wait?"

"We see patients by appointment, not first come, first serve."

"So I have to sit in here a lot longer."

"Only until Brady is ready for you."

"Fine, but I'm not happy about this." Mrs. Freedland turned around in a huff. Kinsey noticed that the woman had sat down next to her son, who shot Kinsey an apologetic look.

She would have appreciated the expression if he'd done anything to settle his mother down. As it was, he'd brought her in early and was being very quiet while his bossy mother was being very impatient.

Kinsey slid the glass partition closed and stood up to move just out of sight. Unfortunately, even the partition wasn't giving her enough of a break. Sometimes a person needed to take a minute for a breather.

She'd just sat down again when Brady appeared with his patient. Noticing her expression, he frowned. "Everything okay, Kins?"

"Yep."

"You sure about that?"

"Yes. I'm fine." Taking a deep breath, she summoned up her best perky demeanor. "All set, Mr. Hanna?"

"Yep. What do I owe you?"

Looking up from his paperwork, she smiled at him. "Nothing. Your insurance took care of everything. And...we already have your appointment made."

"Good. I'll see you in six months."

"Yes, sir. See you then."

Turning to Brady, who was still standing in the hall, Kinsey said, "Mrs. Freedland is ready whenever you are."

Understanding dawned on his features. "She came early again, huh?"

"Oh yeah."

"All right. Give me five minutes to get set up."

"Will do." Just as another person walked through the office door, Brady stepped closer.

"Hey, Kinsey?"

"Yes?"

"What are you doing for dinner tonight?"

"I don't know—why?"

He folded his arms over his chest and lowered his voice. "How about we grab something after work?"

He was asking her out. Dismay warred with disappointment as well as a good amount of fluster. "Thanks, but I don't think that's a good idea."

He tilted his head to one side. "Why not?"

"I don't want to mix my social life with work." Hoping to cut off any further discussion, she picked up a pen. "I'm sure you understand."

"I don't."

"No?"

"I mean, if it's Doc you're worried about, I'm sure he won't mind. I'll explain everything to him."

Annoyance filled her again. Like she wanted Brady to speak about her to Dr. Martin! Reminding herself that Brady was a longtime employee and she was the new girl, she said as patiently as possible, "Thanks, but I'm not comfortable with you doing that." She had no desire to go out with Brady.

Just as importantly, she needed Dr. Martin's faith in her. "I'm sorry."

Brady looked hurt but nodded. "I'll be back in five."

"Thanks." Feeling flustered yet again, she slid open the glass in order to greet the new arrival. "Hi, Ronnie. How are you?"

"I've been better. I'm going to be sitting in that chair for a while today."

Glancing down at the schedule she saw that he was there to get a cracked filling repaired. "I'm sorry that you're going to be here so long, but your tooth will be happier."

Ron laughed. "I'm glad you're here, Kinsey. You are always putting a positive spin on things."

"I'm only trying to look at the bright side. Let's see. Tina should be out to get you soon."

"Thanks, doll."

Luckily, Brady collected Mrs. Freedland without saying a word about dinner, and nothing of note happened in the next four hours. At the end of the day, Tina and Brady left. Only she and Dr. Martin were in the office.

At half past four, Hunt showed up but didn't

touch base with her. Instead, he and Dr. Martin seemed to have a lot to catch up on.

She was just shutting down the computer when Dr. Martin stopped by to say good-night.

"You did a good job today, dear," he said. "More than one person was singing your praises."

Suddenly all of her frustration with the day vanished. She was getting better at managing bossy patients, and she'd let down Brady without causing a scene. "Thank you. I'm trying my best."

He patted her arm. "I know that some of the patients can be a handful. Especially Jessica Freedland."

"I hope she's easier in the exam chair than she is in the reception room."

"Oh, she is. We have her contained there, you see," he joked. "Plus she can't talk."

She smiled at his dentist joke. "I need to learn to be more patient with her."

"No, you need to stick to your guns and show them who is in charge. You did that."

"Thanks, Doc."

"You're very welcome. Now, go on and get out of here."

"I will."

He lowered his voice. "I might have heard something about Brady asking you out."

Oh no. How could that have spread? "It was nothing to worry about."

"I'm not worried. But, ah…if you want to do that, I wouldn't mind."

"I don't want to go out with him, Dr. Martin. Even if we both didn't work for you, I wouldn't have wanted to do that."

He raised his eyebrows. "I see. Well, I guess that settles that, hmm?"

"I hope so." There had been a glint in Brady's eye that signaled that he was up for a challenge. She hoped he didn't think her no was playing hard to get.

"Oh, to be young again. Enjoy it, dear. I'll see you tomorrow."

"Bye!" She knew he was only teasing, but she didn't think dating was all that exciting.

Of course, perhaps she would if she'd dated a lot more than she had.

After Dr. Martin left the building, Kinsey double-checked her computer, the messages, and the pulled files for tomorrow's appointments. She knew that most offices did everything digitally, but she was grateful to have those folders to arrange and organize. If they had a power surge or something, she wasn't going to have to worry about any of the dentist's records.

"Of course, if there was a power surge, we wouldn't be seeing patients," she mumbled to herself as she triple-checked that everything was in its proper place in the reception area.

Then she spied an abandoned jacket and a forgotten book in a corner of the room. After putting those in lost-and-found drawer, she decided to straighten all the magazines, too. And then decided to throw out the ones that looked like they were in the worst shape.

"Oh, hey," Hunt said.

"You caught me again." She noticed that he was holding a bucket and a screwdriver. "What are you working on today?"

"I'm replacing interior doorknobs and hinges."

She peeked in the bucket. The new ones were going to be black. "Ooh. I like those."

The side of his lips turned up. "Glad to hear it, because there's going to be a lot of them."

"I'll get out of your hair," she said in a rush. "Just give me a minute to toss these out in the recycle dumpster in the back."

"No need." He held out a hand. "I'll do that for you."

"I don't mind."

"There's no need for you to go out in the alley. I'll do it."

"All right. Thank you."

He stuffed his hands into his pockets. "Hey, are we good now?"

"Yes, of course."

He peered at her closely. "Are you sure about that? Because I got the feeling that something was off between us on Saturday, but for the life of me I don't know what it was."

The image of Hunt holding the bag of donated food flashed in her mind. It was her reminder that she shouldn't expect him to always be kind and considerate.

Though he sure was being that way now.

"I'll see you later."

He frowned. "Yeah. All right."

Pleased with herself for not saying anything more, she grabbed her purse and hustled out the front door.

She needed to go home, order a pizza, and veg out in front of the TV. This weird day of hers needed to end.

CHAPTER SEVEN

"WAIT!" HUNT CALLED OUT.

Feeling impatient, she turned around. "Look, I just want to go home. Don't worry about anything I said. It's okay if, you know, you don't want to be my friend."

Hunt looked as taken aback as she felt. "I didn't know you wanted to be. We can be friends if you want."

Could this awkward conversation get any worse? "Look. Don't worry about it. We don't have to be anything." Growing more embarrassed by the second, she added, "and now I sound as young as you probably think I am."

"You're twenty, right?"

"I am not." Kinsey lifted her chin. "I'm twenty-six."

"Is that right?"

She bit her lip, then blurted, "Sometimes I say too much. I should be nicer. Especially…" She shut her mouth.

"Especially…what?"

"Nothing."

"Kinsey, just say it."

His light blue eyes were piercing. She could hardly look away. Why, a truth serum had nothing on him. "I…uh, I'm just saying that I should have been more considerate."

"About what?"

"It's really none of my business."

"Okay."

"But, um, if you do need something, I hope you won't hesitate to get help."

"Help with what?"

"I don't know." She was miserable. Trying to change the subject, she added, "Did you enjoy the bread?"

"I did. It went great with the lasagna Edna gave me."

"She gave you lasagna?"

"Did she give you any?"

"No, but, um, I don't need any help."

"What do you think I need help with?"

"Nothing. I should probably go."

"Wait." A new expression flickered in his eyes. "Hey, Kinsey, did you think I was there for food?"

What could she do? She didn't want to lie. "Yes. But there's nothing wrong with needing a helping hand."

"I agree. There isn't a thing wrong with that. Not at all. But I was there working on Edna's office. She made a big lasagna last night for her and

Wayne and gave me half because I'm not much of a cook. I wasn't there for food."

"I see." She'd seen a sack of food, tossed in a preconception about a grumpy handyman, and come up with her own convoluted idea about someone she didn't know and something that was none of her business.

Go, her.

Hunt's eyebrows rose. She braced herself, sure he was about to give her the talking-to that she deserved…when she noticed that the usual cold, hard note in his eyes wasn't there. He didn't look amused but maybe not mad.

"How was the lasagna?" she whispered.

He chuckled. "It was good. Terrific."

"I'm glad."

"Kinsey, you are a piece of work," he teased.

"I'm so sorry. I don't know why I put two and two together and got twenty-five."

He laughed again. "It's all right."

She looked at him more closely. Could he really be taking everything as well as he seemed? That was hard to believe. "It's okay if you hate me now." It wasn't okay, but she couldn't really blame him.

"I don't hate you. You…well, you amuse me, and I'm not even sure why. The stuff you do. The way you watch out for Doc…it makes me smile."

"I don't know if I watch out for him. But someone needs to. Some of his patients are really pushy."

"I have no doubt you'll keep them in line."

"I bet he told you lots of stories about when I was his foster kid."

"A few."

"I...well, I was a lot to deal with."

"Some might say you had a lot to deal with, too."

She shrugged. "Everyone does. I owe Dr. and Mrs. Martin a lot. More than they'll ever know. Please don't tell them that I completely messed up with you."

"You didn't."

"Are you sure?"

He nodded. He studied her a moment, then he seemed to make up his mind. Stepping closer, he held out his hand. "I think we got off on the wrong foot. Let's start over again. Hi. I'm Hunt Vargo. I'm going to be working here for the next couple of months, painting and refurbishing some things around the office."

She slipped her hand into his. As she expected, his hand engulfed hers. His skin was rough with callouses, and his grip was gentle. Like he was taking special care not to scare her off. "Hi, Hunt. I'm Kinsey Zaleski. I'm Dr. Martin's new receptionist. It's nice to meet you, too."

When his hand slipped away, she felt its loss. That was a shock, but maybe she should've expected it. Everything about their interactions had been out of character and surprising for her. He made her uncomfortable.

"I better get to work."

He sounded impatient. Why did that bother her? This was his default setting. "Yeah," she said quickly. "I had better get on home."

CHAPTER EIGHT

ALMOST ANOTHER WEEK had gone by, and she was almost positive that Hunt Vargo was back to his old tricks. All she wanted to do was leave, but he was being a jerk again. She could've gone home five minutes ago, but he'd told her to stay out of the staff break room until a quarter after six.

She would've just gone home except that three of her special root beers were still in there as well as her favorite travel cup. Good stuff had a habit of walking out, and no way did she want anyone drinking her root beer or helping themselves to her expensive travel cup.

Now it was twelve minutes after six, and she couldn't take it anymore. Pounding on the door, she called out, "Hunt, let me in. I need to get my stuff."

"It's not a quarter after yet."

"It almost is. Let me in!"

"*Almost* doesn't count for much in the real world, Kinsey."

Huh? "This is the real world, and *almost* counts just fine."

"I'm talking about things that matter."

"Such as?"

"I don't know. Football," he said through the door. "Almost getting a first down means nothing when you're trying to score."

"I still don't know what a first down even is," she bit out. "Plus—"

"*First down* means you get another four downs to get another ten yards."

"What? Hunt, that's the worst definition I've ever heard in my whole life." She couldn't believe she was arguing with him through a door. The man drove her nuts!

"It's not. It's a great definition. Thirteen words. It's succinct. It's perfect."

Thirteen words? He was seriously counting the words he said to her? "It might be succinct, but it's not perfect. It's lame."

"Lame?"

"Yeah."

"Nobody says *lame* anymore."

"Oh, yes they do. They do if they're trying not to say it sucks." Feeling pretty good about that comeback, she propped a hand on her hip.

That was when he threw open the door.

She barely stepped back in time. "Hunt, be careful."

"How was I supposed to know you were practically leaning against the door?"

"You know how. I've been yelling at you through

this stupid door for ten minutes." She gripped his arm before he could lift up his watch and show her the correct time. "Don't even think about correcting me."

He stilled.

She dropped her hand. For a split second, she was sure he looked at her lips. "What are you doing on Saturday morning?"

"Huh?"

"Saturday morning. Do you have plans?"

Hunt was looking at her intently, like her response mattered to him. "I'm not sure. Sometimes I volunteer at Loaves of Love. Sometimes I go to the farmer's market." Remembering how she'd spent last Saturday afternoon napping in the sun, she smiled. "Sometimes I don't do a thing."

"Do you like dogs?"

"Yes. Um, why?"

"If you ever need something fun to do, you might want to go over to the animal shelter."

"The animal shelter?"

He stuffed his hands into his pockets. "Yeah. I go over there a couple of times a week and either play with dogs or take them for a walk. If you ever feel like it, you ought to go."

"Um, okay." Here she was, sounding rude again. "I mean, yes, that does sound like fun. Where is it?"

He leaned over her desk, picked up a pen, and pulled off a Post-it note. She watched him write down the address in painstaking, perfect print. “Maybe I’ll see you there sometime.”

It was almost like he was asking her out without actually doing any asking. Trying that on for size, she decided that she didn’t hate it. “When do you usually go?”

“I’ll be there tomorrow around nine.” He blinked. “If you get bored, you should think about going over there.”

“You know what? I might do that. Thanks for telling me about it.”

He rapped his knuckles on her desk twice in some kind of man-army-guy gesture of approval.

Or maybe it was his way of deciding that their conversation was over? Whatever the reason, after those two raps, he turned around and walked back down the hall. Kinsey was pretty sure that he’d already put back in his AirPods before he disappeared from her sight.

What in the world had just happened? Somehow she’d managed to embarrass herself, kind of put him down, become his friend, and now had a date with him at an animal shelter.

Her mind was spinning.

Quickly, she put the pen and Post-it notes back where they belonged, scanned the area, and then grabbed her purse and got out of there.

She needed some space and time to process everything.

And maybe think about shopping. All of her

T-shirts were kind of faded and stretched out. It might not be a bad idea to trade one of them for something that fit her and didn't look like she'd bought it five years ago.

It wasn't for Hunt. Not at all. It was just to make herself feel better.

Maybe by Saturday morning, she'd actually start to believe that.

CHAPTER NINE

IT WAS A quarter to nine, and he was sitting in his truck while he waited for Kinsey to show. It hadn't occurred to him to get her phone number or to give her his. So because of that, he had no idea if she was still going to show up.

He wouldn't be surprised if she didn't. He hadn't exactly invited her. It was more like a thrown-out comment that he'd hoped she'd catch.

In addition, his offer had been out of the blue and he now knew her well enough to realize that she would've had a hard time refusing the invitation to his face because she was nice.

She was nice, and that niceness acted like a thin veneer over a scrappy personality.

Doc had mentioned enough things about her over the years for Hunt to also know that she had a big need for order. He was no psychologist, but he was pretty sure that a kid being forced to constantly move into new homes had to have craved that. He would've.

Shoot. Order and precision were two of the things he'd actually enjoyed about military life. He'd liked things he could count on. Now, after spending so many weeks and months either recovering from surgery or suffering through physical therapy, he'd discovered that he'd liked order in his life, but he'd also liked a bit of surprise. Maybe a bit of chaos.

He figured that was why he liked being around Kinsey. She brought chaos into his life. She made him laugh, and not because she did odd things like decide he was hungry but because she looked like she was trying *not* to boss him around. She would've been a fantastic drill sergeant.

For someone else besides him, though. He'd always appreciated a sergeant who knew when to hold his or her tongue. At least for a few minutes.

He didn't think Kinsey could any more stop herself from spouting an opinion than he could stop his knee from aching in the morning.

He drummed his fingers on his steering wheel. Started to tell himself that if she didn't show up he didn't need to be disappointed.

And then, there she was. Zipping into her parking spot in her trusty old Honda. He stayed in his truck as she opened the door, seemed to psych herself up, and then stepped out. Today she had what looked like a fanny pack crossing diagonally across her chest.

And she was wearing a pair of shorts that showed off a great pair of legs. Which he probably shouldn't have noticed.

And then, just before she straightened to scan

the parking lot, he saw a flash of insecurity in her eyes. The same sort of self-doubt that he'd watched dozens of men and women in his care in the army exhibit. He knew she wasn't worried about walking dogs. She'd been too excited about the prospect for that.

She was worried about seeing him. Nervous.

He'd put it there by being continually crabby whenever he saw her. Yep, he'd put up a wall between them. He'd needed it because he was still trying to get himself back together, and she needed that wall because she'd likely been hurt by all her years in foster care.

He needed to be better.

"Hey!" he called out.

Kinsey's head popped up just seconds before a smile appeared. "You beat me here," she called out as she approached. Glancing at the phone that she held in her hand, she added, "I'm two minutes early, too."

"They call this army time."

"How so?"

"When I was just a lieutenant, one of my jobs was to work with a master sergeant to make sure everything was all good. We made sure needs were met and every possible contingency was addressed." Realizing that he was acting as if his experiences and love for protocols would mean something to anyone out of the military, he shrugged. "Suffice it to say that getting to a meeting early is key."

She moved to his side. "I guess so."

"You ready to see some dogs?" he asked, taking care to match her stride so she wouldn't have to struggle to keep up with his longer legs.

"I am, but I'm a little worried that this is going to make me sad all day. I know you're a big, bad former captain and all…but do you usually leave wishing that you could do more for the animals in here?"

What she didn't realize was that he didn't see her concern as a liability at all. He thought it was sweet. "Sometimes I wish that, but then I remind myself that I can't adopt all the dogs here. And even if I could…another one will show up tomorrow. It's the way of the world, I guess."

"That isn't making me feel better, Hunt."

Kinsey was obviously joking, but he heard worry there, too. "How about this, then? If we weren't here, then they might not be getting as much attention. We're making them happy for a little while."

"I can live with that."

"Good to hear." He opened the door for her and allowed her to proceed him.

Kinsey's eyes widened as she looked around, then grinned. "It's so cute in here."

"Yeah. I guess it is." Scanning the reception area, he caught sight of the old elementary school–

style bulletin boards decorating the walls. All five of them had colorful borders, a bold header saying *GOTCHA DAY*, and showcased artfully arranged photographs of dogs and owners.

Honestly, it looked like a twelve-year-old's school project, but it was heartfelt and done with care. And it didn't even matter anyway, because the photos of the happy dogs were the stars of the displays.

Just as Hunt was about to point the photographs out, Kinsey stood in front of the board closest. "This is the best, isn't it?"

"Dogs finding homes? Yeah."

"I've lived here in Medina for almost my entire life. I can't believe I never stepped foot inside."

"I wouldn't have until a physical therapist told me about this program." Doug had told Hunt about the program when he'd suspected that Hunt's difficulty in recovery had as much to do with his mental condition as his physical injuries.

"I'm glad they did."

"Yeah. Me, too."

"Hey, Hunt! You here to sit and play or walk?" Hannah, the director of the shelter, said as she walked through a pair of doors in the back.

"I brought a friend, so whatever we can do together."

"The weather's nice and we have a pair of seven-month-old pit bull pups who could use some exercise. How does that sound?"

"What do you think, Kinsey? Are you ready to take a puppy for a walk?"

"I'm beyond ready to do that."

Hannah smiled. "Come on back with me, then. Kinsey, I'm going to need you to fill out a form. While you do that, I'll get Hunt here to help me put the pups in vests and harnesses."

"Sounds good."

It was difficult for Hunt not to watch Kinsey hurry over to Hannah's side. She looked adorable in her shorts and tennis shoes and long-sleeved T-shirt. She also had her honey-colored hair in a ponytail today. It swung in an arc with every step she took, making her look even younger than she was.

"That okay with you, Hunt?" Hannah asked.

When he met her eyes, he felt his neck heat. It was obvious that she'd noticed him watching Kinsey. "Yeah. Sure."

"Here's your clipboard, Kinsey," Hannah said. "We'll be here right about the time you finish."

Kinsey frowned at the papers. He knew from experience that they asked a lot of questions—some about their homes in case they wanted to adopt a dog.

"You still doing okay?" he murmured. Maybe she didn't like telling strangers about herself.

Her expression softened. "I'm fine. Don't worry about me."

He continued to think of her smile as he followed Hannah into one of the meet-and-greet rooms. She handed him the leashes and halters before leaving to get the pups.

Five minutes later she was back, holding a puppy in each arm. When they spied Hunt they wiggled so much, Hannah barely had time to set them on the ground before they bounded to his side.

"This is Betty and he is Chip," she explained.

He kneeled down so they would feel more comfortable. "Betty and Chip?"

Hannah chuckled. "We go through the alphabet when we name no name dogs," she said as she picked up one of the squirming pups and wrangled a halter on him. "Obviously we're back at the beginning again."

"Gotcha," he said as he did the same for Betty. After attaching the leads, Hannah slipped *ADOPT ME* vests on each before handing both dogs' leads to Hunt.

"I'm glad to see you brought a friend today. I keep telling people that most dogs enjoy walking with other dogs. Plus, it's good for them to practice. It helps them get socialized."

"I bet." He nodded. "Kinsey likes dogs."

"She seems sweet. Pretty, too. Have you two been together long?"

"We aren't together. She's just a friend."

"Oh. Of course. Sorry."

"I bet she's waiting for me."

Hannah led the way, opening doors as Betty and

Chip walked cautiously by Hunt's side. "Here they are," she announced. "Kinsey, Betty is the white-and-tan puppy and Chip is the gray one."

She sat on the ground as both puppies hurried to give her licks and playful nudges. "Oh my gosh. You two are adorable! So cute! Yes, you," she cooed to Chip. "You, too," when Betty yipped.

When Kinsey lifted her chin to meet Hunt's gaze, it was hard to hold back a gasp. There was so much joy shining in her expression. It was beautiful to see.

"I put the clipboard on the table," Kinsey told Hannah.

"Thank you. Hunt might have told you already, but two hours is a good time limit for these walks. Chip and Betty will get tired, and they'll need water breaks, too. Here's your care package for them."

"It has a water bowl, two treats, and some poop bags," he explained.

"I'll put it in my pack" Kinsey said as she continued to pet both puppies.

"Thanks."

Finally, they were off. As expected, the pups had no idea how to walk on leads and wanted to smell and taste nearly everything they came in contact with. Kinsey had nothing but patience for their antics.

They walked down the shelter's front sidewalk, then turned down a quiet street with less cars. Before long, the pups got the hang of things.

"You're doing a good job with Chip," he said.

"He's a sweetheart. They both are. I'm so glad you asked me to walk with you."

"I'm glad I did, too." Realizing how that sounded, he rushed to correct himself. "I mean, I'm glad you're having a good time."

"I am. I can't wait to come to the shelter again." Frowning at the dogs, she added, "It's going to be hard to make them go back into their cages."

"I know, but you can't think about that. At least you're doing this. Plus, based on all the admiring looks we've been getting, I bet at least one of them will get adopted soon."

"I hope so." Her voice was quiet.

Making Hunt feel like a blockhead. "Hey, it never really occurred to me until now that you might be having a hard time with this."

"Because I was a foster kid who didn't get adopted?"

He swallowed. "Yes."

"Don't worry. I know this isn't the same thing."

"I know, but..." He couldn't say it.

"But yeah. I do know what it's like to not have a permanent home," she said softly. "It's hard."

"I bet. I'm sorry you had to go through that."

Kinsey's eyes widened seconds before tears formed.

"Hey," he said as he reached out. "What did I say that hurt you?"

"You didn't hurt, Hunt. Not at all. It's…it's silly, but not a lot of people say things like that."

He was still mystified. "I must be a blockhead because I still don't understand."

She sniffed. "I try not to wear my past on my sleeve, but sometimes, when I share that my mom and dad died suddenly in a car accident and I then had to go directly into the foster care system, people get uncomfortable."

He nodded. "Because they know it's awful."

"Yeah. And I get it. I do. But there's been moments when I want to say that my story might be hard for them to hear but it was really hard to live. Especially because I was just a little kid. It's almost like they don't know what to say so they gloss over it."

"Which makes you feel like you shouldn't have said a thing about your past in the first place."

"Yeah." Bending down, she rubbed Chip's coat. "Thanks for… I don't know. Acknowledging me?"

Her words broke his heart. "Anytime you want to talk about the past, just talk. I'll listen."

"You get it, don't you?"

Hunt pointed to his knee. "There's a reason I rarely wear shorts. My right leg has so many scars on it, it's hard to see anything but the roadmap of red-and-white lines crisscrossing my calf and knee."

"You know what it's like to lose everything you counted on."

"One roadside bomb changed the trajectory of my life. I'd planned on being a career soldier."

"I'm sorry that you were hurt so badly."

"Me, too. But I'm glad that I'm still living."

"I am, too." When one of the puppies yipped, she laughed. "I think Betty's trying to tell us that sidewalks are for walking, not standing."

"Let's go, then."

They walked for another ninety minutes. In the middle of it, they stopped at a cart near the park and bought ice-cream cones for them and pup cups for Betty and Chip. The warm air made the ice cream melt too fast. It was a sticky mess.

It was also perfect. Hunt didn't remember the last time he'd been so happy. It had been years.

The only shadow during the entire afternoon had been when Kinsey had bent down to pick up a tired Chip and she froze for a split second.

"Everything okay?" he'd asked. He was pretty sure she'd gone a little pale.

"Yeah. Everything's fine," she'd replied. "I thought I saw someone I knew."

She was gazing at the line of people at the ice-cream cart. There had to be almost twenty people standing there.

"Do you want to go over there and see what everyone is so interested in? I've got time."

A shadow darkened her eyes. "No. Let's go on back. I think it's been two hours."

Hunt didn't argue, but he knew she was lying. He just didn't know what she was lying about.

CHAPTER TEN

EVEN AFTER SHE'D been home for ten minutes, Kinsey was still shaking. She couldn't believe that she'd seen him again. Dillon. Dillon Carpenter, the absolute worst person she'd ever met in her life.

Ironically, she'd also been made to call him her foster brother when she was just eleven years old. Even now, every time Kinsey thought about her brief stay in the Walkers' home, she felt like throwing up. She had a feeling that she always would, too.

Hunt wasn't the only one who had PTSD from a traumatic event. Only her reactions didn't come from getting injured by a roadside bomb in a foreign country. Hers came from being bullied by a kid two years older than her while living in her first foster home.

He'd been awful, and she'd been so scared and suffering from grief. Looking back, Kinsey knew that she'd been in shock, too. One morning she'd kissed her parents goodbye and hopped on the bus for school. Hours later, the principal had come to her classroom, walked her into a private conference room, and ruined her entire life.

The hours after he'd told her about the car accident, the ambulance, and the phone calls about next of kin were still a blur. But the pain felt as raw as if the man had taken out a razor blade and sliced her skin. Her parents had been raised in Serbia. After they married, they'd wanted a better life. A safer one. So, they'd left their country against the wishes of their families and eventually become American citizens after spending years working toward their citizenship.

Even though she'd been young, Kinsey had been proud of her parents' drive and determination. They hadn't had a ton of money, but Kinsey didn't remember ever wanting for anything. She'd had her own bedroom, a few toys, and plenty of food.

Eventually, their extended family had begun talking to them again, but her mother used to say that the close bonds they'd shared had been broken.

After her parents' deaths, Stephanie, her social worker, had shared that she and the policeman in charge of her case had attempted to reach out to one of her uncles. He'd been distraught about her parents' deaths but had no interest in taking in their daughter.

Kinsey hadn't been surprised. Serbia was very far away, and her parents' families were strangers. All that did matter to her was that her parents were dead and there was no one who wanted her.

No one to help her. Even though a couple of her friends' parents had volunteered to have her for a few days, the police and the social workers hadn't deemed that to be the best option. After a very brief stop at her house to get the few items that would fit in the tote bag they'd provided, she'd left everything behind.

The next day, following a night in a hotel room with the social worker, she'd been taken to the Walkers' house. Stephanie had attempted to prep her about how things were at the Walkers' residence, but Kinsey had been in a fog. Nothing Stephanie said made much sense at all.

Looking back, Kinsey knew that Stephanie hadn't said very much about the couple because they weren't very nice. They'd been matter of fact and made a point to tell her all the rules in gruff voices. The three other fosters in the house had simply stared at her while she'd sat rigidly, trying not to cry.

Only later, after she was given a twin bed and a drawer, did the other kids tell her about what life there was really like. Well, her roommate, Jessie, and the kid named Nate had. Dillon had simply smirked.

Thinking back to those days, she felt tears fill her eyes. He'd been sneaky and scary. She'd never known anyone like him. She soon realized that even Mr. and Mrs. Walker were a little afraid of him.

He'd left after three months, most likely been moved to another house to become another set of foster parents' burden to bear.

But by then, the damage had been done.

He'd marked her. Hurt her. Pushed her down so hard she'd broken her wrist, then had dared her to tell the Walkers the truth.

Of course, she hadn't. She'd made up a story about running and tripping, which had earned her a lecture about following rules from Mr. Walker.

Dillon had made her so afraid to be alone with other sets of kids that everyone had teased her and called her a ghost.

Four years later, when she was sixteen, she'd met a girl that had the same shell-shocked expression that Kinsey had worn for years. One night they trusted each other enough to share what had happened. They'd gripped each other's hands tight when she'd mentioned Dillon's name.

When it had been time to move again, they'd told the social worker the truth. Eventually, Kinsey had even been asked to speak to someone higher up about her experience. She'd been told that Dillon's behavior had escalated and they were building a case against him.

That had been the last she'd ever heard of him. She hadn't thought about him in years. Years.

Which was why seeing him across the street

in downtown Medina had been so shocking. At first, it hadn't made sense. She'd stared. Studied him. Tried to wrap her head around exactly what she was seeing.

Which was why when she met his eyes again, he'd smirked. He'd remembered. He'd known who she was. And when that sunk in, Kinsey had been sure that he'd started laughing. But maybe that had been her imagination.

Whatever the reason, the urge to flee had been too strong to ignore. After helping Hunt return Betty and Chip to the shelter, she'd waved off his invitation to go to the Blue Door Café and get a coffee and a pastry. Kinsey had felt bad. She didn't want to hurt Hunt's feelings, and she would have also loved to sit in that little café and finally try one of the scones that they were so well known for.

But the need to feel safe was too strong.

So she'd made a poor excuse, pretended she didn't notice the dismay in his eyes, hurried to her vehicle, and driven home.

And then, just as if she was eleven again, she'd curled up in a ball and tried to pretend that everything was going to be okay.

Unfortunately, this didn't work at twenty-one any better than it had ten years previously. Two hours later, after a fitful nap and making a list of ideas about what to do, Kinsey finally felt a little more like herself.

She decided to call the sighting a fluke. If she

didn't see Dillon again, she would do her best to put him out of her mind. She'd done it before; she could do it again.

But if she did see Dillon, she would talk to Claudia. Mrs. Martin was older now and hadn't had a foster. But she was still the wisest woman Kinsey had ever met. Claudia was the type of person who listened carefully and then did something about the problem.

She used to love to say that words only helped in the middle of the night. Otherwise, actions mattered.

Kinsey needed Claudia's matter-of-fact nature more than ever.

Feeling better about her decision, she got up, drank a tall glass of cold water, then called Hunt. They'd exchanged phone numbers during their walk with the dogs so they could volunteer at the shelter again.

Kinsey wouldn't have imagined that she'd call him so soon, but she didn't want to put up another wall between them.

Knowing that she was going to have to be truthful to keep their friendship but vague because she had no desire to share the complete story, she pulled up his phone number.

He answered on the first ring. "Kinsey?"

"Yeah. Hey."

"Is everything is okay?"

"I think so." Forcing herself to continue, she

added, "I wanted to apologize for taking off so fast."

"It was your choice. No apology needed."

Hunt's voice was deep. Steady. As if he had no expectations from her. As if he was used to not expecting anything from anyone. Which might've been the case. But even if it was, she couldn't allow him to believe that she'd treat him like that.

Not after their rocky start and the time they'd spent together with those sweet puppies.

She cleared her throat. "Actually, I think there is an apology needed. See, when we stopped next to the light. Just before we turned..." Kinsey gathered herself together. No way did she want to get all emotional.

He filled in the gap. "I remember. Just before we headed back to the shelter you tensed."

"Yes," she replied, glad that he'd gotten her started. "You see, I thought I saw someone across the way."

"You said that. It was no big deal. There were a lot of people around."

"There were, but this man? Well, I knew him. I mean, I thought I did." She closed her eyes in shame, hating that she was a grown woman but was reacting like the insecure child she used to be.

Hunt was quiet on the other end. She could hear him breathing, letting her know that he was listening but wasn't going to press her to hurry up. As if he was on her timeline. Following her lead.

Few things had ever felt so reassuring.

And it gave her the confidence she needed to say the words. No, to give him the explanation he deserved. Taking yet another fortifying breath, she plunged forward. "It sounds silly, but, um, I was afraid of him when I was a little girl."

"How come? What happened?"

Too much. "It's hard to talk about."

"I'm sure it is, but I need to know something more than what you told me. What did he do?"

"He…" She stopped. Took a breath.

"Did he hurt you, Kinsey?"

"Yes."

"I wish you would have pointed him out to me."

His voice was low and cool. Like iron. "I wasn't a hundred percent sure it was him. You see, it was a shock."

"You haven't seen him in years?"

"I haven't seen him since he left that house." Kinsey forced herself to continue so Hunt wouldn't be forced to keep asking her questions in order to get even the smallest semblance of a story. "He was at the first house I was in."

"When you were a baby?"

"No. No. I mean, he was in the first foster home. It wasn't in Medina. It was farther out in the county."

"All this was right after your parents died, right?"

"Yes. I spent the first night with a social worker. Then they placed me there. My parents had only been gone for a couple of days. In that time I'd been in a hotel room with a social worker, had attended their funeral—which wasn't much at all, and had been taken to my house." Needing to share the memories, even though they'd happened ten years ago, she wanted Hunt to understand just how hard a time it had been.

Forcing herself to continue, she said, "The social worker brought me to my room, handed me a tote bag, and told me that I could only take enough that could fit inside."

"Oh, man. Kinsey, that had to hurt."

"I remember just staring at everything. My clothes. My bed. All my stuffed animals and the books and my jewelry. The art projects and the dolls. I didn't know what to take and what to leave." It had hurt more than he would ever know. It hurt more than she would ever allow herself to admit. Even after all these years, the callousness of the moment, the all-encompassing realization that her life was over as she'd known it, still stung.

She drew a fortifying breath. "Anyway, this guy, he was at my first foster home. I was so scared and confused."

"That was natural. Your whole life had been taken from you."

"It really had been. I didn't know what to do. And the family we were with? Well, they were all about rules." She laughed softly. "Rules and the money they were making from taking in kids."

"Wow, Kinsey."

"I know. They weren't the nicest couple I lived with. I was afraid of them. Of course, I was afraid of just about everyone back then. The other kids thought it was funny. They teased me. But he… he had been cruel. He'd scared me. And…and I hadn't gotten tough yet."

"You were just a little girl, right?"

"I was eleven. Probably old enough to have been tougher than I was."

"Don't say that. No one would've handled that well. No one should, you know?"

"I guess."

"I know. No one, no matter if they were older, would have been okay."

Hunt's sweet acknowledgment wrapped up in his scratchy, gruff voice, did more for her than she'd ever thought was possible. "Thanks for saying that."

"Aww, Kinsey. Honey, I'm sorry you're so upset."

"I'm okay." She needed to be, too. Clearing her throat, she pulled herself together. "Anyway, that is who I saw and why I was so rude. I saw his face, and all the pain of that time came rushing back. All I wanted to do was run away. I couldn't face him."

"You weren't rude, Kinsey. You don't need to put on company manners with me."

She smiled at the phrase. "Maybe not, but I didn't want you to think worse of me."

"Not at all. I thought that I did something. I wasn't sure what."

"No, you did everything right. It was me. All me."

"What are you going to do now?"

"About what?"

"This guy."

"About Dillon? Nothing. I'm hoping it was just a fluke. Like I said, I haven't seen him in a long time. A decade. He must have been in Medina to go to the farmer's market or something. I bet I'll never see him again."

"I hope you don't, but what if you do? I mean, you said he was looking at you, right?"

"Yeah."

"Sorry but you need to have a plan of action."

"You sound like we're in the army. Like I was one of the soldiers under your care."

He chuckled. "If we were in the army and I was talking to you, I wouldn't have sounded like that."

"No?"

"No. I sounded much grumpier."

In spite of herself, she smiled. "For some reason that doesn't surprise me."

"Yeah, I bet not. So, what are you going to do if you see him again?"

"I don't know," Kinsey admitted, though she was pretty sure it was a lie. There was a very good chance that she'd react the same exact way that she just had. She would run and hide.

"Kinsey, sorry but that isn't a very good answer."

It was said in a low drawl. It was sweet and gave

her goose bumps. "I know, but it's the best I can do." *Please don't press me on this*, she mentally called out.

"You know, back when I was in the army, my job was to fix things for my officers. I had a major that I worked with a lot. He and I got along real well, and he relied on me to smooth things over so he could do his job better. I was good at it. So good that half the time he hadn't even realized that things could've been different."

"Sounds like he took you for granted."

Hunt chuckled. "He did, but I didn't care because all the soldiers and junior officers knew the truth." He lowered his voice. "And after I got hurt and had to leave, he reached out to me to say that I was darn good at what I did. That he'd been grateful for my service and honored to have worked with me."

"Wow."

"Kinsey, I didn't tell you all this to seem better in your eyes. I'm trying to let you know that I might have a limp and I might only just do handyman stuff now but I'm still me. I can help you."

"I never thought you were just anything. And thanks for that. I appreciate the offer."

"I'm hoping you'll take me up on it."

"I'm hoping I'll never need to."

After a pause, he replied, his voice sounding a little scratchier than it had. "I'm sure you've heard this before, but it doesn't mean it's not true. Hope is not a solution."

"I know. I once knew a girl who said *hope* was the worst four letter word she knew."

He chuckled. "It can be. Of course, others could make the argument that hope is the only thing that can lead someone out of the abyss."

"Amen to that," she whispered. "I'm glad I called you."

"Me, too. I'm real glad, too, Kinsey. I'll see you on Monday, yeah?"

"Sure."

"If you need something beforehand, let me know, though."

"Thanks, I'll do that."

When she hung up, Kinsey sighed. Analyzed her feelings. Realized that she was still reluctant to run into Dillon but that maybe she didn't have to be as afraid of him as she'd been.

After all, she wasn't alone anymore.

CHAPTER ELEVEN

HUNT WALKED NEXT door to see Claudia and Larry on Sunday. Larry had mentioned that they were going to go to church on Saturday night so they could do some chores around the house on Sunday. Claudia was going to organize the pantry, and he had a lot of yardwork to take care of.

Hunt figured he could help him trim some bushes and maybe mow his lawn. Larry was still capable of doing a full day's work outside, but he was getting older.

Besides, when he'd mentioned helping out to Claudia, she'd offered to make him breakfast as a trade.

She'd gone all out, too—biscuits, sausage patties, eggs, and sausage gravy.

"Claudia, this is the last thing my cholesterol needs," Larry griped.

"Don't worry, dear. I made you a fruit parfait."

"You don't expect me to ignore all this and eat fruit?"

"I think you need to do what makes you happy,

honey," she said with a sly wink to Hunt. All three of them knew that Doc would likely eat both.

Hunt grinned at her as he heaped his plate full of Claudia's amazing cooking. "This looks terrific. I haven't had sausage and gravy in years."

"I don't make it very often. Obviously," she added with a meaningful look at her husband. "But I remembered this was your favorite. And it's been a while, hasn't it?"

"Too long."

"We should make plans to eat together more often. Breakfast, lunch, dinner, coffee..."

Hunt smiled at her. "Agreed." Digging in, he barely stopped himself from moaning. The biscuits were light, the gravy was perfectly seasoned, and the scrambled eggs were fluffy and sprinkled with cheese. It was the kind of breakfast he used to dream about when he was deployed. Filling, over the top, and made with a dash of Claudia Martin's kindness and love. "Everything is as good as I remember."

"Thank you, Hunt."

"I'll help you with the dishes."

"Okay."

Larry guffawed. "You didn't give the boy even a second to take back his offer."

"That's because I might miss cooking for him, but I don't miss doing all the dishes."

That seemed as good of a segue as he was going to get. Still thinking about his conversation with

Kinsey, he said, "I never heard how you ended up taking Kinsey in."

Claudia set her fork down. "As our foster daughter?"

"Yes. Did you two just decide to do it?"

Larry and Claudia exchanged glances. Larry looked as puzzled by Hunt's question as Claudia probably was, but didn't say anything.

"No, it wasn't anything like that," she said after a moment. "We heard about Kinsey through a mutual friend."

"Really? I just assumed you started to wish you had a child."

"I did. But I'm not the one who made it happen. It was Larry."

The man sipped his coffee. "It all started because I knew Stephanie Burnett, Kinsey's social worker. I'd been her dentist for years."

"Plus we went to the same church," Claudia explained.

"For the last year, she'd been telling us about a little girl under her care who she was worried about." Doc waved a hand. "She couldn't tell us her name or anything. Just the basics." He frowned. "Stephanie was really worried about her."

"She had said she had a little girl under her care who was fading away," Claudia added. "None of the homes she'd gone to had been a good fit."

Remembering the pain etched on Kinsey's face when she'd talked about the shock of entering foster care, Hunt said, "She told me that she'd had a really hard time."

Claudia nodded. "She'd been grieving her parents' loss, and some of the homes she'd been placed in had been difficult."

"I'm not trying to say anything bad about the other foster families," Larry added. "It's a hard vocation and a lot of people are incredible. But, well, it's hard on the kids, you know? Some adjust and some don't."

"Kinsey didn't," Hunt said.

"Not at all." Larry stared off into the distance, remembering. "Kinsey was a sweet little thing and kept retreating more into herself." After taking a bite of a biscuit, he said, "Anyway, one day I was visiting with Steph after she got her teeth cleaned, and she got emotional."

"She started crying," Claudia explained.

"She said that Kinsey's situation was keeping her up at night. That she felt she needed a home."

"Kinsey had started changing."

He hated to hear that. "Changing how?"

"Some of her sweetness was fading," Larry explained. "She got more closed off." He motioned with a hand. "Kept most everything to herself."

"She was learning how to fit in," Hunt said. "Survive."

"Yep. It would seem so." Exchanging a look with Larry, Claudia continued, "The day Stephanie brought Kinsey over was one I'll never forget."

"She was like a scared dog. We could sense that she wanted to trust us but didn't dare," Larry said. He flashed a smile. "Boy howdy, was she a handful."

"But she was sweet, too." Chuckling, Claudia continued. "Those first four months she was here, I must have called Stephanie every other day."

"Kinsey was that bad?"

"Not *bad*. It was more like she was hot and cold. One moment she'd offer to help me wash dishes, and she'd stand at the sink without a complaint. Then, the next moment she'd refuse to bring her laundry downstairs so I could do it."

Hunt leaned back in his chair. He loved hearing all these stories about Kinsey as a little girl. He thought they were adorable. And hysterical. "Sorry, but it's hard to picture her being like that."

"If you hadn't been busy with your own life, you would've seen it. Your parents were half afraid of her!" Larry said.

"So what happened?"

Claudia shrugged. "We made it six months, and then Stephanie came over to speak to her."

"And offered to take her to the mall."

"All Stephanie had wanted was to see how she was doing." Her voice softened. "But Kinsey was sure that Steph was about to take her from us and put her into another home. She threw a fit."

"She ran right over to me and wrapped her arms around my waist and promised that she'd do the dishes every night if we'd let her stay," Larry said. "It was the most heart-wrenching thing I'd ever heard in my life."

Hunt had a lump in his throat. "Oh, man. I would've lost it."

"I'm not gonna lie—I did lose it. Even though I was a grown man, I started crying and got on my knees. I hugged that girl back and told her nothing was going to pull her out of this house. Nothing. She was ours."

"And that's all it took," Claudia said with a pleased smile.

Hunt was impressed. "Really?"

She chuckled. "Oh goodness, no. Not really. She still had her moments."

"She'd throw a fit if things that she'd planned on couldn't happen," Larry said. "And boy, that girl could cuss."

"Things did get better after that," Claudia said. "By the time she was with us for a year, Larry and I knew we'd be heartbroken if she left. We even asked Stephanie about adopting Kinsey."

"What happened?"

"Kinsey didn't want that. She said she didn't want her parents to think that she forgot about them."

And…there was that lump again. "I guess I can see that."

"I never could," Larry said. "I wanted to be able to say she was 'our' girl. But then one night she confided that there was a part of her that couldn't handle really knowing her parents were dead."

"The principal had told Kinsey the news, you see. And even though Stephanie took her to the funeral, there wasn't much to it and they'd been cremated."

"So she never got closure," Hunt said.

"She never did." Claudia dabbed at her eyes. "Boy, I haven't thought about all of that in a while."

"Thanks for sharing with me. I won't say anything to Kinsey."

"Oh, you can. She knows that we've told her story before. We talked at a fundraiser years ago for the county. That's something you can say about Kinsey—she's never shied away from her past."

"Why are you so curious, Hunt?"

"We've kind of become friends. She met me at the animal shelter on Saturday, and she shared some things with me."

"But you didn't want to ask her more yourself?"

"It hadn't occurred to me to ask, if I'm being honest. But, ah, what got me thinking was that she got spooked."

"What happened?" Larry asked.

"She thought she saw some guy who she used to know in one of her foster homes." After debating a second, he added, "I think she was scared of him."

"Did you see him?"

"No. She didn't let on that she saw him. I thought

maybe I'd said something wrong. But she called to apologize later that night."

"Oh, dear."

"I'm not sure what to do, you guys. I think she's really scared about seeing him again."

"She thinks she will?"

Hunt nodded. "A part of me wants to reassure her that it was just a coincidence, but she said he was staring right at her. And smirking. It really rattled her."

"What did you say?"

"I said that if she saw him again to let me know. Maybe I can go talk to him or something."

"That poor girl. She's worked so hard to put the past behind her."

"Let us know if we can do anything."

"I will, though she might talk to you about it first."

"Maybe," Claudia said in a soft tone. "But I'm just not sure that she will. I've always gotten the feeling that she doesn't want to be any trouble for us."

"Hunt, you seem pretty concerned. Why? Are you dating her?" Larry asked.

"No. We're just friends."

"Hmm," he said. Then before Hunt could say anything else, he stood up. "You know what? I do believe that yard of mine isn't going to get fixed up on its own. How do you feel about mowing some grass today, Hunter?"

“I’d be happy to do that as soon as I help Claudia with some dishes.”

“There’s a lot of yardwork, Claude.”

“There’s a lot of dishes, dear,” she said as she stood up as well. “You go start pulling weeds. I’ll send out Hunter soon. Is that okay with you, Hunt?”

“Yes, ma’am.”

“That’s what I like to hear.”

For the next hour he handwashed pots and pans while Claudia stacked the dishwasher and wiped counters. Neither of them said much.

He had a pretty good idea why.

It was a lot to think about.

CHAPTER TWELVE

SHE'D ONLY HAD to work a half day on Monday. Twice a month, Dr. Martin had his assistant, Victoria Geary, come in to help with insurance claims. It was a thankless job and could often be both time-consuming and difficult. Some insurance companies were a lot easier to deal with than others.

The first time Doc had relayed that he didn't think she was experienced enough to handle some difficult accounts, Kinsey had been a little offended. She might not have earned a bunch of diplomas, but she was pretty good with paperwork and very organized.

However, after witnessing the amount of hoops and minutes on hold that Victoria had to handle, she'd changed her tune. Now whenever she had a half day off, she tried to do something fun. Try out a new restaurant, go to the library or a bookstore. Go walking or have lunch with Claudia.

After spying the menu at a new deli just two blocks away from the Root Candle Factory, Kinsey walked in the door of the establishment with her mind on corned beef. She didn't know why, but she really liked Reuben sandwiches. She just wasn't sure whether she should order a full-size sandwich or just a half. She was hungry, so half a sandwich didn't sound like enough. But what if she didn't finish it? Did she want to stick sauerkraut in her refrigerator?

As she waited in line, she kept debating the options, changing her mind every couple of seconds.

"May I help you?"

"Yes. I'll have a half Reuben, please," she said, still looking at the small menu in her hand. "With chips and a pickle, too."

"You've gotten so proper and polite."

Her head popped up, and she stared at the man behind the counter. "Dillon."

He grinned. "Ah, so you do remember me."

"What are you doing here?"

"Working." Taking a glance over his shoulder, he added, "That'll be seven dollars."

Kinsey felt like running, but there was a line of people behind her. Quickly, she pulled out a ten-dollar bill. "Here."

"You know, I wasn't sure it was you when I saw you across the street. You look great."

A chill skittered up her spine. "Thanks."

"Here's your change and your order number."

Instead of setting the cash on the counter, he had it resting on his palm. She did her best to retrieve it without touching him.

She pocketed the change and glanced at the number: twenty-eight.

"Twenty-three!" the manager called out.

Kinsey moved a few inches to her right. She had five more to go. She bit her lip. Why had she come in here today? She should've just gone home.

"So, Kins…do you live near here?" Dillon asked.

She felt at least four people staring at her. Waiting for her response. Her cheeks started to heat. "Kind of."

"We should get together. Catch up. What do you think?"

She thought she'd never see him again. She couldn't believe it.

"Kinsey, what do you think?"

"Ah." She froze. Just stood there.

"Dillon, stop talking and move on!" the manager called out. "Twenty-four!"

That pulled Kinsey out of her trance at last. Without looking Dillon's way, she moved farther down the counter.

"Give me your number, and I'll call you," he said.

All she seemed to be capable of doing was shaking her head no.

Dillon looked disappointed. Even as he took the next person's order, he continued to sneak glances her way.

"Twenty-five!"

Three more numbers to go. Kinsey watched the three people behind the counter make sandwiches.

Tried to see which one looked like a Reuben. All the while, she continued to feel Dillon watching her. Just like he used to do when no one else was around.

"You know, at first I thought it was kind of cute how he was so taken with you, but now it's getting a bit much, isn't it?" the woman who'd been behind her murmured.

"Kind of," she admitted.

"Don't worry. I bet he's the type who probably says those things to a pretty girl at least five times a day."

Kinsey certainly hoped so. It would be a relief if he wasn't actually being as creepy as she thought he was. She smiled weakly.

"Twenty-eight!" the manager called out.

"That's me," Kinsey said as she quickly approached the window.

"Enjoy," the manager said.

"Thanks."

Taking her bag, she hurried out the door. Pushed aside her plan to eat on one of the park benches nearby. Instead, she rushed back to her apartment.

She needed to get inside, lock the door firmly behind her. And try to come to grips with the fact that Dillon really was in Medina.

And even worse than that… Dillon had not only not forgotten her, but seemed determined to see her again.

She couldn't think of anything worse.

CHAPTER THIRTEEN

USUALLY EDNA ENJOYED getting deliveries for Loaves of Love. The food pantry and community kitchen was doing so well, she often felt like it had taken a life of its own.

But that morning, as she stared at the growing pile of expensive pans, all she felt was dismay.

Her husband noticed. "Edna, you've been quiet all morning. What's going on?"

"I'm starting to feel like these muffin pans are a huge mistake." She frowned as she unpacked yet another box of six commercial-grade muffin tins for the Loaves of Love kitchen.

Wayne looked up from the invoices he was attempting to organize. "How could they be a mistake? These are top of the line. They'll last years and years."

"That's the thing. Because they're top of the line, they were expensive. And I bought twenty-four of them. And what if no one wants to make muffins? Then they'll just sit there on the shelf."

"I doubt that's going to happen."

"But it could. And if it does, I'm going to feel

horrible. I'll have wasted money that could've gone toward actual food."

"Edna."

"Sorry, but you know I don't want to take advantage of anyone's trust in me."

"You haven't taken advantage of anyone."

But she was on a roll. "Wayne, people who donate expect me to be a good caretaker of the funds." She knew she was nitpicking, but it felt important.

"Are you trying to say that spending money on muffin pans is different than on rolling pins or measuring cups?"

Picking up the scissors, she cut a slit in the bubble wrap that the pan was wrapped in. "Maybe. You know I came up with the idea to bake dinner rolls on a whim. I probably should've just stayed with what we were doing, right?"

"No."

When she realized he wasn't going to expand upon his answer, she winced. "Wow, that was firm."

Reaching over, Wayne collected the bubble wrap and tossed it into the trash bag. "I hope so. Listen, darling, I know it's your job to be a good steward of everyone's donations, but we're not using money to go away for the weekend. You bought muffin pans." Holding one up, he tilted his head to one side. "Pans that are too big to fit into our oven at home."

"I guess you're right."

"I know I am." Reaching for her hand, he linked his fingers through hers. "Now, how about you tell me what's really going on?"

"Nothing."

"Mm-hmm. How about telling me again."

"Fine." She lowered her voice. "I had hoped that something would've happened between Hunt and Kinsey by now."

Wayne groaned. "Edna, you have to stop meddling."

"I'm not meddling. I've been matchmaking, and it isn't going very well. I thought when I suggested to Hunt that he ask Kinsey if she'd like to walk dogs with him something would've happened by now."

"Such as what?"

"Oh, stop. You know. Like they'd be going out to eat together. Or I'd see them at the farmers market." Feeling as frustrated by his questions as she was with the couple's progress, she waved a hand. "I thought that something would've happened between them. But nothing has."

"Nothing has happened that you know about."

Setting the latest tin she'd unwrapped on the counter, Edna studied his face. "That I know about? What is that supposed to mean?"

"Only that their relationship is their business, not yours."

"I'm not in their business. All I want to do is help them."

"You want to help them by getting into their business." He squeezed her hand. "Honey, I'm not trying to tell you that you're being too involved, but you do seem awfully emotionally invested. Your heart is in the right place, but sometimes you have to let people make their own mistakes, you know."

Edna opened her mouth to argue but closed it just as quickly. Because he kind of did have a good point. She was emotionally invested. Then there was the fact that every relationship had its own timeline.

That was it! Hunt and Kinsey were in a valley right now. Things would move along in the right direction soon. "I think I need to be more patient."

"I think that's a great idea." He winked.

She pretended not to notice. "Back to these pans, I suppose you're right. We'll use them."

"We will. The volunteers are going to have your back and be thrilled to make cloverleaf rolls."

Wayne's words stayed with her as she later carried the pans to a commercial sink that they'd recently installed. Here, there was more than enough space to wash multiple sets of mixing bowls, bread pans, and measuring spoons and cups. Seeing Chloe Winner-Smith, a frequent volunteer and recent bride of Jamison Smith, she said, "Would you feel comfortable organizing a team to wash these?"

"Of course."

"Thank you, dear. Before you leave, I realized that I haven't touched base with you."

"About what?"

"Madison and Cope." Maddie and Cope might've been just out of high school, but they were another one of her relationship success stories. At least, she hoped they still were.

Chloe smiled. "They're terrific. In love."

"Just like you and Jamison," she prodded.

"Yes," she replied with a laugh. "Just like Jamison and me."

"I trust things are going well? The first year of marriage can be difficult..."

"It's going very well. Great." Chloe was starting to look a little guarded, like she was worried that Edna was going to start asking even more personal questions.

She didn't intend to do that. Not too much anyway. "I'm glad," she said simply.

Turning back toward the door, Edna reminded herself about what a success story Chloe and Jamison were. And even though their relationship wasn't about her, she had been a little bit responsible for making the match.

Wayne had been right. She needed to count her blessings and stop taking it as a failure if everyone she attempted to get together didn't actually get together.

Feeling better about that decision, she decided that it was time to head out. Wayne wanted to watch the ball game on TV, so that would give her a perfect opportunity to visit the cute new accessory store that had opened right off Main Street.

Yes. That's what she needed to do. A little bit of retail therapy, followed by a lazy afternoon in her screened porch with a good book.

Just as she was about to head out, the front door opened. Kinsey stepped inside.

"Hi, dear," she said with a smile.

"Hey, Edna."

Even though Kinsey was wearing a bright yellow sundress and darling white sandals, the young woman didn't look like her usual bright self. In a softer voice, Edna added, "Hey, is everything okay?"

"To be honest, I don't know."

"I'm sorry." Scanning her face, Edna debated about what to say. She didn't want to overstep but also didn't want to inadvertently lead Kinsey to believe that she didn't care. She settled with giving the young woman a little pat on her arm. "Let me know if I can help in any way."

"Actually…"

The poor girl's brown eyes were so troubled. It broke her heart. "Ask away, dear," she encouraged. "I meant what I said."

"I hate to ask you this, but would you happen to have a minute to give me some advice?"

"Of course. And I can even give you two." *Glad to be feeling needed again*, Edna thought quickly. "Let's get out of here and go to the Blue Door Café. We'll be able to take our time. They're so good about letting everyone linger at the tables for as long as they want."

"Thanks. I can't tell you how happy I am to see you. I don't know what I would've done if you weren't here."

Wrapping an arm around Kinsey's shoulders, Edna pulled her in for a quick hug. "Believe it or not, I kind of feel the same way about seeing you."

"Really?" Kinsey's eyes were filled with hope.

"Oh yes. I wouldn't lie about that." As they started for the door, Edna added, "It's been quite the day. Let's head down the street, and I'll tell you all about it."

CHAPTER FOURTEEN

"My goodness. What a lovely day, Kinsey!" Edna exclaimed as they walked along the sidewalk in downtown Medina the following morning. "I'm so glad we're going out for coffee."

"Me, too." Kinsey knew that it might've seemed strange, but she often thought of Edna as her adopted grandmother. Whereas Larry and Claudia Martin had become her almost-parents, Edna had become her almost-grandmother. She supposed it was a normal thing to have happened. What else could she do when she had no family around?

Whether it was normal or not, she was grateful to have three people in her life to depend on. Especially at moments like this, when she really needed some good advice about something very personal. She didn't like to think about the four years she'd spent in various foster homes before landing at the Martins' home.

If she wasn't careful, her brain would flip a switch and she'd return to the girl she'd been after her parents died. A scared, confused girl who wasn't sure where she fit in the world. She'd stop sleeping again. Forget to eat. Descend into depression. Some people might've liked to analyze every little thing that had happened in their past, but she was the opposite. She did her best not to think of anything before she'd turned sixteen. Sure, it wasn't healthy, but neither was chocolate cake, and no one in their right mind would refuse a slice of delicious homemade cake if it was placed in front of them.

After they entered the Blue Door Café, ordered coffees and scones, and then eventually found a place to sit, Edna relaxed against her chair. "This place makes me happy. Every time I come inside, I wish I came here more often."

"I feel the same way. I love the black-and-white photos on the walls and the old jazz standards they're always playing. It's cozy in here."

"And bright and cheerful," Edna said with a nod. "Plus, I always see friendly faces here."

"That's probably because everyone is in a good mood when they walk in the door."

"I agree," she said with a smile.

That little conversation was why Edna was so good to be around, Kinsey decided. No matter what the topic, she made it easy to discuss.

Which was probably why her gut had told her to reach out to Edna. She needed this woman's help in talking out her problem. "Thanks for joining me spur of the moment."

"No reason to thank me. I like coffee and I like

you, Kinsey. I always have. Now, how about we stop procrastinating and you tell me what's on your mind?"

"Sorry. I'm trying. It's not easy for me to talk about it."

Edna ran a finger along the side of her ceramic mug. "This sounds serious. I'm guessing it's either about work, a relationship, or something in your past."

"You're right. It's the last one." Taking a fortifying breath, she said, "Edna, I saw that guy from one of my foster homes again. Do you remember I told you that there was one boy I hadn't liked at all?"

Immediately Edna's gray eyes softened into concern. "Maybe it's time you told me about him. Is he older or younger than you?"

"Older. Two years older." Boy, just saying this much was so difficult. Even though she had the urge to rub her hand along the raised scar on her leg, Kinsey forced herself to continue. "His name is Dillon."

"When and where did you see him?"

"I saw him downtown. I was walking shelter dogs with Hunt, and when we stopped, I noticed Dillon staring at me from across the street."

"Staring, how?"

"Staring like a smirk." Pushing herself, Kinsey added, "Staring like he'd found me on purpose and he was happy."

"Happy?"

"Happy because he knew how I'd react. He knew I'd be upset."

Edna stared at her for a long moment. "And let me guess—he wasn't one of your favorite people."

Kinsey shook her head. "He wasn't. Not by a long shot. I was afraid of him."

"How come?"

It took some doing, but Kinsey made herself be completely honest about Dillon. "He was at the first house I was placed in. It, ah, didn't have the best reputation."

"The foster parents weren't good people?"

"They were okay, I guess. But, well, it was like they did the minimum."

"Hmm."

"My social worker, Stephanie, had told me that I'd only have to stay there for a short period, until she could find a better placement."

"I don't like that she put you in a home where she knew you'd be unhappy."

"I don't think she had a choice, Edna. She had to place me somewhere." Forcing herself to continue, she added, "After living there two months, something happened."

"What happened?"

"I can't talk about it. All that matters is that Stephanie moved me to another home. I learned later that they moved Dillon to someplace else, too."

"Stephanie didn't tell you?"

Kinsey shook her head. "Kids don't learn things like that. All that mattered to me was that I never saw him again. I even tried to forget about him."

"Were you able to?"

"Sometimes." Crossing her legs, she added, "I thought I had made peace with what happened. I mean, if he was in foster care, too, he'd probably also been through some trauma. But when I saw him at the deli today, everything he did to me came rushing back. I think I'm still afraid of him now."

Edna's usually bright expression turned serious. "I think I better hear the whole story."

After taking a fortifying sip of her drink, Kinsey dived in, giving Edna the abbreviated version of the story she had told Hunt. It was sad, but even this second telling didn't ease her nerves. She couldn't shake the uneasy feeling that Dillon appearing in her world had brought.

"I don't know what to do," she admitted when she finished. "I don't know what I'm going to do if he starts showing up everywhere that I am. I want to avoid him as much as possible."

Edna's eyebrows rose. "You've got a big problem on your hands."

"I really do. I was hoping you might have some ideas about how I should deal with him."

Looking apologetic, she added, "I wish I could, but I'm not sure that I'm the best person to give you good advice. I don't want to say the wrong thing."

"I understand." She did, too. Edna didn't want to dip a toe into her past. She likely had her own problems to worry about. "Thanks for listening."

"Hey, not so fast. Just because I don't have an instant answer doesn't mean I don't want to help you." She took a sip of her drink, studying Kinsey over the rim of the cup. When she put it down again, she spoke. "Kinsey, dear, tell me the truth. Are you going to be on edge all day if you're just hoping and praying that he won't want to talk to you again?"

"Yes."

"Hmm." She took a bite of scone. Closed her eyes in delight as she chewed. When she set down her fork again, she had a more determined look on her face. "I think what you need is a plan of action. You can't just wait and live in fear."

"I don't understand what you mean." Edna was sounding very cryptic.

"I think you need a reason for Dillon to decide that it's not worth his time to bother you. It needs to be something strong and solid."

Kinsey had no idea what Edna was talking about. "I don't know what that could be."

"I do." Edna crossed her legs. Tapped a finger on the table. Then her eyes brightened. "Kinsey, what you need is a boyfriend."

She laughed. "You are acting like I can find one of those at the library or something."

"Oh, I'm not talking about a real one. A pretend one. You know, for show."

"Sorry, but I don't think those are all that easy to find. Plus, I don't even know what the fake-boyfriend thing would entail."

"You are making things seem too difficult. All you two would have to do is be seen in places together. He could hold your hand…look smitten."

"I think you've been watching way too many made-for-TV movies, Edna. No man is going to want to do that. And for the record, having a pretend guy sounds like more trouble than it's worth." Plus, who wanted to start holding some stranger's hand? Eww.

"Do you really think so?" Edna asked. "I can only see benefits."

"Listen, I appreciate you being willing to listen to me. I think that was what I really needed."

"But I haven't helped you."

"You did, though. You let me talk this through. Even more importantly, you listened."

"You never have to thank me for being your friend, Kinsey. Even if you decide to never volunteer at Loaves of Love again or if you elect to not take my very good advice, I'll still be your friend," she added with a wink.

"Thanks. I appreciate that."

Standing up, Edna gave her a hug. "I better get

on my way. Wayne's probably wondering where I wandered off to."

"Thanks again. See you later."

Practically the minute she walked out, Edna's phone rang. Amused, Kinsey watched Edna walk down the street with her phone to her ear. She seemed to be talking as fast as she could. Kinsey had a feeling that Wayne had decided to take things into his own hands and give his wife a call to find out where she was.

That was what she wanted. A man in her life who she could depend on. Who cared enough about her to check in regularly. In spite of herself, she thought about Hunt. Would he be the kind of guy who would encourage her to visit with friends but check in, just to make sure she was good?

Yeah. That was Hunt. There was a seriousness about him that couldn't be denied. She had a feeling that if he cared about someone enough to be her guy, he was going to be all in, too, like Wayne was with Edna. He seemed to be always looking out for her—even when she was on her own, he checked in often and made sure she was happy.

Of course, she and Hunt didn't have that kind of relationship. But he would be like that with some other woman. She knew it.

After checking her phone and not seeing any messages that she had to respond to immediately, she took her half cup of coffee that was now cool and asked the barista to heat it up. Then she sat down to happily finish her scone and coffee.

She decided to scan some of her favorite apps for inspiration for her bedroom, too. When she'd moved in she'd found a bed-in-a-bag set on the sale rack in a discount center. As the weeks wore on, though, she began to hate everything about it. It would be awesome to replace her ugly comforter and sheets with new, soft, pretty ones instead.

"Kinsey, here you go," Angel, the barista said.

"Oh my gosh. Did you make me a whole new drink?"

"I did. You're here a lot. We can't have you sipping cold coffee."

"Thanks so much."

"Of course." Angel smiled as she walked back behind the counter. "Let me know if you need anything else."

Just as Kinsey was about to answer, she noticed that Angel frowned at something in the distance.

Confused, Kinsey glanced behind her and then felt a wave of panic.

Dillon was standing just outside the window. He had a phone in his hand, and at first glance, he didn't look out of place at all. Just a regular guy, probably waiting for his girl or a friend to get out of the coffee shop.

But he was standing too close to the window and staring inside too intently to be anything but disconcerting.

When she caught his eye, he lifted his phone and took her picture. Then he grinned yet again before turning away. Seconds later, he was out of sight.

He'd stood there on purpose until she'd noticed him. He'd wanted to get a rise out of her. To put her on edge.

And made her realize that she wasn't going to be able to hide from the truth anymore.

Dillon had come back into her life, and he seemed pretty happy to be there. Whether she wanted him there or not.

CHAPTER FIFTEEN

INSTALLING THE BRIGHTLY patterned tile backsplash in the dentist office break room was going to be the death of him, Hunt decided. Not only did Doc want the tile to go halfway to the ceiling, but Claudia had chosen tiles that had to line up perfectly and go in a certain order.

It hadn't seemed difficult when he'd first laid them out, but as he progressed, the small job was taking a really long time. Plus, the tiles weren't all that sturdy. So far, three of them had chipped, which messed up the pattern. That freaked him out, too. Claudia hadn't mentioned the tiles being expensive or special ordered. But sometimes she did things like that.

And because it was Friday afternoon, Doc wasn't in the office. He'd seen patients in the morning before leaving for the weekend. Hunt was pretty sure he was on the golf course right about now, which meant that he wouldn't be answering any texts.

The only person left in the office was Kinsey,

and he didn't think she had any idea if there were more boxes of tile.

If he chipped any more tiles, Hunt was pretty sure that he was going to have to stop until he could get ahold of both Dr. Martin and Claudia. Dr. Martin would want to know why the break room was still torn up and Claudia would need to get a heads-up in case she had to place an order for more tiles.

Neither were going to be very happy with him about the situation.

"Come on, you," he muttered as he got ready to make a cut in a bright blue piece. "I really do not want to get on the phone. Don't fail me now."

"Everything okay in there?" Kinsey asked from the doorway.

Startling him. And…there went his concentration. And there went yet another tile. He groaned. Shoot. He was going to have to get on the phone.

"Hunt?" Kinsey peeked in. "Did you hear me?"

"Yeah, I did. And no," he added as he continued to stare at broken tile on the countertop, "everything is not okay."

"Oh no." Walking to his side, she scanned the area. "What's wrong?"

"This." He glared at the offending tile in his hand.

"Oh no! Did you get cut?" Before he could tell her no, she reached for his hand and started inspecting it.

She had slim, cool, delicate-looking fingers. So different from his own scarred, rough, calloused ones.

And sure, he wasn't cut. But that didn't prevent him from allowing her to fuss over him for a couple of seconds. After all, he couldn't remember the last time anyone had been so concerned over something so minor.

Or maybe it was simply because this was Kinsey, and he was starting to think that pretty much everything she did was both cute and adorable.

But then he got ahold of himself. Every soldier—both man and woman—in his former unit would be having a field day if they ever saw him acting so childish. It was another reminder that he wasn't the same. He wasn't the man he used to be.

He limped, he had bad dreams, and, it seemed, he enjoyed being coddled. He pulled his hand away. "I'm fine," he said in a far harsher voice than he'd intended to use. "No cuts on me."

"Oh. Sorry."

Realizing that he'd embarrassed her, Hunt attempted to get himself together. "No, I'm the one who should be apologizing. You're trying to finish work for the day, and I've been making a huge racket."

"The noise wasn't that bad."

"It kind of was. When I wasn't using the tile cutter, I've been barking at the tiles themselves."

She smiled. "Did they listen?"

"Not even a little bit."

"I hate when that happens," she joked.

And just like that, his bad mood dissipated. Kinsey had a way about her that he enjoyed, plus she never acted stiff or tense around him. Instead, she seemed to accept him as he was—no matter what he was doing.

As for him? Well, it was getting harder and harder not to ignore how pretty she was. Today she was dressed in a long, loose, floral sundress. It showed off her tan and was completely feminine.

Realizing that he'd been staring, he cleared his throat. Glanced at his watch. "Hey, it's Friday afternoon. You're usually long gone by now. What are you doing here?"

"I'm finishing up. I should be ready to go soon."

Hunt was about to nod and go back to the uncooperative tile when he realized that Kinsey didn't seem like her usual self. She kept fussing with the ends of her long brown hair. "Hey, what's going on?"

"Nothing you need to worry about." She attempted to smile. "Good luck with that backsplash."

It didn't fool him for a second. "Let's try that again. What's going on, Kinsey?"

"I saw that guy again."

Every inch of him went on alert. "Where was he?" he barked before he reminded himself to tone it down a notch.

Kinsey looked taken aback by his tone. "I was in the Blue Door Café drinking coffee. When I looked up, he was standing outside the window watching me."

"What did you do then?" he asked, taking care to keep his voice softer. "Did you go see what he wanted?"

"No." She looked miserable. "I just sat there and got scared. Again."

It was all he could do to not pull her into his arms. "Kinsey, listen. You're a grown woman. Why, I've seen you handle twenty people in the waiting room more than once. You can be tough. He can't hurt you now."

"That's easy for you to say. You're a man who was in the military. You probably know all kinds of ways to put him in his place."

Yeah, he did, and he was also starting to look forward to doing that.

But it wasn't going to help Kinsey get over her fear.

"That's true, but I met a lot of women who were plenty tough. You can be that way too."

"I'm pretty sure there was a compliment in there somewhere, but what you're saying isn't true. I can't be tough with him. Even if I took a bunch of lessons in self-defense, I couldn't. It's like he has a hold on me. Every time I see him, I freeze."

"Did you tell the cops or Doc or someone?"

"Just you. And Edna."

"Edna? Loaves of Love Edna?" He hadn't thought Kinsey and she were that close.

"Yeah. She's a good listener."

"Edna is." He smiled at her encouragingly. Kinsey needed support and encouragement. She didn't have a brother, sister, or even a birth parent to talk to. In a softer tone, he asked, "Did she give you any advice?"

"Yes, but I don't know. It was kind of dumb."

"That doesn't sound like her. She's usually pretty matter of fact."

"That's how I've always thought about her, too." She shrugged. "Her idea was so outlandish I first thought she was joking."

"What was it?"

Kinsey averted her eyes. "That I should get a pretend boyfriend."

"A what?" He had to have misunderstood.

"You heard right." Her brown eyes were bright with amusement. "Edna acted like I had scores of men I was buddies with." Looking away from him, she added, "Even if I did, how could I call a guy I was friends with and ask him to start holding my hand in public?"

Even thinking about some random guy holding her delicate hand in his made Hunt seethe. "What did you say?"

"Not much." Kinsey fussed with a pleat in her dress. "I mean, I knew Edna was trying to help. But, Hunt, it was such a bad idea."

"How come?"

"Because even if I could find a guy who was willing to help me out, Dillon would know I was faking in a heartbeat."

He could hear it now. The tension, laced with the threat of tears. She was scared to death. Walking away from the mess of tiles on the counter, he reached for her hand. "Hey," he said in a soft voice. "We'll figure this out, Kinsey."

"I don't think so."

Pulling her out of the room, he walked her to the front waiting area. Turned on a light. "Come on. We're going to sit down and try to come up with a plan."

"It's not that easy, Hunt. He's not a nice man."

"Before you saw him at the deli, when was the last time you spoke to him?" he asked in a soft tone.

"It was years."

"What? Like five?"

She shook her head. "No. I didn't see Dillon again after he left the house."

"So…the last time you saw him was when you were eleven? Twelve?"

"Eleven."

Hunt fought to keep his expression blank. But inwardly, he winced. Kinsey looked like she was trying not to cry. After all this time, even the memory could bring her to tears. "Tell me about that girl," he said.

She frowned. “What girl?”

“The girl that was in that home when she was eleven. What was she like?”

“Like? Oh, wow. I was in a fog most of the time. Scared.”

“You were grieving, too.”

“Oh, yes. I cried every night. I missed my mom. My dad. I missed my room. My stuff. My life.” Lifting her eyes to his, she added, “It was the hardest time in my life.”

“I’m sorry to make you think of that, but my point is that you’re thinking of this guy through that lens.” When she stilled, he added, “Your grieving, in-shock, eleven-year-old lens.”

“So…that memory I have of him might be completely different than how he really was?”

“Maybe.”

“So, what? You think that there’s no way he really was that bad?”

“I’m saying that he might have been bad, but you were a little girl in a vulnerable place. That’s not who you are now.”

Kinsey stared at him. “You’re right. I’ve been freaking myself out. In my head, he was big and strong and harsh. I didn’t know how to deal with him.” She swallowed. “But I got tougher.”

“I think you did.” He shot her a smile. He hoped it looked encouraging instead of goofy.

“So, what do you think I should do?”

“I think the best thing to do would be to confront him. But if that doesn't feel right, then Edna's advice isn't half bad."

"Do you really think if Dillon sees me with another guy that he's going to back off? That's all it's going to take?"

"I don't know, but I guess it would be a start."

Gazing down the hall, she stuffed her hands into the pockets of her dress. "I'll think about it." She wrinkled her nose. "Sorry I made you sit here and listen to all my problems. I'm so sorry."

"You didn't make me do anything."

"Still… I'll let you go. Have a good night."

All night, he was going to be dealing with this stupid tile. He'd had way better evenings—that was for sure. But no matter what, he wasn't going to be walking to his car afraid. Or going into an apartment scared that some guy who used to terrorize him was lurking around.

So he knew what he needed to do. "Hey, wait."

"What?"

"You know what? I think that Edna's idea might not have been all that stupid. She's right. Sometimes all a guy needs to know is that something won't be as easy as he'd thought it was going to be."

She shrugged. "Like I said, I might have considered it if I had a handful of guy friends who I could ask. But I don't."

"That's where you have this wrong, Kinsey."

"How?"

"Because you don't need a handful of guys to volunteer to be your pretend boyfriend. All you need is one."

"What are you saying?" she whispered.

"You have me."

When she gaped at him, Hunt didn't know whether to grin or be a little offended that she looked so shocked.

Then he decided it didn't matter. He'd made up his mind.

"I'll be your boyfriend, Kinsey. I'll be your guy for as long as you need me to be."

CHAPTER SIXTEEN

AFTER HUNT HAD dropped his bomb, he'd walked away.

Kinsey had hurried after him, because no way was Hunt going to say all that stuff and just leave.

But now she was wondering if following him down the hall had been a good idea. Because now that they were standing in the break room, among a bunch of broken tiles, staring at each other, Kinsey felt as shattered as the tile on the floor.

Or maybe it was like something else.

Like one of Mrs. Martin's beautiful vases that she displayed on a table in her living room. Like the green glass one that had been Kinsey's favorite.

It spurred a memory of when Kinsey had offered to help Claudia put daisies in the vase. But she'd been so excited, she'd moved too fast…let it slip out of her hands. She'd gasped in horror. So afraid that Claudia was going to send her away. Only to watch in amazement when that pretty glass vase fell at her feet without so much as a hairline crack.

Because it hadn't been delicate crystal at all. It had been something far more durable.

Claudia had hugged her tight when Kinsey had started to cry. Saying that there wasn't anything in the house that was worth crying over—except the three of them.

She'd been so relieved and shocked and thankful, Kinsey had stared at Claudia in wonder.

That was how she felt right now.

Hunt was volunteering. Hunt. Mr. Grumpy. Mr. *Get Out of My Way Even Though You Aren't in My Way* Hunt. Mr. Difficult.

Except Hunt wasn't really like that. He wasn't all that grumpy all the time. He'd been the complete opposite around the puppies at the shelter. There, she was pretty sure the animals could have bitten him and he wouldn't have even raised his voice.

So…he wasn't like a lot of things she'd first believed he was.

He rolled his eyes. "Come on, Kinsey. Stop looking like that. I know I'm not your dream man, but I'm not that poor of a candidate, am I?"

"Hunt, of course not. But… I don't know." Pretending to be Hunt's girlfriend meant that they were going to have to spend a lot of time together. Touching and maybe even kissing.

And she wasn't sure how she was going to react to that. Because there was an attraction between them. She felt it. But there was also a very good chance that it was only one-sided.

She couldn't think of too many things that would be more awkward than that. No doubt, she'd start being too open. Too touchy-feely. He'd regret ever offering to help her.

And then she would be no closer to getting Dillon out of her life. But there was a good chance that it could backfire and she'd lose Hunt by the time everything was said and done.

That meant that there was only one thing to say to him. It hurt, but it was the right decision. "No."

"What are you going to do, then?"

She didn't know. "I'll figure it out."

"Why do you need to figure anything out? Do you not trust me?"

"Of course I trust you, Hunt. But it's more than that."

"Listen, think about it some more. Give it a day, okay?"

Even though she was pretty sure she wouldn't change her mind, she nodded. "Okay. I'll let you know my answer tomorrow."

"Okay. Fine. So, are you ready to get out of here?"

"Yeah. Thanks for, uh, listening. And for volunteering."

"Come on." He reached out a hand. Obviously for her to take.

"What are you doing?"

"I'm going to walk you to your car, and don't even try to tell me no." When she still hesitated, he wiggled his fingers. "Come on." Like she was just going to start holding his hand in the middle of the dentist's office.

"Oh. Well, let me get my stuff. It's on the counter." He followed her into the reception area, waited while she did her usual double and triple check, then opened the front door for her as she walked out.

"Take my hand, Kinsey. Let's do this."

"Wait. I need to lock up."

"I'll do it. After I walk you to your car." When she still hesitated to put her hand in his, he made an impatient noise. Kind of a grumble in the back of his throat. "My hands are clean and unsweaty. Come on."

"Did you think I was worried about holding your sweaty hand?"

"Maybe."

Only then did she notice that the corners of his mouth were curved up. He was teasing her.

Well, she could give as good as she could get. "Fine. Here." She slipped her hand into his. Attempted to ignore that little bolt of energy that passed between them as he clasped her hand and walked by her side.

"Could you not look like you're being forced to do this?"

"Sorry." She smiled up at him. "I guess I do

kind of look like I'm back in sixth grade and we had to learn square dancing."

"Hold on." His steps slowed. "Did you really have to learn to square dance?"

"Yes, I really did. The second house I lived in was out in the country, and the PE teacher was from a town called Killeen in Texas. We spent a week suffering through do-si-dos," she explained as they stopped next to her car.

He held her things as she unlocked her door, then stood close as she got settled inside and finally turned on the ignition. The whole time he'd been looking around the area. Scanning to see if anyone was standing nearby.

"Do you see anyone?" she asked.

"No," he replied in a low voice. "Only you." He flashed a smile. "I'm going to be thinking all night long about a little Kinsey square dancing."

"Please, don't. I wasn't cute and I wasn't very little. I was twelve."

"I'll think what I want." He leaned closer. "Have a good evening, Kinsey. Text me when you get home, okay?"

"I've been getting myself home for a while now, Hunt. There's no need for you to worry."

"Do it anyway."

His voice was so serious and military-like, she was caught off guard. "Hunt, what's going on? Are you joking?"

"Not even a little bit." When she continued to

stare at him, he softened his voice. “Look, just humor me on this, will you? Text me when you’re inside your apartment and your door’s locked again. I just want to know that you’re safe. I’ll worry if you don’t.”

“I will. And Hunt?”

“Yeah?”

“Thanks.”

“Anytime.” He nodded as he straightened and backed away. Remained in the parking lot until she reached the street and drove off.

The entire time Kinsey tried to tell herself that she was grateful Hunt had walked her outside and made sure she was in her car safely. She was grateful, too.

But that wasn’t the only thing she’d been feeling. There was a little part of her that had felt a little special. Okay, maybe a little bit giddy, too. Maybe even something a little bit more.

CHAPTER SEVENTEEN

HUNT WAS FINISHING a set of a hundred push-ups when his phone rang. He was tempted to ignore it—he really hated push-ups and wanted to get them over with—but there was always a chance that it could be Kinsey calling.

"Yeah?" he said as he finished push-up number eighty-eight.

"Hunter, what's wrong?"

"Hey, Mom. Nothing's wrong."

"Oh no. Is your knee bothering you again? I bet you've been overdoing it."

It was like he hadn't said a word. Already wishing he'd waited to answer the phone, he blew out a breath of air. "I'm fine, Mom. Hold on."

After taking a sip of water, he leaned back against the wall and tried to catch his breath. "You still there?"

"I am. And I'm still concerned. I heard you breathing heavily. What in the world are you doing?"

"I'm working out. You caught me in the middle of a string of push-ups."

"That's it?"

"Isn't that enough?" He felt like rolling his eyes. For some reason his mother was always sure he was doing something crazy—and what "crazy" entailed was anyone's guess. One day he was going to make up something really outlandish to tell her—just to see what she would do.

"I suppose. I didn't know you still did push-ups."

"I do. A hundred sit-ups followed by a hundred push-ups every morning. Any special reason you called, Mom?" Because he'd also lifted weights. He was sweaty and starving. He needed a hot shower and something more to eat than the apple he'd had with his first cup of coffee.

"I actually do have a reason. Dad and I have our plans finalized for our trip to Medina. We'll be arriving next week."

"Next week?" He didn't bother to hide his surprise. "Mom, I thought you weren't coming for a while."

"I know, but the funniest thing happened when I started telling folks that we were going to be in town," she said, her voice bright and cheerful. "Word spread like wildfire. It feels like every one of our friends wants to see us. The phone's been ringing nonstop. I've been getting texts, too."

"I'm not surprised. You have a lot of friends here."

"I told Stewart the same thing. So, we made a

slight change in plans. Instead of only staying for seven days, we're going to stay two weeks. Isn't that something?"

"Yeah." Two weeks. Two weeks of his parents back in their house, inspecting it. Chatting about what he'd done and hadn't done with the lawn. Making small talk over breakfast. Wanting to go out to lunch. Two weeks of them sleeping in the guest room because "*it was your house now*" but making sure he realized that the shower wasn't as good as the one in the main bedroom.

Two weeks of hoping that his nightmares didn't wake them up and biting his tongue when each of them commented on his preference for working from three in the afternoon until midnight or one in the morning.

"Did you just say yeah?" After a pause, she added, "Honey, did you hear me?"

"I'm sorry. Yes, ma'am."

"Oh, Hunter, you aren't already stewing about us being houseguests, are you?"

"I'm trying not to." That was as honest as he dared to get.

"Oh. Well, we can stay in a hotel if you'd rather."

Hunt bit back a smile. His mother had said the word *hotel* like most people said *hospital*. A hotel was absolutely not where his mother wanted to be.

He didn't want her in a hotel either. "This is your house, Mom. Of course you and Dad are staying here."

"Don't do anything special. We don't want to be in the way."

"You won't be. Everything will be fine." Of course, things would have been a little better if they were only staying for seven days and not fourteen.

"I think so, too. Dad and I have already talked, and we're going to do our best not to get into all of your business."

"I would appreciate that. I'll try not to get into all of your business, too."

Sounding more relieved, she added, "Hunter, I spent many nights staring at the news when you were deployed. All I want to do is spend some time with you. You're the most important person in our lives. We love you. You know that, right?"

"Yes, ma'am. I feel the same way about you and Dad. I love you both."

"If that's the case, then there's nothing to worry about, son." Laughing softly, she added, "We're going to love reconnecting with Kinsey, too. I'm tickled that you two are spending so much time together."

No way did he want to go there. "I'm sure she'll love to see you, too, Mom."

"How are things going with her?"

He didn't know, but he sure wasn't going to share that. "Sorry, but that's 'getting into my business' territory."

"So you're not going to tell me anything?"

"Nope."

"All right. So, how is your knee?"

His knee was also "getting into his business" territory. "Mom, as much as I'd love to chat with you, I've got to go."

"I know. You're always busy. We'll talk soon. Bye!"

"Bye, Ma. I love you." After they disconnected, he sat down on the couch, propped his leg on the coffee table, and counted to ten. He hoped his mother was right and that everything was going to go smoothly.

It was really too bad that he'd learned in the army that there were as many ways for things to go wrong as there were for things to go right.

He'd learned that lesson over and over again.

HE WAS STILL thinking about that a few hours later when he was painting the inside of a storage closet at Loaves of Love.

To be honest, he'd been a little confused about why Edna had wanted him to paint it. It had been packed full of boxes and extra baking pans and utensils and had been kind of a pain to empty. But once the space was empty, he could see just how dingy the area was.

"What... Oh, hello, Hunt!" Edna called out. "I didn't know you were going to tackle this today."

"No time like the present, right?"

She grinned at him as she peeked into the closet.

"Wow, would you look at that? That fresh white paint is making the other three walls look gray. What a difference already."

"I agree, though I didn't think I was ever going to get this place cleared out. You had a lot stuffed in here."

"I know." Edna stared at all the boxes. "It's like a clown car, isn't it?" Bending down, she opened up one of the boxes and pulled out a set of brand-new plastic measuring spoons. "Look at this. I think there are fifty sets of measuring spoons here."

"Why so many?"

"People donate them. About a year ago we needed some new mixing bowls. When word got around that I could use some donations for bowls, measuring cups and spoons, all of this came pouring in." She frowned. "It's almost more than we can ever use, but I don't know what to do with them."

"I bet some volunteers might like them."

"I think they would, too. But not every volunteer is here for food, and I couldn't give these supplies away to someone who didn't need them."

"Which is why they're taking up all this space," Hunt said.

"I'm afraid so." After closing the box back up, Edna stood up. "Any ideas? You dealt with logistics back in the army, didn't you?"

"I did." He was just about to tell her that his

experience had nothing to do with her storage problem when he remembered that the guys in the relax-and-recreation tent in one of his deployments had the same problem with donated paperbacks. There had been a month when someone back in the States had mistakenly sent their unit fifty boxes of books instead of five.

Someone had first suggested burning the extra, unwanted books, but that idea hadn't sat well with Hunt. His mother loved paperbacks. They'd gotten him through more than a couple of sleepless nights, too.

So…he'd developed a whole library system for soldiers to check out the books…and then pass them onto people in other less-literary-blessed units. One of his corporals suggested writing a note on the inside cover to the future reader.

To everyone's amazement, that idea had caught on like wildfire. Pretty soon everyone was combing through the stacks of books, writing notes, and sharing them with other soldiers around the world.

"Edna, how about if we start switching out the used supplies once a month and then 'gift' the used supplies to anyone who wants them…along with a recipe for bread?"

Edna brightened. "That would allow the items to be used for Loaves of Love but become useful to other people, too." She beamed at him. "I think that would work."

"I think so, too."

She patted his arm. "Hunt Vargo, you are a gem. Thanks for the idea."

"Anytime."

"I'm going to speak with Valerie and some of my other volunteer receptionists. They can start organizing it next week. Just think. Before long, I'll be able to actually see what's in here instead of just trying to avoid opening the door."

Afraid that Edna was about to ask him to start sorting the boxes right that minute, he lifted up his paint roller. "I better get to work now."

"I know. And I need to go tell Wayne my good news." She winked. "I'm always telling him that the best things happen when one doesn't expect it. Now I have proof."

Hunt grinned as he walked back into the closet and dipped the roller into the paint. He was pretty sure that the storage-room solution wasn't the only unexpectedly good thing to happen in Medina. His relationship with Kinsey was, too.

CHAPTER EIGHTEEN

IT WAS MONDAY. The first day of her new life as Hunt Vargo's pretend girlfriend. Kinsey felt giddy about it, which was both confusing and awkward. Had it been so long since she'd dated anyone that she was now reduced to getting excited about relationships that weren't even real?

She really hoped that wasn't the case.

Forcing herself to get a grip, Kinsey put on her favorite black pants, a tan tank top, and white fitted blazer. She'd bought the outfit soon after Dr. Martin had hired her, thinking it would make her look a little less like a teenager and more like a working professional when she was sitting at the reception desk.

The white blazer had seemed to do the trick. Though most of Doc's clients still thought of her as a "young girl" they did seem to listen to her more carefully when she had her snazzy blazer on. She'd already decided to get another blazer in black for the fall and winter.

The added bonus about her new "professional" clothes was that they were comfortable. Plus, she could take off the jacket if she went outside to eat her lunch.

Her new goal was to look like hunky Hunt Vargo's girlfriend, so Kinsey put on a little bit of makeup. Just as she was applying a second coat of mascara to her eyelashes, her phone rang. Concerned it was Dr. Martin, she rushed to answer it—and saw that it was Hunt calling instead.

Maybe he was excited about everything, too? "Hi, Hunt," she said the second she connected. "How are you?"

"Good. You got a second?"

He was all business. Feeling a little deflated, she pulled herself together. "Sure. Is, uh, everything okay?"

"Yeah. I just need to know your schedule today."

"Oh. Well, I'm home now. I'll be going into the office about half past eight."

"You doing anything for lunch? Do you have lunch plans?"

"Not really. I might go to the park. I usually bring my lunch."

"What are you doing tonight?"

"I get off around five. It all depends when I get the filing and paperwork ready for the next day."

"What are you doing for dinner?" He fired off the question, still sounding very businesslike.

She was starting to get annoyed. "I don't know, Hunt. I'll dig something out of my freezer, I guess. Why?"

"Because you're supposed to want to see me, Kinsey."

He sounded kind of impatient. "Oh. Yeah. I thought maybe you'd walk me to my car like you sometimes do?"

"Does that sound believable to you?"

She was starting to feel like he was giving her a pop quiz. "I don't know. What do you think?"

He sighed. "I think you're a cute girl, Kinsey."

"Um, thank you?" Feeling flustered, she walked into her kitchen and started shuffling through the pile of junk mail on the counter.

"What I'm trying to say is that we're supposed to be a devoted couple, right?"

"Right?" She had no idea what he was expecting her to say.

"Well, don't you think we'd want to spend time together?"

"I guess we would, wouldn't we?" Why hadn't she thought about that? "Um, but you're going to be working when I'm home from work."

"About that… I decided to rearrange my days a little bit."

How could that be? "I thought you like to work at night so you don't have to deal with a lot of people."

"It's still my preference, but I think I can handle spending time with you. I think we should go out to dinner a lot. That way everyone will see us."

Hunt wanted to go out to dinner with her. Often.

Kinsey felt like her eyebrows had ridden up so high they were practically brushing her hairline. "We can't go out to eat every night." No way could she afford that.

"I agree. Sometimes I'll have to come over to your place." He paused. "And other nights you can come over to mine."

Not only was he sounding very un-Hunt-like, their situation was turning out to be way more sticky than she'd imagined. Boy, she wished she could see his face. It would tell her a lot about how he really felt.

Since that wasn't possible, she kept attempting to explain herself. "Hunt, I feel terrible that you're rearranging your life just to make mine easier."

"Don't feel terrible."

That was such a Hunt way of responding, she smiled. But even if she didn't feel terrible, she'd still feel like she was taking advantage of him.

She drew a fortifying breath. "You know what? Maybe we can come up with other things to do together that wouldn't inconvenience you so much. Or, ah, Edna might have an idea of who else I can ask to pretend-date me." Preferably it would be someone who she wasn't starting to have feelings for.

"No. That wouldn't make sense. If this Dillon guy has been watching you, he's going to be suspicious of someone suddenly showing up in your life." After a brief pause, he added, "It wouldn't be believable. Besides, he's already seen us together."

"I get that a random guy showing interest in me probably wouldn't be believable, but there's got to be a middle ground for us. Eating supper together every night seems like a lot."

"We don't have to do it every night. Let's come up with a schedule when we're together tonight. But no matter what, plan on going to the dog shelter with me on Saturday."

He wanted to see her on the weekend, too? Firmly ignoring the part of her heart which was completely on board with that idea, she blurted, "I already planned to bake bread on Saturday at Loaves of Love."

"Okay. We'll do both."

"It's that easy? You'd be willing to do all this for me?"

"Why wouldn't I?"

There were dozens of reasons, ranging from he had a life of his own that she was disrupting to the fact that she was a grown woman who should be able to, at the very least, have a conversation with a guy who she hadn't seen in ten years without being scared to death.

But the main one, the one that she thought counted the most, was the reason she admitted to Hunt: "Because we hardly know each other."

There was silence for a few brief seconds before he replied. "Are you saying we aren't friends, Kinsey?"

He sounded a little offended. "No," she replied slowly. "But what I'm trying to say is that we're friends but not *good* friends."

"What do we need to do to be better friends?"

He wanted to be closer to her. For real. She was getting flustered. "I don't know," she said as she tried to think. "Maybe we could spend more time together?"

"Well, that's what we're going to do, right?"

Even though it wasn't proving her point, she nodded. "Yes, but—"

"Hey, stop. We've got nothing to fuss about. You and I are already friends. We already enjoy each other's company. We're going to spend time together." He lowered his voice. "We're going to become good friends, Kinsey. Stop overthinking it."

"I'm trying to. It's just that I'm going to owe you so much. I feel bad." How could she ever repay him?

"Don't. All you have to do is say thank you."

"Thank you, Hunt."

"You're welcome. Now, go have a good day."

She was smiling so big. "Thanks. And… I'll see you later?"

His voice lowered. Turned almost sweet. "And yeah, honey. I'll see you later."

He disconnected before Kinsey could dissect the whole "honey" thing.

That meant she was left feeling a little fluttery in her stomach. She was pretty sure it was because Hunt was doing so much for her, but there was also the chance that she was starting to feel something for him that had nothing to do with safety and friendship.

And everything about being something more.

CHAPTER NINETEEN

HUNT HAD SPENT a lot of time over the weekend thinking about plans for their proposed fake relationship. No matter how many ways he tried to organize and sort them, one thing had become clear: None of the logistics made sense.

He and Kinsey hadn't discussed what was permissible, what wasn't, or their goal. Well, not beyond the obvious one, which was that her former foster brother Dillon would remove himself from her life.

But even that goal seemed nebulous.

It didn't sit well with him. None of it did. He was fake-dating without guidelines or proper protocols, and it made him feel like he was free-falling out of a helicopter at fifteen thousand feet. He'd done that. It was scary and nerve-wracking. Even when the parachute lifted him with a jerk, nothing about it had felt good.

Back in the army, he'd usually been the go-to guy for logistics. He was excellent at plans and was good at presenting them in clear and precise ways. One colonel had even referred to him as his unit's fix-it guy. If orders didn't make sense, Hunt would streamline them. If someone had developed a strategy that had loopholes, he would be asked to make a list of possible ways to fix them.

Hunt had been more than competent at doing that. Just weeks before his accident, he'd been told that he was so good at what he did that he was going to be included in more planning meetings with the top brass.

Then, of course, his Humvee had gotten hit and everything in his life changed. Although he was very grateful to only sustain injuries to his leg, he had felt as if part of him had died. Until now. There had been something about Kinsey that had woken him up and spurred emotions that he'd assumed were long gone.

After doing a small job for a framing store, he headed over to the Doc's office and returned to working on the tile in the break room. Claudia had been able to order another box, so he hoped to finish laying the tile by the time Kinsey was ready to leave.

When Dr. Martin walked in the room, he looked delighted to see him. "How're you doing, son?"

Putting down the tile he'd been about to place on the wall, Hunt turned. "Fine, sir."

"It's a shame that I'm seeing you more at the office instead of on my front porch."

"I agree, though I'm glad I'm remodeling rooms instead of having you work on my teeth," he joked.

The lines around Larry's eyes deepened as his smile widened. "I can't argue with that."

"I'll stop by sometime soon."

"I'll ask Claudia to set something up. That way it gets on our calendars."

"Sounds good." Noticing that a couple of rags had fallen on the floor, he bent down to pick them up.

"I bet you're ready to get this job finished, Hunt."

"Only the tilework."

"Claudia hadn't realized how delicate these tiles were when she picked them."

"Yeah, she told me the same thing. I do feel bad about breaking and chipping so many."

"Don't worry about it. Believe it or not, I wanted sturdy white subway tile here. She's the one who thought we needed something fancier. She said everyone who works in this office is surrounded by stark white and metal and that the break room should have a more comfortable feel to it."

Standing at Larry's side, Hunt surveyed the tilework. "She wasn't wrong. It looks pretty good."

"I think so, too. You're doing good work."

"Thanks. I'm almost done."

Dr. Martin walked over to the refrigerator. "I came in for a drink. Do you want any of these seltzer waters?"

"Sure. Thanks."

"Here you go," Larry said as he handed him a can. "Well, I better get back to my patients. Kinsey is going to come find me if I don't get a move on." Grinning, he said, "That girl would've made a good soldier, Hunter. She's keeping everyone in line out there in the reception area."

He chuckled. "I've told her almost the same thing. If she deepened her voice a notch, she could probably make a private shake in his boots."

"Don't tell her that," Larry joked. "She'll be trying out that voice on me!" Just as he was walking out, he said, "I heard your parents are coming in soon."

"Yes. Sometime at the end of the week."

"If they get to be too much, they're welcome to stay with us for a few days."

"Thanks, but they'll be fine. We get along well."

"I know, but you know what they say about fish and houseguests..."

"Noted. I'll let you know if I need some reinforcements."

"I hope so." Seeming to need another moment, Doc leaned against the doorframe and sipped his water.

"Dr. Martin?" a voice called from down the hall.

"I'm on my way, Amanda!" he called out as he hurried out of the room.

As Hunt finished the tile and started prepping another wall to paint, he listened to the conversations in the hallway and chatted for a moment or two with different members of the staff who came into the break room. There was a rhythm there that was entertaining. So much so he realized that he didn't miss his AirPods. Eventually people started to leave just as he was cleaning up.

When Kinsey ran into the room about an hour after Dr. Martin had left, she drew to a stop when she caught sight of him. "Hunt."

"Kinsey."

"I didn't know you were in here. Have you been here very long?"

He shrugged. "Most of the afternoon."

Her eyes widened. "Wow. You should've come up to say hi."

"I knew you were busy. Besides, I wasn't sure if I should."

"Why not?"

"We never really went over any 'do's and 'don'ts' for our dating," he admitted. "I think having some parameters would help us both."

She blinked, as if formulating dating rules had never occurred to her. "How about we play it by ear?"

"Huh?"

She shrugged. "I don't know how your past relationships worked, but with mine, we just did whatever we were comfortable with. I'm comfortable with you coming up to say hi to me whenever you feel like it," she added softly.

She made sense. And...yeah, she was also being pretty adorable. "Noted." When her gaze warmed, he added, "Ah, besides, I had to get this tile work finished."

"Oh. Right. It looks nice."

"Thanks. What are you doing?"

"I ran in here to go to the bathroom." Her eyes widened again, like that was something he wouldn't want to know about.

It amused him. "Don't let me keep you."

She rolled her eyes but did walk into the bathroom and lock the door. When she walked out again, Kinsey seemed a little more unsure of herself. "I'm almost done. Do you still want to go out to eat?"

"Yep. I'll get cleaned up, put this stuff in my truck, and then come get you. Where you want to go?"

"Anywhere is fine. As long as it's fast."

"All right." It was odd, but he felt kind of disappointed about that. There had been a part of him that hoped she would want to spend more time with him.

But that wasn't what they were about. She only wanted him around so Dillon would go away.

Fifteen minutes later they were on their way. "Have you decided on a restaurant?"

"No. Is there someplace you like to go?"

"I told you, it's your choice."

"That's the problem. I don't go out to eat much. I'm on a pretty tight budget since all my money has been going to my apartment."

She was so young. Kinsey had such a spark inside her, he sometimes forgot just how big their age difference was. Seven years might not be a lot when two people were in their forties, but the difference between twenty-six and his thirty-five was significant.

He'd still been in college and marching around a back field in ROTC when he was twenty-one. So naive and green. Full of pride and so optimistic about his future.

So different from how he was now. "How about Barney's Pub? Have you been in there?"

"No. Places like Barney's haven't been in my budget."

"I've been here with my parents when they come into town. They have great shepherd's pie. What do you say?"

"Sounds good."

He parked his truck in one of the nearby spots, then walked around to help her down. Right before she darted in front of him, he held her back with an arm to her side. "Hold on, now. We're a couple, remember?"

"Oh. Yeah."

"Give me your hand, girl."

Her eyes lit up, but she didn't argue. Instead, she slipped her hand into his. He tugged her closer as they started walking.

When he decided that she still looked kind of nervous, he said, "This only works if you look like you're into me. Stop acting like I'm your big brother helping you walk across the street and you can't wait to get free."

And just like that, everything changed. Her lips curved into a beautiful, bright smile. And the look that appeared in her eyes was sweet and flirty and pretty much took his breath away.

"How am I doing now?" she whispered.

"Good. Real good." He, on the other hand, was feeling shell-shocked.

Because a big part of him wished that the look she'd just shot him had been real.

He was in trouble.

CHAPTER TWENTY

EVERYTHING WAS GOING so well their date almost felt real. That was the thought that kept running through Kinsey's mind as she sat across from Hunt and tried not to forget that everything about the two of them was make-believe.

But it was hard to do. Real hard. Because Hunt was looking at her as if she was special. Speaking to her in a soft, caring voice. Leaning in when she spoke.

Added to all that was the fact that it was this new and improved version of Hunt.

The grumpy Hunt, the man who'd gotten on her last nerve, seemed to have gone on sabbatical. And in its place? It was Hunt Vargo. Shiny, almost sweet, new and improved Hunt Vargo.

The guy-who-suddenly-had-company-manners Hunt Vargo. The guy who lettered in multiple sports when he was in high school and graduated near the top of his class. Who'd earned an ROTC scholarship to the University of Dayton and done so well that he'd risen up the ranks practically the moment he'd entered the army.

Sure, all that background info was from his doting parents years ago, but who could blame them? He was a pretty special guy. Someone she was impressed with.

And here she was, staring at his blond hair and sky-blue eyes and perfect jaw. Being charmed by his polished, officer-candidate-school manners. What girl wouldn't want to be on the receiving end of such things? If there was one, she didn't want to know her.

Then, there was his good looks. His athletic build. She was pretty sure that when Hunt looked in the mirror he only saw a myriad of scars on his leg. But if he only saw that? Well, he was missing out. His whole package was notable. She might've been biased, but Kinsey thought Hunt was handsome in a way that few men were.

The only snag was their reality. And that reality was chock full of red flags for both of them. For her, because it would be so easy to let herself believe that at least some of what he was doing was real.

His problem was so much more. Because while former military captain Hunter Vargo might be a catch, she absolutely was not.

She hadn't made any dean's lists, never stayed at a school long enough to earn a varsity letter in anything, and was lucky to be working for a former foster parent as a receptionist.

Plus she had the added bonus of having a creepy guy from her past stalking her.

She was nobody's catch, least of all Hunt's.

"Hey, you okay?"

Her eyes darted to his. "I'm fine. Why?"

"No reason. Other than you started to look like you were about to cry." He frowned. "Did I miss something? Did you see that loser guy again?"

"No."

"You sure?" He tilted his head to one side. As if the new angle would help him figure her out.

She was pretty sure it wouldn't. No matter how anyone looked at her, she was a mess of insecurity and doubts covered up with a bright smile. She didn't know if she was ever going to feel so comfortable with another person that she'd be able to be completely herself.

No reason to dwell on it, though. "What are you thinking about ordering?"

"The shepherd's pie."

"I should've guessed."

"It's good, and it's not like I can make it at home. What about you?"

Looking down at her menu again, she scanned the items, and came up with the three least expensive. "I was thinking of the soup."

"I saw that. It looked good. What else?"

"Just soup. It has broccoli and cheese and comes in a bread bowl." The bread bowl was plenty for her. Plus, the price was right. She had to watch her pennies since she was determined to put money into savings every month.

"Okay, if you're sure."

He looked like he thought she wasn't getting enough, but it didn't matter what he thought anyway. When the server approached, they placed their orders and handed off their menus.

And then they were alone again.

"Tell me about going to the University of Dayton," she blurted.

"College? Well, okay… I majored in international relations."

"And you were in the ROTC, right?"

"Yes. I was awarded an ROTC scholarship. I always wanted to be an officer in the military. My grandfather had been a major in the air force. As long as I can remember, he and that rank were one and the same." Folding his arms over his chest, he added, "It was hard to think of him in any other way."

"Did you want to be a major, too?"

"Nah. I didn't care about the rank all that much. I mean, not beyond the bump in pay. How many bars on my chest didn't matter to me. It was what being an officer in the army signified. It showed the world that I cared about something more than just myself." He looked away. "I thought it was something to be proud of."

He seemed kind of bitter. She hated seeing that. "Hunt, being a captain was a pretty big deal. Plus, you served for years. Are you not proud of what you accomplished?"

"Oh, no. I am." His eyes met hers before they darted away again. "This probably isn't going to sound right, but I'm not as upset about getting hit by that IED as I am that it changed the course of my life."

"Sorry, but isn't that the same thing?"

"I don't think so. The injury tore up my knee. At first no one thought I'd ever walk again."

"But you do walk just fine."

"You're right, but not well enough to stay in the military. My leg is never going to be good enough for that." He frowned. "That's my problem. I keep wishing that I would've gotten injured in another way."

"What?"

He waved a hand. "I know that doesn't make sense. But I can't help but think if I'd only lose a spleen or a kidney or just been cut up, I would have still been able to serve." He swallowed. "I loved being in the military."

"I'm sorry about your leg but I'm glad you still have all your body parts, Hunt."

"Don't worry. I know what I sound like. Ungrateful. I should be waking up every morning glad to be alive, not wanting to play some dumb head game about 'better' injuries."

"I could be wrong, but I believe thinking that makes you human, not ungrateful."

"Yeah, but I could've died, Kinsey. I should be counting my blessings every day."

"Do you wish someone else in your unit had gotten hurt instead of you?"

"No. Never."

"Then give yourself a break."

His eyes lit up. "Is it that easy?"

"Probably not." After taking a sip of water, she added, "You still didn't tell me much about college life."

"What do you want to know?"

"The fun stuff. Did you go to games? Did you join one of those fraternities? Did you live in the dorms? Did you have to study all the time?"

"Whoa. You do have questions. Let's see. I had a good enough time, I suppose, but I had a lot going on. I took a full class load plus ROTC. So no, no fraternities for me. And I did go to some basketball and football games occasionally, but it's not a big sports school. Not like Ohio State." He was thoughtful for a moment, as if running through her list of questions. "And yes, I lived in the dorms, and yes, had to study a lot. I was on scholarship."

Now she felt a little silly. Sure, she'd known he'd probably studied and written papers and such, but she'd also imagined him hanging out with a bunch of friends and going to parties. "See, Hunt, you have a lot of stuff to be proud about."

"Why are you so interested? Are you thinking about going to Dayton?"

"Oh, no. I already did all the college courses I plan to do."

"Hmm."

Luckily she was saved from telling him anything more about herself when the server brought their food. She was gratified to see that her soup was just as filling as she hoped. And delicious, too.

"How is yours?" Hunt asked.

"Wonderful. It looks like you're pleased about your order, too."

"It's great," he said before taking another bite.

The rest of their meal was uneventful. It seemed they were both tidy, efficient eaters. Neither of them left much on their plates or felt the need to talk instead of eating.

The only surprise was when the server brought the check and Hunt insisted on paying for both of their meals. When the server walked off with his pair of twenties, Kinsey attempted to give Hunt money for her meal.

"Nope. Not taking it."

"We didn't agree to you paying." She lowered her voice. "And don't try to tell me that you'd be paying if we were really dating, because I'd still want to pay."

"Okay. Are you ready to go?"

That was it? He was just going to move on? "No, I'm not ready," she whispered. "Why aren't you listening to me?"

"I'm listening to every word. You just said you

didn't want me to say that I'd want to pay no matter what. So I won't argue. Now, come on. I need to get you home, and then I need to get back to work."

Telling herself that it was just a nine-dollar bread bowl of soup, Kinsey stood up. Then reminded herself that they were supposed to like each other as they meandered through the maze of tables until they were out the door.

The warm air felt good after the pub's air-conditioning. She took off her blazer. "It's so nice out."

"It is," he murmured as he reached for her hand.

As they walked toward his vehicle, she scanned the area. Looking for Dillon.

"Hey, don't worry, Kinsey. I don't see him."

"You already looked?"

He winked. "Army, remember?"

She smiled as he cupped her elbow when she climbed into his truck, then drove her to her car in the back of Dr. Martin's office.

"I'll follow you to your apartment and walk you up."

"Thanks," she said as she climbed into her warm vehicle.

Ten minutes later, they were walking side by side again. This time to the entrance of her building. "I need to check my mailbox."

"Whatever you need, Kins."

He stood patiently while she fished the mail key out of her purse and unlocked the metal box with her loft number on it.

After she got her mail, they walked up the stairs. He unlocked her door and even walked through the space to make sure all was well while she waited at the front.

And then, it was time to tell him goodbye. "Thanks for supper, and for checking out my place…and everything."

"It was my pleasure." Reaching out, he ran a finger along her cheek. "Get some rest. I'll see you tomorrow," he murmured. And then, before she realized what he was about to do, Hunt bent down and brushed her lips with his.

She was still staring at Hunt when he turned around and walked out the door. "Lock it, honey," he called out.

Doing as he asked, she shut the door and locked the dead bolt. Thought about that fleeting kiss.

And realized that whether they were a real couple or not, she'd liked it. She wouldn't be opposed to him doing that again. Maybe she'd even look forward to it.

It was only later, when she was tossing and turning and trying to get to sleep, that Kinsey realized there hadn't been a single person around who would have witnessed that kiss. If that was the case, why had he kissed her?

Maybe he'd forgotten that small detail. She doubted it, though. She was learning that he didn't forget much.

CHAPTER TWENTY-ONE

Hunt had now been Kinsey's pretend boyfriend for several days. It wasn't all that easy. Actually, it was a lot harder than he would've ever thought. The problem wasn't him, though.

He might not have had a great track record when it came to serious relationships, but he knew how to act like a halfway decent boyfriend.

Nope, the problem lay with Kinsey, because she was too much. Too cute. Too bubbly. Too entertaining. To make matters worse, Kinsey was far too pretty for her own good.

He really wished he could find more things wrong with her. That would make it easier at night when he was trying not to think about her. If she had more faults, he could concentrate on those instead of how many things about her were so right.

But because he couldn't seem to think of anything to dislike, he was stuck thinking about all the things he liked about her. There were so many, he might as well have been counting sheep.

So, that was an issue.

The far more pressing problem, unfortunately,

was that his acting skills were pretty bad. He'd learned at the Irish pub that pretending to only pretend to like Kinsey was next to impossible. In fact, the mishmash in his head was so mixed up that it put him in a bad mood and set his nerves on edge. Honestly, his head felt like it was about to explode.

Which, again, was Kinsey's fault. Because every time she tossed an adoring look his way or touched his arm, he wanted to pocket the memory. Like it was special.

But it wasn't. It was just an act so the creepy guy from her past would stop following her around. He knew that. Knew it.

Unfortunately, he found himself responding to her playacting like he'd been waiting for it all of his life. Before he could stop himself, he would touch her, too. Press his hand to the small of her back when they went out to eat. Gaze at her lips until he lightly kissed her good-night. *Every* night. He knew he should stop doing that, but he didn't want to.

Which was another problem.

He needed a break from her. That was why, instead of planning yet another dinner with her, Hunt went to the animal shelter. He had to either get his mind off of her or come up with a plan so he didn't do something crazy, like start falling in love with the girl.

Feeling pretty proud of himself, he walked inside the shelter and was immediately hit with the smell of antiseptic, dog, and grass. "Hey, Courtney."

"Hi, Hunt. I didn't expect to see you today."

"It was a spur-of-the-moment thing. I figured one of the dogs might like a walk." Noticing Courtney was brushing one, he moved closer to see who it was.

Courtney was one of the shelter's newest employees. She was in her late thirties, had a sweet voice with a hint of southern drawl, and was so calm and collected that all the animals seemed to instantly relax whenever she was nearby.

Except for maybe Benson. Benson was a Collie mix, and had no trouble letting his displeasure be known as Courtney attempted to brush his tangled fur.

"You came at the perfect time." She sighed as the dog whined and squirmed from her ministrations.

He was a big dog. "Do you need a hand with him?"

"No, I've got it, but I'd appreciate it if you stay right here." Running a hand along the Collie's neck, she explained, "He hates getting groomed but puts up with it if he's around other people. It's like he needs everyone to give him sympathy while he's getting these knots snipped out of his fur."

Hunt put his hand near Benson's nose so the dog

could reacquaint himself with his scent. "I heard getting beautiful takes a lot of time, buddy. You ought to let Courtney work her magic instead of fussing."

"See, sweetheart?" she asked. "All your caterwauling isn't making anything easier. Hang in there a little longer. It's all for your benefit."

Whether it was because Hunt was now standing there or Benson was simply giving in, the dog finally settled down and stopped whining.

"Good dog."

He wagged his tail.

"Oh my gosh, you're helping! Keep doing whatever you're doing," she said as she picked up the nail clippers. "Paw up, Benson."

He lifted his paw.

Looking pleased, Courtney began to carefully clip each toenail. "I'm surprised you're here alone, Hunt."

"Why is that?"

"The last two times you've been in here, you've been with that pretty brunette with the big smile. How are things going with her?"

"Okay, I guess."

Courtney glanced his way before moving to Benson's other side. "Paw up," she instructed. When she started clipping another set of nails, she said, "Just okay, Hunt?"

"Yeah. Everything's fine. I mean, it's as fine as I could hope for it to be." Hearing his words, he frowned. He wasn't just bad at having a pretend girlfriend, he wasn't any better talking about her. He sounded flustered and confused.

"Hmm," she said.

"What does that mean?"

"Nothing," Courtney said quickly. "I just thought there was something more between you. My bad."

"How come you thought that?"

She shrugged as she released the front paw and moved onto the back. "Paw up." After Benson complied, she said, "It just seemed like you and that woman clicked. Like you two seemed to enjoy each other's company."

"We do. She's great. I like being around her." Clearing his throat, he tried to save himself from sounding like a complete fool. "Like I said, I just decided to come in today on my own."

"I'm glad you did." Courtney smiled at him as she exchanged the clippers for a brush again. Benson growled under his breath as she concentrated on an especially tangled section of fur near his neck. "Settle down. I'm not hurting you. Remember? This is all I've got in my hand," she soothed as she held the brush in front of the dog's nose.

After a couple of sniffs the dog seemed to ease and sat down.

"I'm always amazed that you get these strays to listen to you so well."

"It doesn't always go well, but we think Benson here was once pretty well taken care of. He's a smart thing, too. Once he sees what he's dealing with, he's a lot calmer." She winked. "Like I said, he's a bit of a character with his whines in front of an audience. He should've been on stage."

Hunt wished Benson could give him a couple of tips. "Most things are like that, I guess. Still, you make grooming dogs look easy."

Looking fondly at the collie, Courtney said, "Caring for these animals is the easy part. It's everything else that gets overwhelming." Standing up, she led the dog into a carpeted enclosed area and then went to the front desk. "Sorry for making you wait."

She glanced down at a sheet of notebook paper. "Looks like you get a choice today, Hunt. You can either walk an eighteen-month-old pittie who is in need of some serious exercise or you can spend time with three or four senior dogs who haven't had much attention lately."

"As much as I'd love to hang out with the seniors, I was hoping to take a walk. I need the exercise. Is that okay with you?"

"It's better than okay. I'll go get Pop-Tart."

"Pop-Tart?"

"I don't name 'em. The director is on a diet. She keeps naming all the new dogs after treats she's trying to stay away from."

"Sounds counterproductive."

Courtney chuckled. "I kind of thought the same thing, but no way am I going to tell her that."

When he caught sight of Pop-Tart, he decided that the puppy's name suited him perfectly. He was wiggly and ready to play. After getting his harness on, Hunt took him on a walk to the park.

Pop-Tart pulled a bit at first but eventually settled down. He even decided to take a little nap in a spot of shade in the park.

Since Hunt's knee was doing a little bit of barking of its own, he sat down on a nearby bench and stretched it out. Smiled when he realized that his quest to not think about Kinsey had been a success. He'd hardly thought about her at all the entire time he'd watched Courtney groom Benson or when he and Pop-Tart had been out walking.

"I need to be around you more often, Pop-Tart," he murmured.

The puppy popped its head up and sauntered toward him.

Hunt laughed. Looked like it was time to walk some more.

Just as they left the park, his phone rang. Glancing at the screen, he frowned. "Hey, Dad. What's up?"

"What's up is we're at your house and you have next to nothing in your refrigerator."

Hunt drew to a stop. "I thought you were coming in at the end of the week. Like, on Saturday." At the earliest.

"Your mother texted you yesterday that we were going to be early."

"Oh. Oh, yeah." He'd been so consumed with all things Kinsey, he'd forgotten. "Sorry about the lack of food. I'll stop by the store on the way home."

"Don't worry about it. Mom's making a list now. We'll head out and get everything we need. What do you think about grilling steaks tonight?"

"Sounds great, Dad."

"Excellent. We'll get potatoes, too. Oh, hold on." After a second, he added, "And salad and corn. It's going to be a feast."

Hunt could hear the smile in his dad's voice. His father lived for "steak night." "I can't wait. Thanks for picking it all up."

"Oh, you know your mother likes fussing in her old kitchen. It's no trouble at all. We'll see you when we see you."

As they headed back to the shelter, Hunt reached down and rubbed Pop-Tart's head. "Sorry you can't come home with me, buddy. I have a feeling that you'd love steak night, too."

The pup's sweet expression and wagging tail gave him a moment's regret before he pushed aside his thoughts. One day he'd be settled enough to finally give one of the shelter dogs a home. One day, he'd find the right woman, she'd feel the same way about him, and then they could start their life together. Maybe she'd even be willing to move into the house he'd lived in since the moment his parents brought him home from the hospital.

Then they could adopt that dog. Eventually have a kid or two. He'd teach them to play all the sports he'd loved. Try to be as good of a dad as his own was. Make sure they knew that few things were ever going to matter as much as the people living in the house.

And just like that, Kinsey jumped right back into his thoughts.

And that was just where he intended for her to stay.

CHAPTER TWENTY-TWO

THERE WERE TWO words that kept repeating in Kinsey's brain all week long: *Only you.* Well, that wasn't exactly right. It was more like six words, which included her asking Hunt *Do you see anyone?* and his reply, which had been *Only you.*

She couldn't seem to stop thinking about that moment. The way he'd sounded, all gruff and honest. The way his expression had appeared so sincere when he'd met her gaze. It had been the stuff of daydreams. The kind of thing that only happened in television movies. Or to other girls.

Certainly not to her.

Kinsey didn't think she was much of a romantic. Living in foster care during her teens had taken care of that. Usually, she tried to see the world with every flaw visible. That way she didn't get too disappointed if something didn't turn out to be as good as she hoped.

Unfortunately, that view hadn't gone over real well with her girlfriends in junior high and high school. While those girls were imagining their first kiss with stars in their eyes, she'd held no such illusions. She'd known that a guy could pretend to be nice in front of adults but vicious when no one else was around.

She had Dillon Carpenter to thank for that.

As life went on, she'd learned that all boys weren't like Dillon and that some guys were actually good to be around. Eventually, she'd even learned that getting close to a guy wasn't scary. She now liked to think that she had a far more healthy view of relationships.

But that was because she'd learned to block out anything that was unpleasant. She was excellent at it. With hardly any effort, she could neatly compartmentalize a bad experience into the do not disturb part of her brain. Even better, she could keep those bad memories there for years. Sometimes she could almost believe they'd never happened in the first place.

She didn't need a counselor to tell her why she'd picked up this habit when she was twelve. Losing everything, being thrown into a harsh environment, and then having to fend off Dillon had been traumatic. Learning to almost erase bad memories from her life had helped her survive.

But now she was an adult. A responsible, independent woman. It was a lot harder to block out things she didn't want to think about. Actually, she wasn't doing a very good job at all. It was like a seal on a freezer that wasn't quite right. No matter how hard she tried, embarrassing memories kept seeping out.

It was uncomfortable.

"Kinsey?"

Startled, she glanced up to see Dr. Martin gazing at her with concern. Tension rose inside of her. How long had he been standing there? "Yes, Doctor?"

His kind gray eyes didn't soften. Instead, they seemed to zero in on her. Just like he did when he had a drill in his hand or was examining X-rays.

Kinsey clenched her hands so she wouldn't squirm in her seat. "How may I help you?" she asked. She smiled, pleased with how professional she sounded.

Unfortunately, Kinsey didn't fool Doc for a minute. "I came in to ask where Judith's records were. I can't seem to find them."

"Um, let me take a look." Well, she would. As soon as she remembered Judith's last name.

"It's Judith *O'Connell*, Kinsey."

"Yes, sir." Wiggling the mouse in her left hand, she said, "I'm pulling them up now."

But instead of walking away like she'd hoped he would, Doc continued to stand nearby. Arms folded over his chest. Watching her every move.

He was making her nervous.

Luckily, Kinsey's training kicked in and she was able to quickly search through emails for the records Judith's former dentist had sent to the office, download them, and add them to her file. When her computer emitted a light ding, she breathed a sigh of relief. Dr. Martin had only needed to wait for two minutes. Looking up at him, she said, "Judith O'Connell's records have been downloaded now. I'm sorry I didn't take care of this earlier."

"Thank you, Kinsey."

"Of course."

Right before Doc moved away, he hesitated. "I think we need to talk, dear. Do you have plans for lunch?"

And just like that, her sense of ease vanished in an instant. "Not really. I was going to eat the turkey sandwich I brought from home in the break room."

"You can join me, then. We'll leave as soon as we close the office at one."

Meeting him for lunch wasn't all that unusual, but this wasn't an invitation. It was a request, and that hadn't happened before.

Doc looked really serious. What had she done wrong? "All right," she said, swallowing a gulp. "Thank you."

She doubted Dr. Martin had heard, though. He was already down the hall by the time she'd replied.

Dread filled her. Had she just made another bad mistake? Was she about to get fired over a forgotten file?

Worry settled in like an unwanted guest. Maybe it wasn't just about a missing file. Maybe she'd done a *lot* of things wrong and she'd been so consumed by Dillon and fake dating that she'd messed everything up.

As the morning passed, Kinsey worried. All her imagined mistakes snowballed. Biting her lip, she scanned Doc's appointments for the day and started checking and double-checking that everything was taken care of for each appointment.

"Kinsey, do you need a break?" Amanda, Doc's assistant, asked in her usual kind way.

"No. I'm fine."

"Sorry, but I'm going to say that's not true. Go take ten minutes. I've got this."

Feeling like she was once again missing something, Kinsey stood up and went to the break room, only to be greeted by the sight of the now completed tile work over by the coffee machine.

Hunt had finished it long after she'd left.

Deciding Amanda was right, Kinsey poured herself a cup of hot coffee, snagged one of the specialty doughnuts from the nearby shop that Amanda had brought in, and sat down. She needed to get it together before she went back to the reception desk. Amanda could handle things, but scheduling patients and answering questions about the office wasn't her forte. She was much better behind the scenes.

Victoria came in a couple of times a month to handle new patient and tricky insurance claims. Getting the "right" answer from a claims department took a ton of patience, since it often involved waiting five or ten minutes for an actual person to get on the line. It also took a lot of finesse, which Amanda had in spades.

She took another sip of coffee, then realized she'd taken her cell phone with her. And remembered that she now had Hunt's phone number. Needing something to take her mind off of the upcoming lunch, she took a chance, pulled up his number, and sent him a picture of the tile, with the coffee maker and box of doughnuts now resting on the counter in front of it.

It looks so good! she texted, then pressed Send.

To her surprise, a little line of dots appeared almost immediately. I'm glad it's almost done. Ha.

That had to be a joke in Hunt-speak. Amused, she responded, I'm sorry I didn't get to witness all the fun you had arranging the design.

I made sure the building was empty. Cussing might have been involved.

She giggled. She would've never thought that Hunt was a texter. Just as she was about to head back to the front, he sent another message.

Is this your break time?

No. I don't usually take mid-morning breaks on Friday. I needed one today.

You okay?

Yeah. There's just some things going on. I'll tell you about it when I see you.

See you later

See you later. Kinsey wasn't sure why that phrase made her feel so warm and fuzzy, but it did. Maybe because she knew Hunt didn't say—or text—things lightly. If he said he would see her tonight, he would.

Not for the first time, Kinsey wondered what it would feel like to be his *real* girlfriend. She hoped the woman he eventually decided to *really* pursue would be worth his time. Kinsey would want to beat her up if she broke his heart.

She almost choked on her coffee. *Beat her up? Oh, brother.* It seemed one could take the girl out of foster care but it was next to impossible to completely take foster care out of the girl. For better or worse, Kinsey was pretty sure that she was always going to be a little rough around the edges. Her parents would probably not know what to think about that.

After washing her hands, she hurried back to the front. "Thanks, Amanda."

"Anytime. Nothing wrong with taking a break every now and then. Things can get stressful around here." Tilting her head toward the waiting room, she whispered, "Get ready. Mr. Morelli is here."

Mr. Morelli didn't like much, and he wasn't shy

about telling whoever was in earshot about his feelings.

"Oh, man. Things are sure to get interesting."

Three hours later, she was sitting across from Dr. Martin at a popular Mexican restaurant and feeling worse than ever. She probably shouldn't have eaten two doughnuts or the giant cup of coffee during her impromptu break. Her stomach was in knots, and nothing on the menu sounded good.

When the server came, she ordered a small plate of two ground-beef tacos. It wasn't very fancy, but hopefully Dr. Martin wouldn't notice if she didn't eat very much.

"I haven't eaten at Taco, Taco's in ages. Have you?" Dr. Martin asked after they ordered.

"No. Not since you, me, and Claudia ate here."

He frowned. "That had to be almost a year ago."

"I think so." He looked so puzzled, she felt like reminding him how she'd been saving her money for years to get her first apartment and be able to live on her own. Going out to eat wasn't a usual occurrence for her.

"Well, this is a treat for both of us, then," he said as he grabbed another chip.

"It's nice of you to take me out."

"It's my pleasure. Let's plan on doing this more often," he added with a warm smile. "Next time, let's ask Claudia to join us."

"I'd like that." She smiled weakly as she took a sip of her soda.

"Aren't you going to dig in? You used to love these chips."

"I still do. I'm, uh, just waiting for lunch. I don't want to get too full." Of course, the real reason was that she didn't think she could swallow a mouthful of anything. She was too worried about why he'd asked her to join him for lunch. Doc might've been claiming that he hadn't asked her out for any other reason but to catch up, but she knew him well enough to know that wasn't the full story.

"That's probably wise." He lowered his eyebrows, though, as if he couldn't imagine being too full to eat a meal after having a few chips and salsa. "So, I guess you're probably wondering why I asked you to lunch."

"Yes." Unable to help herself any longer, she said, "Did I do something wrong?"

"Wrong?" He tilted his head to one side. "Of course not. Why would you think that?"

Because it had felt like his invitation hadn't actually been an invitation. More of a nicely worded order. Plus, it was right on the heels of her forgetting to prep a patient's file. But she didn't want to mention either of those thoughts. "I don't know."

He raised his eyebrows. "Are you sure?"

"I was a little worried about messing up that file this morning."

"I'd completely forgotten about that, dear. You should have, too."

"I like to do as good a job as I can for you."

"You do. I'm glad I hired you."

"Oh. Well, that's good."

"I guess I better get to the point before you get even more worried, hmm?" Before she could answer he said, "All right. I've heard through the grapevine that someone has become interested in you. Someone out of the blue."

Everything shifted inside her as things began to make sense. He'd heard about Dillon. Unable to help herself, she ran a finger along the raised scar on her leg. "Yes. It's been a surprise."

"You know, I was a little relieved when I heard the news," he said in a kind tone. "Kinsey, I've noticed that you haven't seemed yourself. I wondered what was going on. It never occurred to me that it was boy trouble."

She chuckled. "I think I'm a little too old for 'boy trouble,' Dr. Martin."

"Perhaps. But it is trouble, right?"

"I think so. I'm not sure." How could she tell for sure when she hadn't allowed Dillon to say much to her? Maybe he wasn't as bad as she remembered. There was still a small part of her that worried she was making a big problem out of a couple of chance sightings.

"Kinsey, you might be my employee, but you're far more than that to me. How can I help?"

"I don't think there's anything you can do." Sure Dillon was scaring her, but she was pretty sure that he was going to lose interest now that she was with Hunt all the time.

"Sure I can." He leaned back, then smiled as their server approached. "This looks wonderful, doesn't it, dear?"

Her tacos were exactly how she liked them. "It sure does."

When the server left, Doc added, "Would you like me to talk to him for you Kinsey? I'd be happy to tell him to leave you alone."

She stared at him. "How would you do that?"

"Very easily." He sipped his water. "I wouldn't mind, dear. I'll remind him that you're young. You shouldn't have to worry about being bothered at work. Or bothered anywhere else, for that matter."

"Thanks, but you don't need to get involved." He was making a confrontation with Dillon sound so easy. It wasn't, though. What would she do if Dillon hurt him?

"I do, though. After all, it's because of me that Hunt is working at the office."

Hunt? He'd been talking about Hunt?

They'd been talking about two different people. Replaying the conversation in her head, Kinsey released a breath she hadn't even realized she'd been holding. Then, unable to help herself, she started giggling. "Oh my gosh. You've got it all wrong." Leaning forward, she said, "Doc, I thought you were talking about Dillon. Not Hunt."

"Who in the world is Dillon?"

Still trying not to dissolve into a fit of giggles, Kinsey was more honest than she normally would be. "He's…he's a person I was in foster care with. He's working at a sandwich shop in town. Then later, I saw him from a distance. It's rattled me."

He frowned. "I had forgotten all about him. He's back in your life?"

"Kind of." As succinctly as possible, Kinsey told him about the few times Dillon had been watching her.

"Do you want me to get involved or something?"

"No. I think it's getting better. But, that's why I was so confused. I thought you were asking me about Dillon. Not Hunt."

"So…you're okay with Hunt's attentions? He's not bothering you?"

"He's not bothering me at all. He and I have become close."

Kind of.

Picking up his fork, he breathed a sigh of relief. "I'm so glad we talked. Claudia and I were worried about you."

"That's sweet. I can't believe you were really going to warn him away from me, Doc."

He looked a little affronted. "Why would you think I wouldn't?"

"Because Hunt is your neighbor. He's one of your best friend's kids. You've known him all his life."

"That's true, but we know you pretty well, too."

"I'm just saying that I know you're close to Hunt. I would never want you to worry about hurting him."

"Kinsey, you might have only entered our lives when you were sixteen, but Claudia and I consider you to be our daughter. There's nothing we wouldn't do to help you. Nothing," he added with a tap on the table for added emphasis.

"Okay."

Not seeming to notice that tears were forming in her eyes, he added, "Plus, you've been through enough pain and drama. I certainly don't want to add to it."

"Thank you."

"If I can make your life easier, I will. Besides, you do too good a job at work for me to lose you," he teased.

"I'm glad you think I'm doing a good job."

"Everyone thinks you're going great, kiddo. Don't doubt that. Now, eat up. Hunt's parents are in town, and I've got a golf game set up with Stewart."

"You certainly don't want to be late for that."

Appreciation lit his eyes. "I'm glad you understand."

"Thank you, sir." Finally picking up one of her tacos, she dug in.

CHAPTER TWENTY-THREE

THE REST OF Kinsey's day had been uneventful. Bolstered by Dr. Martin's compliments and energized by the tacos, she'd been all smiles the rest of the afternoon. One of the delivery drivers who stopped by had even teased Kinsey, saying that her pretty smile should be used in Dr. Martin's next advertising campaign.

She'd laughed, of course. No way would Dr. Martin start placing ads in magazines—he was too old school for that. And if he did, he certainly wouldn't pick her. But honestly, that guy could've complained to her about a dozen things and it probably wouldn't have dimmed her mood. She was going to be floating on air, thanks to Larry revealing that he and Claudia thought of her like a daughter.

When she was finally satisfied that everything in the office was organized and ready for Monday morning, Kinsey did her usual routine, wiping down the waiting room and shutting down her computer. When she'd walked to the break room to retrieve the sandwich that was still in the fridge, she paused to gaze at the tiles.

She was a little disappointed that Hunt hadn't showed up but reminded herself that he was in the middle of several jobs, and his parents were in town, too. His mom probably wanted to spend some time with him.

Plus, she shouldn't start counting on Hunt to be at the dentist's office every day when she was leaving. No matter how much she was starting to develop feelings for Hunt, it was unlikely that he'd ever feel the same way about her.

There were too many obstacles between them, the least of which was their age difference. She might've been mature for her age, but she was still seven years younger than him. And not only was there a big gap in their ages, but there was a huge difference in their life experiences. She might have experienced a devastating loss when she was a kid, but Hunt had been in a war. He'd said that he'd seen and done things that had marked him.

Plus, he had been all around the country and the world. She'd never left Ohio. How would she ever keep his interest?

But…maybe he wasn't looking for scintillating conversation. Maybe he was just looking for a friend.

Her mind still on Hunt, she turned off all the lights in the office, locked the door, and headed to her car.

Dillon was leaning against it.

Stunned, she stopped in her tracks. She had no idea what to do.

"I was starting to think you'd never get out of there," he said. "I almost got tired of waiting for you."

Frantically, she scanned the area. Hoping against hope that she'd see Hunt's truck parked nearby. Or, shoot, anyone who could offer a helping hand. But the majority of the vehicles that usually parked around her were long gone. She and Dillon were essentially alone.

Although a part of her wanted to run away, she forced herself not to do that. She owed it to herself to finally face him.

"What do you want, Dillon?"

Appreciation glinted in his green eyes. "Ah, so you do remember my name. I was starting to think you didn't remember me." He folded his arms over his khaki-colored T-shirt. "That would've been a real shame, Kinsey. I sure have never forgotten you."

She knew better than to respond to that. They both might've been older, but she couldn't imagine that he no longer looked for a weakness to take advantage of. "You need to move."

"No, you need to talk to me. I don't like it when you act as if I don't exist."

Reminding herself that there might not be anyone next to her in the parking lot but there were people walking by in the distance, Kinsey forced herself to hold her ground. "We have nothing to say to each other."

"I disagree. We could talk about old times." He lowered his voice as he stepped toward her. "For example, you could ask me about where I went after you complained about me. Aren't you curious?"

"Not at all. I don't care where you went. Now, step aside. I need to leave."

"No. You need to stand here and listen to me. Because you should care where I went, Kinsey Zaleski. You should care a lot. Because of you, I was sent to a group home."

She flinched. Her social worker had only told her that he'd moved to a new home. Back then, she hadn't known that group homes existed.

He laughed softly. "Ah. I knew you knew." Still smirking, he added, "I'm curious. Since no one ever liked you enough to adopt you, you must have moved around a lot, too. Did you ever get the opportunity to be in one of those?"

In spite of her determination to not give Dillon any ammunition to use against her, Kinsey shook her head.

"Yeah, I didn't think so." He scoffed. "You would've had to do a lot of bad to get sent there. And back then, back when I met you? Well, everyone felt so sorry for you. Even the Walkers did, and

I didn't think they were capable of feeling sorry for any of us kids."

He paused. Pulled himself together. "But you made an impression on them, Kinsey. You'd be upstairs in the girls' room crying your little heart out, and they let you. The rest of us had to give you a wide berth because you were such a 'poor little thing.' So traumatized by your parents dying in that car accident."

No way was she going to revisit those days. Not when she'd kept those feelings locked up for years.

Not when Dillon seemed determined to make fun of how she felt.

"Stop." She blurted it. It came out forcefully. Rough, like the word had been torn from the depths of her soul.

She hated that she was being so vulnerable.

"No." Dillon studied her. Sneered, as if he couldn't find anything about her that was redeeming. "Why should I? No one ever said they felt sorry for me. I never understood why either. Like, how come no one ever thought having two parents in prison wasn't traumatic, too? Why were you, with your long hair, perfect skin, and big brown eyes, the only one to get special treatment?"

"I don't want to talk to you about this." He was bringing up too many memories. Too many things that she'd worked so hard to forget. Her hands were starting to feel clammy.

Dillon inhaled sharply, like he was attempting

to control his temper. "Okay. Fine. We can talk about that another day."

"No."

"Oh, yes, Kinsey. We do need to see each other again."

"Dillon, that isn't a good idea. We don't need to see each other again because we have nothing else to talk about."

His green eyes flickered. A look of remorse settled in as his voice became quieter. "Look. I know you're scared of me, but you don't have to be. I'm fine now. As you know, I have a job and everything." He stepped closer. "And sure, I've still got some issues. I still have some PTSD from some of the things that happened to me, but I won't take my hurt or anger out on you."

He already was, though. Chill bumps formed on her arms. She hadn't felt this trapped since…since they were in the same house together.

He raised a hand. "Oh no, Kinsey. You've got that look. That look that says you're going to cry. Don't. I promise I don't want to do anything but get to know you again."

"No." No way.

"Come on. Don't say no." Brightening, he added, "Kinsey, let me take you out to dinner."

"I can't."

"You can't or you won't?"

What was she going to do? This conversation was lasting forever, and it was as if everything she'd ever learned about standing up for herself had left her brain.

"She means that she can't," a voice said behind her.

No, not a voice. *The* voice she cared so much about. "Hunt," she whispered, turning around to face him.

"Hey," he said back, his expression soft.

Kinsey was so relieved, she felt like wrapping her arms around his middle and holding on tight. Doing whatever she could to keep him close.

But Hunt did one better. He put both of his arms around her middle and tugged her toward him. Close enough that she could feel the bulge of his biceps against her ribs. Feel the heat coming off his body as it warmed her back. "It's okay, Kinsey," he whispered.

Still holding her against his chest, Hunt lifted his chin. "Who are you?"

"Why don't you ask her? She knows."

"I'm asking you, because I want you to tell me."

"Very well. I'm Dillon Carpenter. Who are you?"

"I'm the guy who's not a big fan of my girlfriend getting cornered in a parking lot."

Still tucked against his chest, Kinsey felt her breathing ease. He was acting exactly like she'd hoped he would. So good at pretending to care about her.

"We were just talking. All I want to do is grab some something to eat. Catch up on old times."

The muscles surrounding her tensed up.

"How about this, then?" Hunt asked. "I'm also not a fan of my girlfriend going out with other guys. Especially when I'm not there." Then, just as if Dillon wasn't standing there, Hunt's grip on her loosened. He backed up a step so he could see her face. "I'm sorry I'm late, honey."

Kinsey had never been so happy or relieved. "I didn't know you were still coming."

"Of course I was. But you left the office without telling me, hon," he added as he smoothed back a piece of her hair from her face. "I wish you hadn't done that."

Her insides didn't know whether to melt because he'd called her "hon" or burst into laughter because it sounded so foreign and awkward, she was pretty sure that Hunt had never used that endearment before.

She didn't have to worry about that, though, because Hunt wasn't directing his attention on her. He was looking directly at Dillon. "Let's stop playing games. I'm going to make myself real clear. Kinsey has no desire to reacquaint herself with you. She doesn't want to talk to you or see you. It would be a good idea if you respected her wishes."

"Or what?"

"Or I'm going to have to get involved. And I'll get the police involved."

"Looks like you've found yourself a good little bodyguard, Kinsey," Dillon said. "I'd never thought you had that in you." He shrugged. "Though, like we said earlier, we're strangers now. Neither of us really know what the other person is like now. That's a shame," he added with a smirk before sauntering off.

Shaken by the conversation, Kinsey didn't budge from the safety of Hunt's arms. She'd stayed there even when Dillon crossed the street, turned left, and eventually disappeared out of sight.

The best part was that Hunt didn't move. He didn't seem to mind holding her close for a little longer. Even though Dillon was no longer watching. Just like she didn't mind staying exactly where she was.

It was too bad that just as she had finally calmed down, Hunt stepped away. When his arms dropped, she felt his loss. She wrapped her arms around herself in order to warm up.

"Are you doing better now?" he asked.

"Yes. I'm not sure how you knew to come over here, but I'm sure glad you did." What would she have done if Hunt hadn't shown up? She'd been practically frozen in place. There was no doubt in her mind that Dillon would've been pleased that her long-dormant fears for him had reared up. He would have taken advantage of them.

Meeting Hunt's gaze, she smiled.

But to her dismay, all he did was frown. "Girl,

the question isn't why did I show up. The question is why didn't you call or text to let me know what time you were getting out of the office?"

"I thought you had other things to do."

"I have a lot of things that I could be doing. I had planned on walking you to your car, though. Why didn't you reach out to me?"

Kinsey was confused. Yes, they'd agreed that he would walk her to her car. But he'd never promised to do it five evenings a week.

Certainly not in the afternoon.

Hunt was acting like they had a real relationship. Like she was supposed to be depending on him.

They did not.

"Ah, because I didn't think I was supposed to?"

He frowned. "I've walked you to your car every night this week."

"I know."

"Then?"

She felt like rolling her eyes. "Hunt, I can't read your mind. Plus…" Her voice drifted off. How could she tell him what she was really thinking?

"Come on. Just say it."

He was getting impatient with her. He had so much nerve. "Okay. Fine. What if I get used to it?"

"What about if you do?"

"What will I do when you find something better to do with your time?" Sure, her voice was quiet, because this was right out of her darkest childhood fears. Being replaced with another foster kid. Until the Martins.

"Such as what?"

He didn't get it. He had no idea what she was getting at.

Which made her completely embarrassed. "I don't know," she said at last. "When you meet a woman you like."

Something flickered in his eyes before he blinked. "Kinsey, if I promise that I'm going to help you, then I will."

"Okay."

"Besides, if everything goes the way we hope, this guy will lose interest soon."

His words made sense. They were clear cut. Matter of fact. No frills. No promises. All just pretend.

She should be okay with that. After all, it was what she wanted. Just a pretend relationship in order to make a guy she used to be afraid of move on. When all this was over, maybe she'd be ready to get involved in a real relationship. She could finally feel like she was no longer scarred from her parents' death and all those years in foster care. One day she'd be able to get married. Have a family. Have the life her parents had always imagined she'd have.

"Kinsey, what do you think? Are you good with this?"

"The question is are you good with pretending

to be my boyfriend and maybe even having to deal with Dillon again? Are you up for that?"

"Yes to you, and yes to dealing with Dillon. Besides, he didn't seem that tough to me."

"He might seem that way, but I can assure you that he's not a nice person."

Reaching for her hand, he linked his fingers in hers. "I don't know what you think being in the army was like, Kins, but I promise you, I had to deal with a whole lot of not-nice people when I served. He doesn't scare me."

There was a light shining in his eyes now. Almost like he was going to welcome the opportunity to confront Dillon and put him in his place.

She wasn't sure what she thought about that, but she was very sure that she was very glad she wouldn't have to do it on her own.

It might not be the right way to think, and it was probably against every social norm where women wanted to handle everything themselves.

She'd done that. And handling everything on her own was stressful and exhausting. If Hunt could make her life a little easier for a while, she'd take it.

No, she'd hold onto the opportunity as tightly as she could. She just hoped Hunt didn't grow tired of her before she felt safe again.

"Hey listen, since my parents are in town, we're going to barbecue with Larry and Claudia. Want to come?"

"I don't know."

"It'll be fun. Easy. Say yes."

She should say no. But since the choice was either be by herself or be with Hunt, the Martins, and his parents, her heart wouldn't let her. "All right. Thanks."

"Great. You go home, relax and get changed, and come over to the Martins' around six. Okay?"

She had no idea if they were going to be playacting for everyone or not. She was too worn out to ask.

All she could do was nod.

She really hoped she knew what she was getting into.

CHAPTER TWENTY-FOUR

HUNT WAS STILL trying to wrap his head around it. The news about Kinsey joining them had created a minor commotion in his house. Though it made no sense at all, for some reason his mother decided she had to change outfits. Then she did another inventory of the pantry and refrigerator while she figured out what else to make.

"Ma, the last thing we need to do is bring more food to the Martins'."

"Don't worry about me, Hunt." Making a motion with her hand, she muttered, "Go amuse yourself until we're ready."

Though it was on the tip of his tongue to remind her that he was no longer nine years old, he kept his silence. He also vacated his own kitchen so his mother could continue to make yet another mess.

He sat in his easy chair, turned on the television, and played on his phone while he waited.

Eventually, his dad got home. After barely saying hello, he hurried into the shower so he wouldn't smell like a cigar.

When he appeared again, dressed in a pair of

loose khakis and another golf shirt, Hunt was more than ready to go over to the Martins' and see Kinsey. "You ready, Dad?"

"I am, but Hunter, I'd like to talk about something first."

Everything in his father's stance was sending out warning signals. "What do you want to talk about?"

"This evening."

He was feeling more confused, and more than a little fed up with houseguest parents. They were messy and took forever to do everything. "Okay, but can we do it while we're walking?" He picked up the covered dish his mother had instructed them to take to the Martins'. "I think Kinsey is already over at Doc's."

"If she is, then we need to have a little chat now."

A little chat? His father was notorious for "little chats" that took over an hour. He was going to need some reinforcements. Hunt looked over his shoulder. "Where's Mom?"

"I don't know. Probably in the kitchen gathering everything for s'mores."

"I thought she bought a cherry pie at Heinen's."

"She did, but Kinsey loves s'mores, right?"

"I don't know." He was pretty sure everyone liked s'mores. And was also pretty sure that Kinsey had stopped craving them years ago.

Dad shot him a pointed look. "You should know your girl's favorite foods, Hunter."

"You're being ridiculous. I'm not going to have this conversation, Dad."

"You're right. There's probably plenty of time to learn all her likes and dislikes." He lowered his voice. "But how are things going with her otherwise?"

"Everything is fine between me and her."

"You know, your mother always liked it when I gave her little treats. When was the last time you gave Kinsey flowers?"

By this time Hunt had had enough. He'd already been bullied into putting on a fresh shirt and was currently holding a container of potato salad that could feed a dozen new recruits.

"I don't want to talk about my love life, Dad."

"Don't worry. We won't discuss anything too personal."

What did that mean? "I'm thirty-five, Dad."

"I know. But I don't remember the last time you were this serious about a woman."

He didn't remember either. But then again, every other relationship he'd been in hadn't been make-believe.

Although his feelings for Kinsey were certainly not fake. He liked her a lot.

"Do you recall, Hunter?"

"Um, sometime when I was deployed, I think."

"So it has been a while. You might be rusty."

"I'm doing fine, Dad. As far as I know, Kinsey has no complaints. Now, I'm carrying this potato salad over and finding Kinsey. You and Mom join us whenever you're ready."

Shaking his head at the whole situation, he strode over to the Martins' back door.

Kinsey must have been looking for him, because she opened the door before he could knock.

"I'm glad you're here," she said.

"Me, too." Her hair was in a cute ponytail, and she had on a pair of shorts, a flowy red top, and sandals. Her legs were tanned and toned, and her smile was bright. It was going to be hard to look at anyone else but her. Realizing he'd been staring, he cleared his throat. "So, how's it going?"

Her eyes danced. "I think our acting skills are going to get a workout tonight."

"I've thought the same thing," Hunt muttered, though he was also starting to wonder if any acting was going to be needed. At the moment, he didn't want to do anything but stick by her side.

"Look who I found, Claudia," Kinsey said when they entered the kitchen.

"Hi, Hunt."

"Hi. I've got my mom's potato salad."

"Oh, good. Larry just fired up the grill." Looking just beyond them, she frowned. "Where are your parents?"

"I believe my mom is gathering ingredients for s'mores."

Claudia smiled at Kinsey. “Honey, isn’t that sweet? Joanne remembered how much you liked them.”

Kinsey shared a smile with Hunt. “It’s so sweet.”

He barely refrained from laughing.

It turned out that s’mores were just a hint of what was going to happen during the next two hours. Both sets of parents seemed excited to bring up all kinds of things he and Kinsey had done in high school—even though she’d passed through those halls several years after he had.

“Are you doing okay?” he asked when she volunteered to help him carry their plates inside after they finished dinner.

“I’m fine,” she said with a laugh. “They’re all kind of cute, aren’t they?”

“They’re bordering on annoying.” Taking the plates from her, he quickly rinsed each and put them in the dishwasher. “I feel like we had four sets of eyes watching us every time one of us looked at the other.”

“Well, at least now that dinner’s over, we’ll get to have s’mores.”

Unable to help himself, he wrapped an arm around her. “That is a bonus.” When she leaned closer, it was all he could do not to bend down and kiss her.

“Oh! Don’t mind me,” his mom called out. “I just came in for marshmallows.”

Kinsey tensed, then looked up at him with a wide-eyed expression.

Hunt felt the same way. It was going to be a small miracle if they both survived the night.

CHAPTER TWENTY-FIVE

SITTING IN THE back of the Martins' backyard was one of Kinsey's favorite places to be. Sure, it was lovely and well taken care of, and there was an apple tree that actually grew apples that you could eat. But even if there hadn't been any of that, even if the backyard had been filled with weeds or the size of a postage stamp, she would still love the place.

Because the Martins had made it that way.

From the time Stephanie had first dropped her off there, Kinsey had sensed that Dr. and Mrs. Martin were different. They didn't want more foster kids. Just her. They didn't act as if she was disrupting their routine, they embraced the changes.

And since she'd moved to their house just after she'd turned sixteen, by the time she turned seventeen, the three of them had become a little unit. She couldn't say family, but she did feel like there was something special between them all. She'd stopped walking around on eggshells, waiting to be kicked out. She'd even put away the canvas bag that Stephanie had given her for her belongings.

She hadn't been sure how long the Martins were going to keep her around, but it had begun to be obvious that they weren't going to send her away anytime soon.

And then came her next birthday. Ever since she'd been at the Walkers' house, Kinsey had started counting down the days until her seventeenth birthday. When she was eighteen, she'd finally get to have some control of her life.

So, her seventeenth birthday was a big deal. It signified that she just had three hundred and sixty-five days left. Ironically, Kinsey had started to hope that each day would last a long time.

Claudia and Larry had gone all out to celebrate. Not only had Claudia made Kinsey a cake and put seventeen candles on it, but she'd gotten a big bouquet of balloons. She'd even wrapped seventeen presents for Kinsey.

Not to be outdone, Larry had used her birthday as an excuse to spruce up the backyard. A new patio replaced the old, cracked cement one. A lovely path soon led from the patio to a new firepit complete with Adirondack chairs and side tables. To finish it off, Larry and Claudia had planted all sorts of bushes and flowers. Kinsey had thought it looked like something out of a magazine. It was beautiful.

The only bittersweet moment had come when Larry and Claudia had realized that Kinsey hadn't had anyone she wanted to invite to their party. They'd been surprised, and even a little bit hurt.

Kinsey hadn't understood why, until she'd realized that Claudia thought that she was embarrassed by them. That was when Kinsey had had to tell her the truth, which was that this was the first birthday party she'd had since she was ten years old.

A few of her other foster parents had given her a present and a card, but they'd never gone all out. No one else had made her a cake. She hadn't wanted anyone to come over and make her worried about how to act. Being with Claudia and Larry had been enough.

But then it had gotten better, because Hunt's parents had shown up after sundown with sparklers, graham crackers, marshmallows, and chocolate bars. The five of them had sat in those fancy chairs next to the firepit, roasted marshmallows, and laughed. Joanne had shared stories about their son, Hunter. Hunter had been doing all kinds of heroic things overseas, and Kinsey had been wide-eyed about how amazing he'd sounded.

Before the little party had ended, all four of the adults had sung "Happy Birthday" to her. Claudia had hugged her tight when she'd started crying.

When Kinsey had fallen asleep that night in a brand new pair of pajamas—one of her seventeen presents—she'd thought that it had been the best night in her life. Maybe even more than the birthday parties her own parents had given her, because now she appreciated it so much more.

But as she sat next to Hunt in front of that same firepit with both sets of their parents, Kinsey thought that this evening might be just as special.

"Hey, you're awfully quiet," Hunt whispered as Stewart and Larry traded jokes about getting old.

"I'm fine. I'm having a good time listening to everyone's stories."

"We can get out of here in a little while," he said as he leaned closer. "As you know, the four of them can hang out here all night."

She tried not to notice how good he smelled. "I'll let you know when I'm ready. Not yet, though."

"Hunt, leave poor Kinsey alone," Stewart called out. "You're hovering over her like a nervous mama bird."

Kinsey bit her lip when Hunt straightened—but not before sharing a look with her.

"I'm not hovering, Dad. Just making sure she's warm enough."

"We're in front of a fireplace and it's seventy degrees out here. She's fine."

"Leave him alone, Stewart," Claudia said. "I'm having fun watching the two of them together."

"She's right," Joanne said with a new, dreamy tone in her voice. "Why, how many times have we talked about this happening?"

Kinsey tensed. "Wait, what?"

"Oh, you know. You and Hunter falling in love

and making all of us so happy," Joanne continued. "I must say that the two of you look so cute together."

"Mom."

"Don't fuss, Hunter. Gosh, wouldn't it be something if one day—"

"Mom, I love you, but stop."

"I have to agree with the captain here," Larry said with a wink in Hunt's direction. "We need to let them alone."

"Am I embarrassing you, Kinsey?" Joanne asked.

She was uncomfortable on multiple levels, but what could she say? "Not at all, but I am ready to roast marshmallows."

"Of course you are, honey," Joanne said. "Some things never change."

Stewart held up six metal hangers. He'd been unwinding and straightening them out while they'd all been talking. "Come get a hanger, sweetie."

Just as she was about to stand up, Hunt placed a hand on her knee. "Stay put. I'll get it for you."

When she smiled her thanks, Kinsey was pretty sure she heard both Claudia and Joanne sigh with happiness.

Their reaction was cute, and she knew everyone meant well. But boy, everything that was happening was getting more awkward by the minute.

"Here," Hunt said, handing her a hanger. When he sat down, he added, "Don't think about everything, okay? Let's just have a good time."

"I can do that."

And so, she did. They roasted marshmallows, smooshed them in between chocolate and graham crackers, and ate way too much sugar. She also managed to drip melted chocolate onto her shorts. She did have a great time, though. The night was beautiful, the treat was yummy, and the company was wonderful.

The time flew as she and Hunt helped clean up the trash, wash dishes, and carry casserole dishes back to his parents' house. It was close to midnight when they left. Hunt had decided to drive her home. Larry and his dad were going to drop off her car in the morning.

After she unlocked her apartment door and Hunt walked her in, she smiled up at him. "Thanks for the ride home."

"Thanks for making tonight so much fun."

"It was fun, wasn't it? I was sure it was going to be really awkward."

"Oh, it was. But I had a good time, too. We have great parents."

"Yeah, we do," she said, realizing it was time to finally start thinking about Larry and Claudia Martin as something more than just her fosters. In every way that counted, they were her parents.

"I better go. Get some sleep."

"You, too," she whispered. And when Hunt pulled her into his arms for a hug, Kinsey relaxed against him. His arms were strong, and his body felt like it was all muscle. Somehow, even though their clothes and her hair smelled like a campfire, the scent that she'd come to associate with him was still there. It comforted her.

"Good night, Kinsey," he whispered as he pressed his lips to her brow. He reminded her to lock the door as he strode out.

After she showered and got into bed, Kinsey stared out her bedroom window. Looked at the stars.

And couldn't help but wish that her relationship with Hunt Vargo was as real as the rest of the world believed it was.

CHAPTER TWENTY-SIX

IT WASN'T TOO often that two eighteen-year-olds asked Edna for a meeting, but then again, most teens weren't like Madison and Cope. Standing near the reception desk, Edna watched the pair walk down the street toward Loaves of Love. Cope was holding Madison's hand while she seemed to be talking a mile a minute about something.

Edna couldn't help but smile at the way Cope directed Maddie around a pile of leaves and mud that the girl seemed completely oblivious to. When he stopped in order for a trio of ladies to exit a building, Madison frowned before realizing that she'd been close to running into the women.

Madison really was one of the smartest yet flightiest young woman Edna had the pleasure of knowing.

She supposed she should give the girl a break, however. Madison was going to Case Western and living on campus while Cope was working at the hardware store. They didn't have the opportunity to spend lots of time together.

Which was another reason why Edna had agreed

to this meeting before she had an idea what it was about.

"Edna, was there something you needed?" Valerie asked.

Realizing that she'd been staring off in the distance, Edna shook her head. "No. I've been waiting for a couple people to arrive, and they just did."

Turning to the front door, Valerie smiled as Cope held the door open for Maddie and they walked inside. "They sure look cute together, don't they?" she whispered.

"So cute," Edna whispered back before approaching the pair. "I don't know how you two do it. You both are always on time for everything."

Madison grinned. "I think that's because we're so busy. We have to stay on track, or we'll never get everything done."

"That must be the reason. That and your youth," Edna teased as she hugged them both hello. "Now, you two have a choice. We can go to my office or go to the Blue Door Café and get coffees while we talk. My treat."

After Cope and Madison exchanged glances, Cope said, "Thanks for the offer, but I think it would be best if we met in your office."

He looked so serious. For the first time, Edna began to feel concerned. Maybe this meeting didn't have anything to do with school or jobs or references and was about something far more serious. Schooling her features, she said, "I'm good with that. Let's get to it."

She had a small seating area on one side of her newly remodeled office and a pair of chairs situated in front of her desk. "Have a seat," she offered, deciding to let them decide how casual or formal they wanted the meeting to be.

She wasn't surprised when Maddie and Cope chose the pair of chairs in front of her desk.

Sitting down behind her desk, she pulled out her readers and a pad of paper and pen. "You know what? I kind of like meeting in here. It sure keeps me more organized."

"I like your office, Edna," Madison said. "It looks a lot different than when Aunt Chloe and I stopped by last May."

Edna waved a hand behind her, just like she was on *The Price Is Right*. "That's because I hired Hunt Vargo to install all these built-ins. It gave me enough space to add the little seating area, which has been a lifesaver. Now five or six people can sit in here without the room feeling claustrophobic."

"It does seem a lot more open," Cope agreed. "I like it."

"Thank you. I'm glad." Clasping her hands together on the top of her desk, Edna said, "Now, enough about me. What is on your minds?"

After Madison and Cope exchanged glances, Madison spoke. "I overheard my aunt Chloe say something to Kayla Copeland the other day when I was making bread here."

"We both overheard it, remember, Mad?" Cope asked.

"Oh yeah." She shared a soft look with him before turning back to Edna. "Anyway, after hearing her, it got us thinking about kids in Medina."

Edna smiled encouragingly. Kayla was one of her favorite people—and her first matchmaking success story. "Anything specific?" Edna prodded.

Maddie glanced at Cope.

"Yeah. See, when I was in school, I got free breakfast and lunch," he said.

"Okay…"

"Well, I got real used to eating breakfast and lunch." His lips pressed together. "Dad did the best he could, but sometimes dinner wasn't all that great."

All of a sudden, Edna realized where this was going. "You missed those meals in the summer."

"Yeah." He cleared his throat. "Kayla said that the school district does provide some meals if people sign up, but it's kind of awkward." Averting his eyes, he said, "No way did my dad ever want to fill out the paperwork and then go pick up a week's worth of breakfast and lunch food on Saturdays. Some kids used to help out there for volunteer hours."

"So, if you went there, they would know."

Cope nodded.

"Plus, some of the food is kind of gross, Edna," Madison said. "I mean, it's nutritious and all, but..."

"I get it." Picking up her pen, she said, "While I agree that kids need to eat, I don't think we could do any better than the school district already does."

"I agree," Madison said. "But, um, I was thinking maybe we could offer to make muffins for kids."

"Muffins?"

"Yeah. Kayla said that a couple of times a month volunteers can make dinner rolls instead of bread. Could we make muffins and put them in a cute container or something?" She waved a hand. "Everyone likes muffins for breakfast, right?"

"People do like muffins. I don't know if they're the best choice for breakfast, though."

"I think they're a good choice for any time of day. Who's to say they must be eaten for breakfast?"

"Well, I guess we could do that."

"If someone comes here for food, they could take home a container of muffins. Maybe even if they bake a loaf of bread, too," Cope added. "If they wanted."

Edna grinned. "I like that idea. I like that a lot. Variety is always a good idea, I think. Now, the first thing we need to do is come up with some recipes. Would you two be willing to gather them? And don't forget—blueberry muffins are delicious, but it's not always very easy to buy blueberries in bulk. Plus, they can be expensive, especially when they're out of season."

"Actually, my mom helped me come up with some ideas. She had a muffin recipe that can use jam and jelly in the center. Didn't you say that sometimes people like to give the shelter jars of preserved jams?"

"I did. But I'm not always too keen on giving them to people because I don't know how long they've been in someone's cellar. If you can find a way to make sure the ingredients are fresh, then I think you two are on your way." Looking from one to the other, she said, "Are you ready to spearhead this project? You'll need to gather materials, write down recipes with detailed instructions, then make samples for our volunteers to try."

"I'm game," Cope said. "What do you think, Maddie?"

"I think we've come too far to back down now," she joked.

Edna stood up and hugged them both. "Let me know when you have your first sample batch out of the oven. I can't wait to give them a try."

Madison beamed. "We will."

A few minutes later, the pair were on their way to the grocery store and Edna was feeling better about the world. Sure, her Hunt-and-Kinsey match was moving more slowly than she'd anticipated, but she thought most things worthwhile always were. Even making something as simple as a pan of muffins involved some planning and organization.

She needed to remember that.

CHAPTER TWENTY-SEVEN

HUNT HADN'T BEEN sleeping well. No, that was putting it mildly. After almost a year's absence, his nightmares had returned. They were bad ones, too. All based in foreign countries, all taking him back to the army.

He wasn't sure what had triggered them. He'd thought he'd slept pretty well after the crazy get-together with his family, Kinsey, and the Martins on Friday night. But maybe he hadn't? On Saturday morning when he'd woken up, he'd felt a little out of breath, a little sweaty. He'd blamed it on the summer heat.

Since his parents had plans the rest of the weekend with some friends near the lake, he'd been on his own. He'd spent Saturday cleaning, then had worked in his garage late into the night on a china cabinet. He was refinishing it for a woman who'd bought the thing at a consignment store, then had somehow managed to almost ruin it because she hadn't read the directions on the bottle of paint stripper. She'd called him in a panic, asking if he'd please fix it up for her granddaughter.

He still wasn't sure why he'd said yes. Repairing her damage was painstaking work and took hours of time he didn't really have.

He'd fallen asleep after midnight both irritated with the customer and with himself for agreeing to the project. Maybe he'd breathed in too many fumes and gotten sick. Or maybe his body had just decided that it had been too long without a nightmare. Whatever the reason, when he'd fallen asleep, he'd dreamt about Afghanistan.

He smelled the dust and the grime and the ash and the faint hint of spices. Heat seared his skin. Insurgents mixed in with his soldiers. Panic attacks were followed by whispered orders, bursts of gunfire, and an overwhelming sense of doom.

The dream had ended like it always did, with him yelling orders that weren't clear enough and his vehicle getting hit by the bomb.

He'd woken up at five in the morning screaming, not in pain but ordering two of his soldiers to take cover. Sweat had been pouring off him. He'd felt disoriented. Almost hungover.

Because of that, his morning had been slow and his nap that afternoon had been too long.

To make matters worse, he'd had the same dream the following night. When he'd woken up Monday morning, his hands were shaking. He was so disappointed. He'd thought he'd gotten past this. What if he never did?

He'd known he had to get a handle on himself,

so he stopped by the veteran's center and spoke to a buddy of his. Jared had listened with compassion and reminded Hunt of the things he'd learned when he'd been laid up in bed in Germany after his surgery.

Jared had given him a lot of good advice, but his best had been the reminder that Hunt wasn't alone. He wasn't the only one still occasionally experiencing nightmares, and there were plenty of people in his life to lean on.

Hunt continued to think about Jared's words during the day while he shopped, welcomed his parents back, and then later hugged them goodbye when they headed back to Arizona.

Now he was wiping down baseboards in the waiting room of Dr. Martin's office while he watched Kinsey continually do one more thing for Doc around the office. Hunt wasn't pleased. She'd already stayed an hour longer than she should have, and he could tell that she was tired.

When Doc handed Kinsey yet another folder with a lengthy explanation, her eyes seemed to glaze over. She'd reached her limit.

"Kinsey, are you sure you understand what to say to them about the billing issues?"

"I think so, Dr. Martin."

"Think so?" Looking impatient, Doc sighed. "I suppose I had better go over it again, then. I'm not sure what is going on with you today, Kinsey."

"I'm sorry, Doc. I don't know what's wrong either."

Hunt did. Which meant that it was time to intervene.

Kinsey looked like she was about to cry. That was the excuse Hunt had been waiting for. He walked across the room to join them. "Hey, Doc, did you notice what time it is?"

"Hmm?" He frowned. "Hunt, why are you in here? I thought you were going to paint an examining room tonight."

"I was going to, but I wanted to walk Kinsey to her car first. And now I think I'll paint tomorrow. I'm going to take her to get something to eat."

"Why?"

"Because it's six o'clock, Doc."

Glancing at Kinsey, Doc said, "Is it really? Well, this shouldn't take you too long."

Usually Hunt would stay silent, but the man was clueless and Kinsey looked exhausted. So he gave Doc a pointed look. "You've already kept her an hour late."

"Oh. I guess I did." He looked a little sheepish. "Sorry."

Impatient, Hunt sharpened his tone. "Is she hourly?"

"Hunt, it's okay," Kinsey blurted. "I'm fine."

"No, I don't think it is," he retorted. "You're asking Kinsey to work late with no compensation, and this isn't even the first time this month that it's happened."

"I guess that's true. Sorry, dear."

"She stays late a lot. I don't think it's safe for her to stay this late, don't you agree? The parking lot gets pretty empty. There aren't as many people around."

Kinsey pressed a hand to his chest. "Hunt, stop. I can speak for myself."

"I know you can. You can certainly give me a piece of your mind. But you won't say a word to Doc. Even when he's taking advantage of you."

"He's not."

"No," Dr. Martin interrupted, looking more upset than Hunt could remember him being. "Kinsey, I'm afraid Hunt is correct. You are so competent, I haven't even been thinking about how much extra work I've been giving you to do. He's also right that it never occurred to me that I'm asking you to work more and more hours without compensating you for your time. That was wrong."

"I haven't minded."

"You should, though. Worse, I should've thought about it. I've hired dozens of people for this office over the years. Never did I ever ask them to go continually above and beyond without either a bonus or, at the very least, an extra day off."

Turning to look Hunt directly in the eye, he said, "Thank you, Hunt, for pointing that out."

Hunt nodded but didn't say anything.

"What should I do about all this billing, Doc?"

"Let's tackle it tomorrow. That's soon enough. Go on home."

"Thank you."

Just as Hunt was going to remind her to get her purse and whatever else she needed, Doc sighed. "What time did you get to the office this morning, Kinsey?"

"Eight."

"You've worked ten hours today."

She looked down at the ground. "I suppose."

"And didn't you work later another night this week?"

"Yes."

"And you were here until almost six at least one day last week, weren't you?" When she nodded, Dr. Martin said, "Dear, you and I need to have a real talk. Let's do that on Friday."

"All right. Thanks."

"Thank you, dear."

Before Larry could change his mind, Hunt helped Kinsey gather her things together and then ushered her out the door.

He could tell she wasn't very pleased with him, but he didn't care. As far as he was concerned, Kinsey needed someone to step in and intervene. It wasn't right that Dr. Martin was making her work so many hours.

As they stopped at the crosswalk, she glared at him.

"Go ahead. Tell me what I did wrong."

"That's all you're going to say?"

"Pretty much. Sorry, but something needed to be said and it didn't look like you were going to say a word."

"Larry might have been my foster dad, but he gave me this job, Hunt. I owe him."

"You're right. He took a chance on you. But he hired you for a job, and you've been earning every penny. Any other employee would've quit by now." When something else flashed in her eyes, Hunt realized that he'd overlooked the most obvious conflict of interest. "You think you owe him for more than just this job, don't you?"

"There is no 'think,' Hunt. I do owe him."

"You don't owe him for being your foster parent. Honey, he loves you."

"They changed my life. If it wasn't for them, I would be a very different person."

Larry and Claudia Martin were good people. There was no denying that. But he wasn't going to allow her to give all the credit for her goodness to them. "I agree. They did a real special thing when they became foster parents and took you in. But I've learned that one event or situation doesn't change the trajectory of an entire life. It's a series of events. A bunch of things."

"That's true, but—"

"No, listen. If I hadn't entered the army, I would be different. If I hadn't gotten deployed and my unit had remained stateside, I'd be different. If I hadn't gotten hurt and almost lost half my leg, I'd be a different person. For better or worse, all those things contributed to the man I am today." He lowered his voice. "And the thing is today isn't over yet. Something amazing could happen. Or something bad."

"That doesn't make me feel better," she joked.

"It may not, but it is what it is, right? It's life."

"I really am ready to go home."

"Okay. I'll walk you to your car." When she smiled sweetly at him, he pretended he didn't remember that they were just for show and slung an arm around her shoulders. She was still such a petite thing.

She looked up at him in surprise. "What are you doing?"

"Stop looking scared. I'm your boyfriend, remember?"

And just like that, some of her irritation smoothed out into amusement. "I haven't forgotten."

"If you haven't, then lean into me. Like you like it." He swallowed, ready for Kinsey to have a lot to say about that.

Instead, she did as he asked.

It felt so right.

After making sure she got in her vehicle okay, he said, "Want to grab something to eat before I take you home??"

"Thanks, but no. All I want to do is take a hot shower, eat leftovers, and watch mindless TV."

"I don't mind."

She pressed her palm on his chest. "Thanks again for saying something to Doc."

He pressed his lips to her brow. "Anytime."

He stood there and watched her drive off.

And tried not to think about how she'd smelled like vanilla and peppermint. Or how a part of him hoped this Dillon character would still be around Medina for at least a little bit longer. Because when he was gone, Hunt would have to step out of her life.

Then he'd have no more goofy jokes. No more sweet smiles. No more moments to savor when she tried to get all feisty like one of those terriers at the shelter.

When she was out of his life, everything was going to be quiet and calm and monotonous.

And that was going to sting. It was going to sting real bad.

CHAPTER TWENTY-EIGHT

The first thing Kinsey had noticed when she became Hunt's pretend girlfriend was that other people noticed that they were together, too. One of the patients had smiled at her knowingly when Kinsey had shared that she was planning to go out to eat with a friend over the weekend.

Two girls who she'd known in high school and still got together with occasionally reached out and said they'd heard the news that a certain gorgeous ex-military guy arranged his day in order to walk her to her car after work. They'd thought it was swoony.

Then there was Dr. Martin. He was beaming at her every chance he got, and she knew it wasn't because of the recent raise he'd given her.

All the attention on her personal life was awkward. She didn't think so many people had been this interested in her since her first week at Medina High School.

But things shifted into high gear when Claudia called her up to see if she wanted to go shopping on Friday afternoon. Kinsey loved Claudia. She knew that the woman liked to spend time with her no matter what. But she rarely planned a shopping trip without a specific reason—and this time that reason was Hunt.

Kinsey had easily accepted Claudia's invitation. After all, she knew from experience that it was better to give into her instead of playing games. But she would be lying if she didn't admit to feeling more than a little put on the spot. She and Hunt had fielded lots of not-so-subtle questions about their relationship while eating s'mores in front of Doc's firepit. It felt too soon to answer those same questions all over again.

She supposed she shouldn't have been so surprised about all the attention. After all, it wasn't like she and Hunt were keeping their relationship a secret. Hunt was constantly touching her whenever they were together. Sometimes when he looked at her, there seemed to be genuine tenderness in his gaze.

Every now and then Kinsey almost forgot that he was acting. They were only spending a lot of time together so Dillon would think she had a tall, handsome guy looking out for her. But she was still feeling a little bit like she'd hopped onto a merry-go-round and it had turned into a roller coaster.

Hunt would probably be shocked, but a lot of people knew who he was, and the fact that he walked with a limp and didn't have a fancy job hadn't diminished his appeal in the slightest. As far as they were concerned, he'd already done everything needed to garner respect. He'd been a football star in high school and then had become an officer in the army and served his country. In addition, Hunt Vargo was gorgeous, full of good manners, and was obviously devoted to her.

He was a catch.

She would have been over the moon to be in a legitimate relationship with him. Unfortunately, all it meant to Kinsey was that he was awfully good at playing a role. She was surprised he hadn't joined the community theater.

Maybe it didn't matter. She'd blushed and smiled when patients shared that they were happy for her. She'd written cute, meaningless comments to her high school buddies.

She'd also accepted Claudia's invitation. That had been a given. She not only enjoyed being with Claudia but wanted her advice about a piece of furniture she'd spied in the window of the consignment furniture store she'd gone to in Parma.

"Oooh, I like this," Claudia had exclaimed when she saw the large baker's rack that was still in the window. "You have a good eye."

"I was really just thinking of how I could put it against the wall in my bedroom."

"Your bedroom?"

"You know I don't have a dresser. I thought I could put clothes and stuff on the bottom shelves."

"What about the top part?"

Kinsey shrugged. "I've been thinking about planting cute succulents in little pots and putting them there," she confided. "I don't want a television in my bedroom, but would those plants look odd? What do you think?"

Her expression warmed. "I think you're nesting, dear."

Kinsey laughed. "I don't know about that, but I am excited to try out some hobbies." Suddenly feeling foolish, she added, "You're so good with plants. Would you mind helping me?"

"Of course not. I'm always happy to help."

"Thanks. I don't want to spend a bunch of money on plants and cute little clay pots just to kill them all."

"You won't. I think you can do anything that you set your mind to doing. I'm proud of you."

"Want to go to the plant store next?"

"Of course, honey. I'll be glad to. We'll go to Maria's Gardens. That's my favorite." Eyes lighting up, she added, "Maybe we can go out to lunch afterward. A fun, girly place."

"I'd like that."

"Let's go inside, take a closer look at this baker's rack, and take a peek at everything else."

"Okay, but I think this is the piece I really want."

"If you do, then I'll help you do a bit of haggling on the price."

"That's allowed?"

"I don't know. But we can try, right?"

Sure enough, Claudia stuck to the plans Kinsey had just presented. She circled the store twice, pointed out two other options for the bedroom but backed off immediately when Kinsey nixed those ideas.

Then, to Kinsey's surprise, Claudia stood to the side when Kinsey approached the gruff-looking shop owner and announced that she wanted the piece but didn't want to pay the price because three of the shelves were broken and the door on the left side had obviously been hung crookedly.

The woman had frowned and looked ready to argue...until Claudia very sweetly told her that they also might be interested in a chair and ottoman—if there was a deal on both.

Next thing Kinsey knew, the woman had shaved fifty dollars off the price. And Claudia had whispered that she'd been texting Hunt, Jamison Smith, and Sean Copeland about picking up both pieces and delivering them to Kinsey's loft apartment.

"Everything's going to be picked up on Saturday morning, dear," she announced as they walked out. "Isn't that wonderful? The guys said they'd be happy to help you out."

"That's nice, but I didn't need a chair and ottoman."

"I think you did. Plus, it's going to look perfect when it's been reupholstered and put in the corner of your bedroom."

Kinsey couldn't deny that was true but still felt overwhelmed. "Claudia, I can't afford to get something reupholstered."

"I know. But Hunt could do it."

That seemed worse. "He has jobs that pay money, Claudia. I can't make him do upholstery for me."

"Oh, I'll pay him for the piece. If Larry can hire Hunt to work on the dental office, I can hire him to fix up a piece of furniture." Giving Kinsey a little wink, Claudia added, "Besides, Hunt won't mind giving me a deal on it since it will be for his girlfriend and all." She squeezed Kinsey's arm. "After all, one day he'll probably be using it, too."

Oh no! "Claudia, that wasn't necessary."

"Don't make a big deal out of this. I got that chair and ottoman for a song. And you do need furniture. Plus it's the perfect size. You can curl up when you watch a movie, and Hunt can prop his leg on the ottoman. It's a win-win."

"I don't know if he knows how to reupholster furniture."

"He'll figure it out," Claudia said in her typical breezy way. "After all, how hard can it be?"

"Um, pretty hard?"

"You need to have more faith in Hunt, dear. He might have a bum knee, but that doesn't mean he isn't fantastic at a lot of other things."

"I have faith in Hunt. I don't even think about his hurt knee."

"That's good. I mean, he'd probably be upset if you did think that he wasn't capable."

"I don't think that at all."

"So, yes to the chair?"

"Yes. Thanks."

Claudia gave her a warm hug. "It's my pleasure, honey. I'm just so happy for you. For you and Hunt both. I never imagined that two of my most favorite young people would be getting together. Stewart and Joanne are going to be just as thrilled as we are."

"You aren't going to tell Stewart and Joanne anything, are you?"

"Of course not, honey," Claudia said with another pat on the back. "I'm sure Larry already has."

Gulp. The first thing she needed to do when she got home was reach out to Hunt. They were going to need to come up with a plan as soon as possible. Before Claudia started hinting about wedding dress shopping.

Kinsey had been determined to figure out that plan ASAP. Until she found a note in her mailbox from Dillon. It was short and to the point.

I know where you live, he'd said.

And that was enough to send her in a tailspin yet again.

CHAPTER TWENTY-NINE

HUNT HAD JUST unboxed the first of three ceiling fans for a banker who'd recently moved into a new, bigger house, when Kinsey called him.

Glad he had his earbuds in, he clicked on the receiver. "Hey, Kins. What's going on?"

"Can you come over?"

Something was off in her voice. Putting down the instruction manual, he said, "What's going on?"

"A lot."

"A lot, huh. Well, that tells me nothing." He hoped his teasing tone would ease whatever was bothering her, but the opposite seemed to be happening with him. The moment he'd heard worry in her tone, he'd started to absorb it. "What happened?"

"It's too much to tell you over the phone. I know you are probably working. But is it important?" she pressed, sounding even more stressed out. "I mean, are you busy right now?"

Now? "Honey, is Dillon there?" If so, Dillon had better hope that the police got to her loft before he did. If that guy had put his hands on her, Hunt knew he was liable to hit him hard enough to see stars.

"No, he's not here. But this is important, Hunt. So can you? Please?"

It was eight at night. He had a fan in pieces on the living room floor and two other fans to install. Normally, he'd tell Kinsey that he was in the middle of a job and couldn't take off until it was completed.

But the banker and his wife were in Jamaica and weren't coming back into town for five days. Plus, Hunt had known them for years. Even though he'd told them that he'd be at their house tonight, he could text and let them know that a personal matter needed his attention. He could come back later tonight or even tomorrow.

"Give me about fifteen minutes to clean up, and then I'll be over."

"Where are you?"

"At a house near Weymouth."

"The country club?"

"Yep. Expect me within the half hour, Kinsey."

"Thanks. I'm sorry to make you do this, but I really appreciate it."

"If you need me, I'll be there. Of course I'm going to come over. See you soon."

After shooting a quick text to the couple in case they noticed on the security cameras that he hadn't stayed long, Hunt carefully returned the instruction booklet and the fan back to the box, made sure everything was in good shape, and then headed out.

Her building's parking lot didn't have any visitor spaces available, but he found a spot about a block away. Ten minutes later, he texted as he stood outside the front of her building so she could buzz him in.

Kelsey's apartment was half of the top floor of a brick building constructed in the early 1940s. It had some charming features but was definitely showing its age. When he'd first seen the building, he'd been surprised that she'd chosen to live in a place that didn't have any modern features or a workout facility. Most single people he knew wanted to meet other single people and live somewhere with modern conveniences and even a clubhouse.

But now that he'd gotten to know her better, Hunt realized that this place was far more her speed. She was a loner in a lot of ways. She was also particular about her things and her space.

And even though she seemed to be the friendliest receptionist in town, he was starting to realize that it was because she felt comfortable and safe at her desk behind the glass partition.

She wasn't nearly as relaxed when she didn't have control of a situation.

He'd barely knocked twice when she opened the door with a sigh of relief.

"I'm so glad you're here," she said as she reached for his hand and tugged him inside.

"What is going on?"

"Two things."

He closed the door behind her. "Tell me one."

"First of all, I went shopping with Claudia today."

Okay. Out of everything that had been running through his head about what she needed to tell him, a shopping trip with Mrs. Martin wasn't one of them. "You're going to have to expand upon that, Kinsey."

She stared at him blankly for a split second. "Oh, right. Well, come on. Sit down. I made you decaf coffee like you like. And snacks."

Sure enough, there was a plate on her coffee table with grapes, almonds, crackers, and a block of cheddar cheese. It was sweet, but he was really confused. Maybe a little irritated, too? "Girl, I thought you were in trouble. Or crying. Or something really bad had happened."

A pained expression crossed her face before she playfully popped a hand on her hip. "What are you trying to say? That I can't feed you something while I rock your world?"

A burst of laughter erupted from him before he hardly knew what was what. But he supposed it couldn't have been helped. Kinsey was hysterical.

And, he suspected, she was also biding her time

before telling him the second thing that had happened.

This visit was going to take a while.

After tossing the hoodie he'd been wearing onto one of the barstools facing her tiny kitchen, he strode over to her kitchen sink. "I'll take that coffee now. Thanks."

"Sure thing." She poured two cups, handed him one, then walked to her couch.

As he followed, he took a moment to finally look around. The walls were made of plaster and were painted a creamy white. There were pale gray baseboards and decorative crown molding along the edge of the ceiling. In the back of the space was a tiny kitchen with only about four drawers and that many cabinets. The countertops had been recently updated, though. They were black quartz. To the left of the kitchen was a trio of narrow windows that likely brought in a huge amount of sunlight every morning.

There was a pretty big empty space near the windows, too. Too small for a breakfast nook, but maybe big enough for a bistro table or a small, feminine-looking desk?

In the living room, a pale pink rug lay on the wood floor in front of a pretty big couch that made up in space for what it lacked in comfort. Finally there was a trunk being used as a coffee table and a rather rickety-looking side table painted black next to where she was sitting on the couch.

"I like your place, Kinsey."

"Thanks." She smiled. "It's not much, but when you consider I moved in with just the twin bed I slept in at the Martins' house and a couple of boxes, I think I've been doing pretty good."

"You've got a lot more stuff than I do." His house was spacious and had a great television mounted on his living room wall. He also had a large electric recliner that was roomy enough to sleep in.

But beyond his king-size bed and bedside table and a couple of plastic lawn chairs on the back patio, there was little else. Kinsey, with her limited budget, was putting him to shame.

By the time he'd had a couple of sips of coffee and had eaten a few grapes, Kinsey had shifted, clenched her hands, and somehow managed to look even more uncomfortable than she had sounded on the phone.

He leaned forward. "Talk to me, Kinsey. What happened when you were with Claudia?"

"She asked me about you."

"That's not a surprise. Both your parents and mine were pretty into the two of us being together on Friday night."

"I agree. But she knows more. She knows you've been walking me to my car every night."

"Doc probably told her." He shrugged. "Everyone is supposed to see us together, remember?"

"No, it's more than that. She kind of has stars in

her eyes about it." Looking even more flustered, she added, "Sorry, but I think she thinks we're really serious. Like we're going to get married one day serious."

"Okay…and…"

"And I didn't know how to tell her that everything between us was fake." She closed her eyes for a second. Then blurted, "So I kind of let her believe that the two of us were heading that direction."

"Heading in that direction," he repeated. That wasn't ideal, but he still wasn't sure why she was so spun up. "What are you not telling me?"

Kinsey winced like he'd barked at her. "It wasn't like I had a choice, Hunt," she said in a rush. "We were in the consignment store. She caught me off guard, and I had nowhere to go."

"I get it. You were trapped. So, what did you say?"

"You know what I had to say. I mean, we're either pretending to be a couple or we're not." She took a deep breath. Gazed at him intently with her pretty eyes. "Hunt, what I'm trying to tell you is that it was true. I told her that I like you a lot."

Hunt took care to keep his expression blank. He'd perfected that look in the army, when someone with a higher rank told him to do something stupid. "That isn't so bad."

"What do you mean by that?"

Kinsey glared, like he'd just hurt her feelings

but he wasn't sure what he'd said that was wrong. "Nothing."

Somehow he'd just made things worse, because she drew back as if he'd raised a hand to her. "Kinsey, what am I saying that's got you so upset?"

"You don't know?"

"Obviously not. I'm walking on a tightrope here, and apparently doing a bad job of it." He knew he sounded gruff and irritable, but that was because he was. "Talk to me."

"Hunt, I'm trying to tell you that the conversation I had with Claudia can't be taken back."

"You mean when we're no longer pretending to go out?" He picked up his coffee cup and took a fortifying sip.

Looking miserable, she nodded. "What I'm trying to say is that I was telling the truth. Hunt, I don't think my feelings are fake. I really do like you a lot."

She liked him for real. Only his sudden catlike reflexes (and maybe a prayer) prevented the remainder of his coffee from dripping all over her couch. It did splatter on his hand, though. "Honestly?" he grumbled under his breath as he marched toward the kitchen and turned on the faucet.

Kinsey hurried after him. "Did you burn yourself?" she asked.

"No."

"Let me see." She reached a hand into the cold stream of water. Curved her palm around his fingers.

He felt a jolt. Startled, he pulled his hand away and turned off the faucet. "I'm fine."

"Are you sure? Burns are tricky."

"I'm not burned. I, ah, just wanted to rinse my hand" Glancing back at the living room, he said, "I think your couch is okay, though."

She handed him a dishrag. "It's just an old secondhand couch, Hunt. A splash of coffee isn't going to be the end of the world."

"I know." After a beat, he met her gaze again. "How did you leave things with her?"

"I told her that I didn't want to talk about the two of us anymore because everything was so new. That it was private. She seemed to accept that. But I'd be shocked if she didn't tell Doc."

"Or my parents."

"Yes. I don't know what to say. I'm sorry."

"No. No reason to apologize. None of this is your fault." The truth was that he liked her a lot, too. But was the right man for her? He wasn't sure.

"No, everything is my fault. If Dillon hadn't shown up, and I wasn't so scared, then I would've never told Edna. If I hadn't told her, then she wouldn't have talked to you." She started pacing. "And if you hadn't gotten involved, then we wouldn't have started this whole crazy relationship in the first place."

He shook his head. "No. We're not going to do

that. First of all, Dillon is a jerk. He's been using your fear of him to amuse himself. This is a Dillon problem. Not yours."

"But—"

"I'm serious, Kinsey. Do not blame yourself for him showing up out of nowhere. It's not your fault he's whacked. It's not your fault you were in a foster home with him. It's not your fault your parents died in a car accident and you didn't have any family able to take you in."

"I know I can't change the past, but it is my fault for involving you."

"I willingly agreed to it. I wasn't forced. You know that, right?"

"Right."

She still looked dejected and he knew why. "Hey, for what it's worth, you aren't the only person with real feelings here."

"You don't have to say that."

"I'm not just saying it, girl."

"So…are we now actually going out?"

Man, he wanted that. Pushing aside all the reasons that it wasn't a good idea, Hunt nodded. "I guess we are. But, um, maybe we should take things slow for a while."

"Slow." She nodded, like she was trying to figure out what would make him happy.

"Yeah." Warming to their new relationship, he flashed a smile. " Now, how about you tell me about the other thing?"

"Oh." All the light in her eyes faded. She turned away, went to the corner of her kitchen counter, and picked up a piece of paper. "This was in my mailbox."

He opened it. Read the words. And felt like scooping Kinsey into his arms and taking her back to his house. That or doing his best to figure out where Dillon was living and pay him a visit.

"Kinsey. Honey, are you okay?" When she shrugged, he added, "You should have told me this first off."

"I don't know what to do."

"Want to go to the police station tomorrow?"

"I don't know. The note's not even signed, Hunt."

"Do you have security around here?"

"Yeah. It's not great, but it works."

"Do you want me to take you to the Martins' house? Or to mine? You can sleep in the guest room."

"No. I want to stay here. It's just… I wanted you to know." Looking nervous and miserable, she raised her eyes to his. "I do really like you, Hunt. But even if I didn't, I need you to still be my boyfriend. Fake or otherwise."

"I will still be your boyfriend. And it's real. I'm not going anywhere."

"Thanks."

Needing to see her smiling again, he said, "Anything else happen during your shopping trip with Claudia?"

"Well… I might have bought a baker's rack and an ugly chair that Claudia thinks you might want to reupholster."

"What? I don't reupholster furniture."

"She was on a mission, Hunt. I wasn't going to tell her that you wouldn't do it."

Amused, he said, "I don't blame you. I'll take a look at the baker's rack, though. Where is it?"

"I think a couple of guys we know are going to pick it up and deliver it on Saturday."

"Where are you going to put it?"

"In my bedroom. It's for linens and books and stuff. Right now I'm storing things in cardboard boxes."

"I'll help you get that fixed up."

"Thanks."

He shook his head. "Not a problem. Hey, I hate to do this to you, but I really do need to go. If you're okay."

"I'm okay." Staring up at him, she whispered, "So… I'll see you when I see you."

"Honey, I'll see you tomorrow."

Visibly relieved, she smiled at him. "See you then."

Unable to help himself, he reached out, tucked a piece of her hair behind her ear. And finally leaned down and brushed his lips across hers.

She leaned closer. Gripped his arms with her two small hands.

And so he kissed her again.

"Lock up when I leave," he murmured. Then, before he gave into temptation and kissed her again, he turned around and didn't look back.

But he sure was tempted.

CHAPTER THIRTY

Operation Muffin had taken off like wildfire at Loaves of Love. After Madison and Cope had proposed the idea, Kayla Copeland, since both she and her husband worked in the school system, had spearheaded the program. Next thing Edna knew, at least two workstations at a time were making homemade muffins for kids to have for breakfast. The muffins smelled heavenly, and everyone seemed excited to bite into something new and different.

To Edna's surprise, the project had also brought in new volunteers. More than one person had sheepishly admitted that they'd had no desire to make anything with yeast—it was too daunting for folks who'd never baked more than a frozen pizza.

But this muffin project? Well, it seemed everyone was comfortable making muffins, especially if it was to help give some hungry kids a taste of something homemade.

Actually, it turned out that schoolchildren weren't the only ones who enjoyed peanut butter, banana, berry, and cinnamon muffins for breakfast.

Wayne, especially, had hopped on the Operation Muffin bandwagon. Though he had never minded kneading dough and producing homemade bread, he had never seemed all that excited about it. On the other hand, he could make pan after pan of his favorite muffin—peanut butter and banana.

Just yesterday, an elderly gentleman who'd come in for a couple of cans of soup had left with a six pack of cans, a loaf of bread, and four banana muffins. *These look just like my wife used to make*, he'd said in a soft, whimsical voice. *They bring back a lot of good memories.*

The man's pleased expression had kept Edna smiling the entire day.

Now, if she could only figure out how to make Hunt look a little happier, she'd be set.

He'd come into Loaves of Love to do a little cleaning and carpentry work in the food pantry. And he was doing a bang-up job with the wooden boxes he was building for onions and potatoes. They were going to be as beautiful as they were useful. However, her favorite military veteran wasn't anywhere close to being his normal self. Considering that he wasn't all that peppy on his best days, this was concerning.

Though Edna was tempted to ask Wayne to step in and offer to take him to lunch, she knew that would be a misstep. First of all, Wayne wasn't the type of man to invite people out to lunch for no reason. Secondly, he really wasn't the type to give relationship advice. He'd probably avoid the subject like the plague, which would defeat the whole purpose!

It also went without saying that Wayne joining her in a cozy chat with Hunt was a bad idea, too. Wayne would crack jokes or change the topic if he thought that they were getting too serious.

Prepping him wouldn't help either. Why, Wayne would probably try to talk her out of getting any more involved in Hunt's life than she already was. She could practically hear him say that the man had already served his country. He didn't need to deal with her matchmaking meddling, too.

But she wasn't going to meddle. Just help. There was a difference, right? Feeling better, she made her decision.

It was up to her to help Hunt. She wasn't sure he would be receptive to her efforts, but she knew she had to try. Doing nothing wasn't an option. She cared about Hunt.

After making sure that Valerie had everything she needed at the reception desk, Edna strode down the hall toward the pantry. "Hi, Hunt!" she called out in a bright voice.

He visibly jumped. And almost hit one of his fingers with a hammer, too.

Uh-oh. "How it's going?"

"It was going pretty good until a minute ago," he said with a laugh.

"Sorry. I guess I was a bit too peppy when I walked in. Next time I'll be quieter."

"No, it's okay. This is your place. You can act however you wish."

"You know that's not how I do things." Feeling awkward all the sudden, she leaned against the doorframe. Stared at him.

Setting the hammer down, he turned to face her. "May I help you with something, Edna?"

"Hmm? Oh, no."

He blinked. Looked at the crate that was half-way built. "Am I in your way? Is someone here for food?"

"No."

He looked around the room. "I could work in the back. Would that be easier?"

"You're fine. It's rare for anyone to stop by this time of day."

"Okay…"

She felt like a ninny. "Sorry. I, ah, came in to speak to you about something, but now that I'm here, I'm not sure where to start."

"You might as well just dive in."

"You're right." Pushing aside the last bit of hesitation, she blurted, "I'm worried about you."

"Why?"

There it was. Hunt's usual direct-to-a-fault demeanor. No frills. No softness. No doubt a lot of privates used to shake in their boots when they heard that bark.

And she was suddenly feeling awkward and embarrassed. "Well, you see, I don't think you've been acting like yourself the past few days."

"You don't think so?"

"Um…no."

"How have I been acting differently?"

"You've seemed to be preoccupied."

"That's probably because I have been preoccupied."

Hunt was still looking at her directly in the eye, and she was starting to feel like the most foolish, nosey woman on earth. Or…at least in the state of Ohio.

He might have been right, too. Hunt was one of her volunteers. He was doing some work for her. Neither of those reasons gave her the right to pry into his business.

It was time to retreat.

"You know what? I… I owe you an apology. You came here to work, and I'm acting as if you doing your job is my invitation to get into your business. It's not. Let's just forget I ever came in here, shall we?"

"That's going to be pretty hard to do, given that your coming in here almost made me hammer my thumb and all."

Concerned, she stepped forward. Then spied the twinkle in his eyes. "You're teasing me."

"Well, yeah."

She blew out a burst of air. It puffed up her

bangs, probably making her look even sillier than she already did. "Now I'm even more flustered. I'm going to go on my way now."

"Yes, ma'am." Hunt stood still. Letting her know that he wasn't going to get back to work until she got out of his way.

Before she was tempted to make things even more awkward (which was likely next to impossible to do) she turned on her heel and walked back down the hall.

When she was about five steps away, she heard Hunt's hammer pound against a nail again.

She'd be lucky if he ever accepted another job from her.

"Edna, there you are," Valerie said. "I've been looking for you everywhere."

"Why? Is something wrong?"

"I'm not sure. Someone keeps calling your cell phone." She held it up. "You left it on the reception desk. I hope you don't mind, but I decided to bring it to you."

"Of course not." She was embarrassed that she hadn't thought about her phone in the last hour. "I can't believe I just walked off and left it."

"At least I was there to hear it ringing," Valerie said with a smile. "Like I said, when I heard it ring, stop, then ring again, I figured I better bring it to you."

"I'm glad you did."

Taking it from Valerie, she glanced at the screen

and saw that Wayne had called her twice. What was that about? Was he sick? Hurt? "Thank you, dear. I'm sorry you had to come find me."

"It was no trouble," she said before heading back down the hall.

Stepping into her office, Edna pressed Wayne's phone number. "Is everything okay?" she blurted.

"Hmm? Oh, sure. I was at the store and wanted to see if you wanted some red peppers."

"You called twice about peppers?"

"Well, yeah. They're on sale. So, would you like some?"

"Oh, um, okay."

"How many?"

"I don't know. Two? Three?" Did it even matter?

"Oh, Edna?"

"Yes?"

"I also called to make sure you were staying out of Hunt's business."

She chuckled. "You really know me too well."

"Too well? I don't know if that's possible," he teased. "So…are you leaving him alone?"

"I am now." That was true.

He groaned. "Edna, do I even want to know what you did?"

At last! An easy answer. "Probably not."

"Why don't you come on home? We'll go for a walk, and then we'll have supper. While we walk you can tell me everything you did—or didn't do—to poor Hunt Vargo."

"What are we having for supper?"

"What do you think? Stuffed red peppers."

She could practically hear the smile in his voice. It made her grin. "I'm on my way," she said softly. As much as she wanted to help Hunt and Kinsey, she could only do so much. In the end, each of them was in charge of their own future.

Yes. Getting out of this building and concentrating on her own life sounded like a good idea.

A very good one.

CHAPTER THIRTY-ONE

Hunt knew Edna was a kind woman, and he also realized that her heart was in the right place. But that didn't mean he regretted shutting her down when she'd attempted to have a heart-to-heart about his love life in the middle of a workplace. There was no way he would be okay with that.

The good thing was that she'd gotten that message loud and clear. After their brief exchange, she'd left him alone again and he'd been able to sigh in relief. His feelings for Kinsey were confusing and convoluted. Even if he'd wanted to tell Edna about how he was falling in love with Kinsey, he couldn't do it. As much as his heart was saying that was the right thing to do, his head continued to list reasons why he was the wrong person for her.

Two hours later, he'd finished building the last vegetable crate. The volunteer had been all smiles when he'd handed it to her, which made him feel good. At least he was doing well at work.

After stopping by the animal shelter for some dog cuddling, he went home, cleaned up, and then finally did the thing he'd been avoiding for the last two days. He'd picked up the phone and called his mom.

They'd been playing phone tag, which was normal, due to his erratic work schedule and their three-hour time difference. Every time they'd missed each other he'd felt a little guiltier and a little bit more relieved. But he couldn't put it off any longer.

She answered immediately. "Hunter. Hello."

He mentally winced at her use of his full name. "Hey, Ma. How are you?"

"Well, dear, I'm afraid I'm a lot of things right now."

"Oh?"

"Oh, yes. I'm happy to hear your voice, confused by the phone call I received from Claudia Martin, and a tiny bit hurt that you didn't see the need to tell me that you and Kinsey had gotten even more serious since the barbecue."

Feeling a bit like he was getting dressed down by a general, Hunt cringed. His mother was on fire. "Ma, settle down. There's no need for you to get yourself worked up."

"Did you just tell me to settle down?"

And…he'd just made things worse. Closing his eyes, Hunt tried to get a grip on himself. "I'm sorry. I didn't mean to speak to you that way."

"Yet you did."

He rubbed the back of his neck. "Once again,

Mom, I'm sorry. It's just that Claudia never should have called you about Kinsey and me. That was my news to share. Not hers."

"I agree with you a hundred percent. And I might have even told her that…if I hadn't been so surprised." She took a deep breath. "Why weren't you honest when Dad and I were with you? You know Dad and I would've been thrilled to hear that you found someone. And even though you and Kinsey might have a bit of an age difference, we love that girl. We're happy for you. We're happy for the both of you."

She was really disappointed to be out of the loop. "Ma, I didn't want to say anything to you and Dad because this relationship with Kinsey and me didn't start out as real."

"What?"

"She's got some guy following her around. It's a guy from her past. She was in foster care with him. From what I can gather, he bullied her. She's scared of him."

"What?" Her voice had gone up two octaves. "Hunter, you need to put a stop to that."

"I've already warned him off. I would do more, but he makes sure to be around when I'm not there." Thinking of the note he'd left in her mailbox, he added, "Kinsey can't go to the police because so far he hasn't committed an actual crime."

"He needs something more to do."

Hunt couldn't help but grin. That comment was

vintage Ma. If he'd ever acted bored or had been getting into trouble, she'd start handing him chores left and right. She was probably the reason he'd done so well in the army. He could both follow orders and dole them out with ease. "I think there's more to it than that, Ma. I don't know what his story is. Maybe he just happened to see Kinsey and decided to mess with her for a while. Maybe he has a habit of bothering a lot of people he was in the system with. I don't know."

"Hunter, I can understand that this man is a problem, but I don't understand why you two decided that the solution was a fake romance."

Glad he'd gone on his back porch to call, Hunt started pacing. "It sounded like an easy solution. A friend of ours came up with the idea, saying that sometimes all a guy like him needed was a reason not to bother Kinsey. It seems to be working."

"That's good," she replied. "I suppose."

He chuckled. "Don't sound so disappointed."

"I can't help it. I was sure you'd fallen in love. You deserve that, sweetie."

"Everyone deserves to fall in love, Ma. But that's beside the point. What matters is that you now understand why I didn't tell you anything before."

"I do, but it's too bad. Dad and I like her."

"I like Kinsey, too. I really like her. And as I said, things between us are changing and getting more serious. But I want to figure all this out with

Kinsey, not you and Claudia. She and I deserve to have some privacy, don't you think?"

She sighed. "I do."

"Thank you. Now, tell me about Dad. What's going on?"

"Do you want the good, the bad, or the ugly?"

He grinned as he sat back down on his lawn chair. "I want it all."

"Hold on to your hat, then. First of all, your dad shot a forty-three on the back nine at the country club. Then, right as he was celebrating, he tripped on a club some kid left on the course and sprained his wrist."

Hunt felt like his face was going to be sore from smiling so much. "I'm guessing that takes care of the good and the bad. What's the ugly?"

"Even though your father is wearing a brace and should be taking it easy, he's decided to organize this house. This morning, he decided that I've been doing laundry wrong all this time."

"Uh-oh."

"'Uh-oh' is an understatement. Dad's never run a load of laundry in his life! He is not allowed to have an opinion."

He took a breath so he wouldn't start laughing. "I'm guessing you told him that?"

"Oh, you bet I did."

"And?"

"He ignored me. Hunter, he's driving me up

the wall. I might have threatened to hurt his other wrist if he doesn't stop giving me free advice."

He couldn't take it anymore. He burst out laughing.

"Laugh all you want, son, but living with him has not been fun."

"No, ma'am. I suppose it hasn't."

Her voice warmed. "You know, it would do us a lot of good if you flew out here for a few days. Planes fly in both directions, you know."

"I'd like that. But with everything going on, I can't right now."

"I suppose you're right. Kinsey's safety is more important."

It was, but he also was in no hurry to leave Kinsey for any length of time. "How about this? If Dad is still being a pain in a couple of weeks, I'll book a flight and help you out."

"If he's still interfering with my business, I'll be sending him your way, son."

"I'll be ready. I'll call Dad tomorrow and see if I can talk some sense into him."

"I hope you will." More softly, she added, "And I'll talk to you in a few days, Hunter."

"Yes, ma'am. Sorry for not calling you sooner."

"I suppose I can't blame you. Tell Kinsey hello from us."

"Will do."

"Take care now, Hunt. I love you."

"Love you, too, Ma. Bye."

When he hung up the phone, he realized that some of the heaviness he'd been carrying around had disappeared. He felt lighter. Easier.

Obviously, he needed to call his mother a lot more often.

CHAPTER THIRTY-TWO

NOW THAT THE giant baker's rack was resting against her bedroom wall, Kinsey was experiencing buyer's remorse. The thing was not only bigger than it had looked in the resale shop, but it was in worse shape than she'd realized.

The guys Claudia had rounded up had been as good as their word. Just that morning, Sean and, Jamison had gone to the store, picked up the piece of furniture, then somehow wrangled it up the stairs and into her bedroom. She still had no idea how they'd done that. After they'd placed it against the wall, Sean had asked if she was pleased with how it looked. No way would she have been able to tell him that she wasn't.

Instead, she'd nodded, thanked the two of them about a dozen times and sent them on their way.

Maybe it would have been easier to be honest if Hunt had been there, but he hadn't been able to help. Not only was his knee in too bad of a shape to carry something so heavy up a flight of stairs, but he'd had a call with the banker about more projects for his house. She'd waited impatiently for him to stop by.

Now that he was over, Kinsey was even more worried about her purchase. Hunt didn't look as if he liked it at all.

When another minute passed in silence, she couldn't take it anymore. "Well, what do you think?" she said at last. "Can you fix it?"

"Yes."

His yes was a good sign. But it also didn't give her any indication about whether he was willing to fix the broken cabinet door or its cracked leg. "Yes…what?" she asked.

"Yes, I can fix it."

"And the shelves? Can you make some to fit where they're missing?"

"Yep."

She felt like rolling her eyes. "What about painting it? Is it going to be difficult for you to sand and paint this thing lavender?"

"No."

Folding her arms across her chest, Kinsey tried to control her patience. She hated when Hunt measured every word he spoke like he was doing right now. It made her feel like she was never getting the full story. "Enough with these one-word answers! Tell me what you think."

"Fine. Yes, I can paint it purple. Yes, I can make the shelves, and yes, I can fix all the problems with the thing."

She held up the cardboard color swatch she'd picked up from the paint store. "The color is called 'smoky lavender blue,' Hunt."

"Whatever."

"What's the problem?"

"The problem is that I don't think any of it is a good idea."

"Hunt, you have no idea how hard it was for those guys to maneuver this thing up the stairs. I thought Jamison was going to leave before they were halfway done."

"Oh, I have a pretty good idea how hard it was for them." Tilting his head to one side, he said, "It's really heavy. It was probably close to impossible."

"But they did get it inside, and now it's planted in my bedroom like an oak tree. I don't think I'm ever going to be able to get it out of here."

"I can almost assure you that those guys aren't going to want to be the ones carrying it out." His lips twitched.

She popped a hand on her hip. "That's why we have to make it work, right?"

His eyebrows rose. "We?"

"Fine. You. *You* need to make it work."

"I hear you. But I'm warning you now—I'm pretty sure that even after I attempt to reinforce the leg, fix the crooked door, sand the rough patches, fill in the cracks, and paint the whole thing the *smoky lavender blue*, it still has a pretty good chance of falling apart."

"You think it's in that bad of shape?"

"Yep. You shouldn't have bought it, Kinsey."

"Claudia really liked it. I did, too."

"Since neither of you were planning on fixing it up, I'm going to have to say that your opinions don't count for much."

"That's kind of rude."

"It's also kind of true. Sorry, but this old cabinet you got a good deal on should've gone to its final resting place. The junkyard."

"Hunt, you're so talented. I'm sure you're going to be able to make it look really cute. As good as new."

"Sorry, but your flattery isn't going to get very far."

"All right." For some reason, she was a little hurt. She'd imagined that he might look at refurbishing the cabinet as an excuse to be together. Now she realized that she'd been starting to believe their pretend relationship. Which was a mistake. They didn't have a real relationship. Not really.

She drew a breath. "You know what? It's probably best if we just call it a day. Thanks for coming over and, uh, for giving me your honest opinion. But I'll figure it out from here."

"Kinsey, don't get your feelings hurt because I'm being honest with you."

"I'm not." Which was a lie, because she kind of did have her feelings hurt.

He sighed. "Look. I meant what I said. I'll fix it

up. Maybe I can start working on it in the mornings before I head off to my other jobs."

"You mean, when I'm at work?"

"Well, yeah."

She wasn't sure how she felt about that. As close as they were, it still seemed weird for him to be in her bedroom when she wasn't around.

"You know what? Don't worry about it. I'll work on this myself."

"Sorry, but you can't fix this cabinet's leg, Kins."

"I can try." Of course, she was just spouting words. She had no idea how to fix the cabinet's legs.

Hunt turned to face her. "No."

"No?"

"I'm not going to let you. It's liable to topple over and crush you."

"You're being dramatic. I'll be fine."

"You know what? You've worn me down. I'll get started on it now. Let me go get my tool belt."

No way did she want to sit around feeling guilty about making him fix her furniture. "No."

"I'll be right back."

He was ignoring her. Stunned, Kinsey watched him walk right past her. Out of her bedroom. Into her little living area.

She hurried to catch up.

"Hunt, you just can't walk out that door right now." She said that because yes, he'd already turned the knob and was opening it. All without looking back at her. It was annoying. "Hunt, wait!" She reached for the sleeve of his flannel shirt.

Well, she'd reached for the sleeve, but what she'd actually gotten was his arm. Yep, she was gripping his arm like it was her new lifeline, and boy, was it solid and filled with muscles.

Hunt froze for a second before he slowly turned his head and looked down at her hand. Yep, she was still holding onto him.

"Kinsey, what are you doing?"

His voice had turned husky. Or maybe that was just her imagination. Maybe she was hearing things. Or transferring her feelings to his voice, because his annoyed half whisper sounded delicious to her.

"Kins?"

"I'm stopping you from walking out the door. That's what I'm doing."

"Honey, no disrespect, but your grip on me isn't holding me back."

"No disrespect, but I'm going to do everything I possibly can to get you to listen to what I'm saying."

"Don't be so silly. I'll get my stuff and start making that piece of furniture stable enough for you to use."

"And I'm telling you not to." For good measure, she put her other hand on his other arm. Effectively trapping him in her arms.

He was now facing her. Looking down at her.

Studying her features. No. Scratch that. Hunt was doing one thing, and that was staring at her lips.

She could smell the soap on his skin. He smelled like something woodsy. Sharp. Like aftershave? She didn't know. Her senses were feeling kind of blurred.

She was not alone in this. Not at all. She knew he had feelings for her, too. And their previous kiss had been amazing.

He was still hesitating, though.

She knew he had his reasons. She was younger. He had issues. She had a stalker. Their relationship was confusing and seemed to involve an awful lot of bickering.

She knew all those reasons mattered to Hunt.

She knew all those reasons should matter just as much to her. But all she cared about was what she wanted. And what she wanted was to kiss him again.

And so, before he could shake her off, utter ten reasons why them kissing was a big mistake…she made her move.

She rose up onto her tiptoes and pressed her lips to his.

"Kinsey," he whispered as he ran his hands up her arms. Pulled back.

"No."

Tenderness mixed with worry filled his eyes. "Kinsey—"

She shook her head. "Don't push me away. Stop

pushing me away. Stop acting as if there's nothing there. For once."

"For once?"

She sucked in a breath. Because right there in his eyes was everything she'd never believed could happen. Want, hope. Need. Like he wanted her in his life.

Like he hoped she would want to be there.

Like he needed her as much as he needed air to breathe.

And sure, all those things were probably her imaginings. They were probably figments of her imagination mixed in with a lifetime of yearning to matter to someone.

To matter to someone so much that nothing was going to prevent them from moving heaven and earth in order to have her there by their side.

Her breath caught.

She needed to stop. This was Hunt. Hunter Vargo. Not Prince Charming. Not Mr. Congeniality. Not—

But it didn't matter because he was kissing her. Holding her close. Pulling her against him. Kissing her like this one moment meant so much that he wasn't going to let anything ruin it.

What to do? What to do?

She held on. Moved closer. Kissed him back.

And realized that nothing else mattered. Not her dreams. Not all her insecurities. Not everything they'd talked about.

This kiss? No, it wasn't going to change her life. It wasn't going to make everything that was wrong better. It wasn't everything.

But it was enough.

CHAPTER THIRTY-THREE

Hunt had lived long enough to realize that there were few things in life that turned out to be as good as expected. The first bite of a ripe watermelon on the hottest day of the year. The first hot shower after a six-month deployment. The sense of accomplishment he'd felt at the end of basic training.

But none of those things had ever come as close to perfection as the shy, awkward, beautiful brush of Kinsey's lips. He was certain he would never forget it—he sure didn't want to.

Kinsey making the first move had taken him by surprise. For a second, he pulled away. He'd been so stunned that she'd made the first move. Then, of course, he'd kissed her the way he'd been wanting to. She relaxed against him, holding onto his arms like she could prevent him from pulling away.

So sweet.

And sure. He'd felt pure happiness. Holding her in his arms had felt right. Felt as perfect as he'd imagined. Like she belonged there.

And sure. It had felt so good that he hadn't

wanted to do anything but kiss her some more. Maybe pull her down onto a piece of furniture, hold her close, and kiss her long enough that he'd never remember kissing another woman.

Of course he hadn't done that. But the temptation had been there. Dismayed, he realized that the two moments would be forever intertwined. The desperate longing for a woman he would never be good enough for followed by the soul-sucking knowledge that he'd just done something he wasn't sure either of them were ready for.

Both felt like twin punches in his solar plexus. He could barely catch his breath.

He pulled away. Dropped his hands. Took a deep breath and tried to get himself together. Hunt thought he'd done a pretty good job of it, too… until he noticed that Kinsey was staring at him with a dazed expression. She seemed to be struggling to breathe as well.

It was so cute.

Just as he was about to smile about that, doubt settled in. "Did I hurt you?" he asked. "Did I hold you too tight?"

Her eyes widened before she shook her head. "No."

Needing to keep touching her, he brushed a chunk of her hair away from her face. "Are you sure? I kind of forgot myself for a second. Sorry if—"

"Stop!" she interrupted.

He dropped his hand again. Now what had he done wrong? "What?"

"Oh my gosh." Kinsey wrinkled her nose. "Hunt, I'm fine. Great. Honestly, the things you worry about."

And…there it was. The combination of sass and snark that he found so addictive.

So he gave it right back. "Sorry if my concern for you was irritating."

"It didn't irritate me." She chuckled. "I promise I might be younger than you and a whole lot smaller, but I'm sure not fragile." She averted her eyes. "Besides, it was just a kiss, right?"

"Yeah. Right." He nodded. Tried to look like he agreed completely, but it was a bit of a struggle. Because the fact was that the last ten minutes had felt like more than "just" anything, though.

Just like the first time they'd kissed, it had felt special. Memorable, too.

But maybe he'd just wanted it to be? Things seemed to affect him in different ways than they used to. He was more vulnerable than he used to be. The nightmares, the injury, the discharge from the army…all those things had changed him. For the worse, too. He used to be the most dependable guy he knew. Steady on his feet, never flustered. Always in control. Now it felt as if he was none of those things.

Feeling self-conscious, he averted his eyes. "I should probably get going."

"Are you sure? I thought you were going to stay a while. I mean, I thought we were going to hang out. We could watch tv or something. Whatever you want."

There was so much confusion in her tone, he forced himself to meet her gaze.

Instead, her eyes were filled with shadows now. Obviously, Kinsey was confused. And who could blame her?

He was, too.

His emotions were all over the place. "Sorry, but I just realized that I have a job I need to finish tonight," he lied.

"Oh."

"Yeah. I can't believe I forgot it," he continued, no doubt sounding more unbelievable with every word he uttered. Running a hand through his hair, he said, "I should look at my schedule. And at my notes."

"Notes?"

"Yeah. I've picked up a couple of jobs lately, and I don't think I wrote them all down." Which was a lie. He always wrote his jobs down in the spreadsheet on his desk.

"Hmm."

"Yeah. In fact, I might not have all that much time to work on this."

Kinsey stared at him for a long moment. Letting him know that she didn't believe a word he said. Letting him see that all of her sass had faded into embarrassment.

It was obvious that she was closing up, just like he was. His mouth went dry. "Kinsey, maybe…"

"No. It's all right. Well, thanks for taking a look at it anyway."

He was acting like a jerk, and an insensitive one at that. Giving himself a mental kick in the rear end, he cleared his throat. "Kinsey, ignore what I just said. I'll help you with this. It's not a problem. I…well, I just can't right now. I need a minute."

"A minute?"

"More like sixty of them." Frustrated with his inability to explain himself, he bit out, "Probably more than that."

"I understand. We made a mistake, didn't we?" She shook her head. "I mean, I'm the one who crossed the line. I shouldn't have kissed you again."

"You might have made the first move, but I jumped on that idea. This isn't on you. It's me." And…he'd just sounded like the hero in a stupid made-for-TV movie. "What I'm trying to say is that ever since I got injured, I need a little more time to process things. It really is a me thing. Not you. I liked kissing you, Kinsey. I liked it a lot." He stepped toward the door. "But I need to take a break."

She pulled her bottom lip into her mouth. Bit down. Seemed to come to a conclusion. "See you later."

"Yeah. See you." He walked to the door, let himself out, and slowly walked down the stairs.

Fifteen minutes later, when he let himself into his place, Hunt had a raging headache. Fearing that a migraine was starting, he popped one of his pills, then climbed into the shower, taking care to keep the water hot and the room dark.

As steam filled the space and his body relaxed, he breathed deeply. Reminded himself that he was stateside. He wasn't in danger and his men were fine.

Concentrated on the water pounding against his shoulders instead of how badly he'd just messed things up with Kinsey.

By the time he was dried off and in a pair of gym shorts and an old army T-shirt, Hunt knew he was going to need to stay away from Kinsey for a day or two.

He had no choice. Until he learned to get a handle on himself, he was going to continue to hurt her. She deserved better than a guy who turned a conversation about furniture into a discussion about his inability to handle her kissing him.

She could do so much better than him. More importantly, she deserved better. He couldn't do a lot of things anymore, but he could still protect her from himself.

CHAPTER THIRTY-FOUR

AT TEN IN the morning on Monday, Kinsey made a decision. If she made it through the morning in one piece, then she was going to celebrate by going out to lunch. Maybe get ice cream, too. With sprinkles on top.

Unfortunately, the chances of being able to do any of it looked slim to none. She was stuck at this desk until all the patients in the office had been seen, and so far, not a one of them had.

"Kinsey, have you heard anything yet?" Armour Buck asked as he stood on the other side of the glass partition and attempted to peer onto her workstation.

"I'm sorry, Mr. Buck, but no."

His lips pursed. "That's what you said thirty minutes ago."

"It's still true now. I am sorry."

Mr. Buck's usually patient expression hardened into a craggy scowl. "Saying you're sorry doesn't mean much for those of us sitting in here, dear."

Since she didn't dare apologize to him again, Kinsey simply stared back.

After a fifteen-second battle of wills, Mr. Buck turned away and tottered back to his chair. "Nothing. She doesn't know anything," he told Mrs. Buck in a voice loud enough for everyone in the room to hear.

"I told you to leave Kinsey alone. This isn't her fault." Lifting her head, Mrs. Buck met Kinsey's eyes. *Sorry!* she mouthed.

Kinsey shot Mrs. Buck a weak smile before glancing down at her cell phone again. Amanda had said she'd try to text with updates about the patient whose emergency was so dire that Dr. Martin had met the woman before the office opened and asked Amanda to come in early, too.

The news had come as a shock to Kinsey. She'd been surprised to see all the office's lights on when she unlocked the front door.

That was two hours ago. Again and again, she'd hoped to hear from either Dr. Martin or Amanda with good news, but so far Amanda hadn't sent more than a couple of heart emojis.

Kinsey was pretty sure that meant that the poor dental patient in room two was still in a bad way. She felt sorry for the person. She really did.

But what she really needed was some direction. Even being told to reschedule everyone would come as a relief. Being a receptionist in limbo was a thankless job.

When two kids around five or six started arguing, then crying, Kinsey's head began to pound.

Man, was it going to be a long day. All in all, a horrible Monday. Sure, some people might say that all Mondays were horrible. However, this one actually was.

Not only was it cloudy, cooler than usual, and thunderstorms were looming, but things were not good inside Dr. Martin's waiting room. There were too many people, pretty much everyone was in a bad mood, and there was no end in sight.

Kinsey thought it would be a minor miracle if she survived until lunchtime. The fact was Mr. Buck wasn't the grumpiest grumpy man in the room.

No one in the waiting room was happy. Neither were the hygienists.

But Kinsey was pretty sure that she was having the worst time of them all. After all, she was the messenger, the gatekeeper, and the person to run interference. People were taking out their frustrations on her because there wasn't anyone else available.

When another woman approached, looking ticked off and very self-important, Kinsey tried to think of puppies and kittens in the animal shelter. Anything to soothe her soul and prevent her from snapping at the patient.

"Hey, are you sure you don't have an ETA?" the blonde asked.

"I'm sure. Dr. Martin and one of the hygienists are still with the emergency."

"This is a regular dentist's office. Couldn't that person with the emergency have gone to the hospital? After all, that's what that place is for, right?"

"As I told you when you first walked in, I'm just the receptionist. I don't have a lot of information to share with you."

She glanced at her watch. "I'm going to be late for my meeting." She looked down at her phone and started thumbing through screens. "Even if I went back now, it would be cutting it close."

"You should probably reschedule." Like Kinsey had told her when she'd first shared that she had an important meeting to get to.

"For when?"

"For the next available opening," she bit out.

She rolled her eyes. "And when would that be?"

Clicking on her mouse, Kinsey scanned the next two weeks. Then the next two months. At last she spied a bright pink spot, her addition to the program in order to make all openings stand out. Usually when she saw that little pink box, she felt a burst of pride.

Unfortunately, all it served to do today was highlight just how annoyed everyone was going to be.

"The earliest I could get you in is on September first. At four o'clock."

"That's over two months from now."

"I know, Ms. Atkinson."

"That is inexcusable."

"I know you're upset, but it is what it is," Kinsey replied with a new edge in her tone. "I suggest you take it. I'll also put you on the waiting list in case someone cancels at the last minute."

"And if I stay? Can I get this over with today?"

"I hope so."

"You hope so. You know, I don't think you're being very professional. I'll definitely be telling Dr. Martin about your attitude."

Feeling her bottom lip start to tremble, Kinsey bit on it hard. No way did she want to start crying in front of this crowd. "What would you like to do, ma'am?"

"I guess I'll wait a little longer."

Kinsey nodded. Took a sip of water and tried to calm down. And then, at long last, her phone dinged with a message from Amanda. She grabbed it like it was a life preserver.

Doc is pretty much done. FYI, he called in Mark to assist. His ETA is in five. Tina just came in the back. Let everyone know.

Hold on. What if someone doesn't want to see Mark?.

Doc says we can't give them choices.

Great. Okay. I'll let everyone know.

Glancing at the list of patients, Kinsey said a little prayer. When she walked into the waiting room, the crowd went silent.

"Hi, everyone. I have some news. Doc has almost finished with the patient he's been taking care of this morning. We'll be calling in his next appointment soon."

"How soon is soon?" Mr. Buck called out.

"Soon," she said with a meaningful look in his direction. "I have more good news. We have called in another dentist to assist this morning, so we'll get everyone taken care of as quickly as possible. He's on his way."

"Who is the other dentist?" Someone asked.

"Dr. Mark Ortiz. He's well respected, and we're so thankful that he rearranged his schedule to help us out today."

Mrs. Buck frowned. "I thought he was retired."

"He is."

"So, he's old," stated the blonde.

"I don't want to see him," Mr. Buck said.

"If you don't want to see Dr. Ortiz, then let me know when I call your name." When she spied the gentleman fold his arms over his chest like a stubborn toddler, Kinsey felt like rolling her eyes. Armour Buck really was a handful.

Walking back to her desk, she noticed that Tina had arrived and that Amanda was going to be working with Dr. Ortiz. Bracing herself, she called out the first two patients. One for cleaning and the one who'd needed a filling.

Bracing herself, she said, "Mr. Buck, would you like to get that dental work completed by Dr. Ortiz or would you rather wait?"

"I'm waiting."

"Ms. Atkinson? What about you?"

"I'll take it," she said as she jumped to her feet. "I have got to get out of here."

Now that people were starting to be seen, everyone in the room seemed to breathe a sigh of relief. Kinsey knew she sure did.

As the rest of the day slowly progressed her mood gradually improved. Dr. Martin had gotten a small break and his usual good spirits had returned. Best of all, at long last, Mr. Buck was taken care of and sent home.

Now all she had to do was count the hours until she could go home and collapse. She was starving. She'd barely found enough time to run to the bathroom or get a bottle of water.

When she heard the unmistakable thump of Hunt's work boots she finally felt like things were returning back to normal.

"Hey," he said as he placed a large paper cup on her desk. "I brought you a coffee."

"Why?" Wasn't he upset with her?

"I needed to apologize for what happened on Saturday afternoon," she whispered. "I know I started acting weird."

He had. "What happened? What did I do wrong?"

"You did nothing. You were perfect. It was all me." Looking even more uneasy, he added, "I started overthinking things, and then I thought I was about to get a migraine. I still get those from time to time."

"I'm sorry. I… I didn't know."

"I don't get them much anymore. Only when I get stressed."

Kissing her had stressed him out. "I'm sorry if I did something you didn't like."

"No." He leaned closer. "No. That isn't it at all. You did everything right. Like I said, this is on me." Straightening, he continued. "Anyway, I ran out of there because I thought I had a migraine coming on. Obviously, I can't drive when I get one."

She would have driven him home. Heck, he could have lain on her couch all day. But both options probably hadn't occurred to a guy like him. He was used to taking care of himself—and everyone around him.

"I understand. Thanks so much for this coffee." She picked it up and took a tentative sip.

"It's your favorite. A double shot with a squirt of chocolate and a dash of vanilla syrup."

Taking another sip, she smiled at him. "You even got them to add whipped cream, too."

He smiled. "That was easy. All I had to do was tell the gal at the Blue Door that it was for you."

His blue eyes filled with warmth. "It seems you're a regular, Kinsey."

"Hunt Vargo, you're an answer to a prayer."

Looking pleased with himself, he deposited a small brown sack on her desk as well. "I also brought you two cookies. One oatmeal and one peanut butter."

The news kept getting better and better! "Thank you. I'm so hungry."

"You're welcome. I heard you had quite the day." He moved to lean against the nearby wall.

She loved that he wasn't in a hurry to rush off. As far as she was concerned, he could stay there for as long as he wanted. She didn't even care that some of the patients in the waiting area were having no problem watching her and Hunt like they were their favorite afternoon soap opera.

"It's been awful, but how did you know?"

"Edna."

"How did Edna find out?"

"A patient who was talking about a grumpy man in the waiting room while she was at Loaves of Love." He grinned. "Even Larry gave me a call to say that you'd had a heck of a day."

"It has been," she said as she took another sip of coffee. It was so good, she almost sighed in happiness. "I'm sorry that you had to hear all about it, though."

"I'm glad someone told me. I hate that you were

having to deal with a bunch of angry dental patients on your own."

She giggled. "You're making them sound like a mob. They weren't that. Just a bunch of busy people who wanted some answers."

"I heard it was more than that."

She nodded. "Things did get a little dicey for a minute, but I got through it."

"They shouldn't have taken out their frustration on you, though."

"I think it's part of the job. Today I was the only one available."

"Still…you okay?"

His voice was soft and sweet. Somehow everything seemed better now that Hunt was involved.

"Yeah." She smiled up at him. "Thanks for the coffee, and the cookies, too. It's going a long way toward making the rest of my day a lot better."

"Anytime."

After he talked with her for another few moments, sharing a story about his niece and nephew in Arizona, Kinsey felt almost like herself again. But better, because she now had Hunt in her life.

She really hoped he wouldn't leave anytime soon.

CHAPTER THIRTY-FIVE

HUNT WOULD NEVER have imagined that a cup of coffee could make Kinsey so happy. He had hoped it would, though.

For the last two days, he'd barely been able to do anything besides replay their kiss, their discussion, and eventually the way he'd pushed her away.

Yet, here he was again. Standing against a wall in the reception area of Dr. Martin's office. In some ways it was a replay of the way he'd stood when he'd jumped all over her because she'd inadvertently messed up his painting schedule.

Now, looking back, he wanted to knock some sense into his former self. No one should ever care so much about painting baseboards.

At least he was finally getting his priorities straight when he was around her.

"This is so good," she said as she took another sip of her latte and a nibble of the oatmeal cookie. The look on her face, so soft and appreciative, was beautiful to see. It had been years since he'd been the recipient of a woman's tender look. It was addictive He was already looking forward to doing something to make her smile like that again.

So, even though she was at work and there were more than a couple of interested onlookers watching them in the waiting room, he leaned over and kissed Kinsey's brow. "Are you good now?"

"I'm perfect." She lowered her voice. "As perfect as I can be since I have to stay here for two more hours."

It was a little after three o'clock. "I'm going to let you go."

"Yeah. I guess you should. Doc wouldn't understand if you hung out here for the rest of the afternoon," she joked.

He grinned. "Probably not." Pushing himself off the wall, he said, "I'm gonna head over to that banker's house and switch out some porch lights and then stop by Loaves of Love. I'll be back at five thirty to walk you to your car, though." He paused. "You aren't thinking about working late tonight, are you?"

"Absolutely not."

"Good. Five thirty it is, then."

"Wait." She got to her feet. "Are you sure you have time?"

"I'm positive." Fighting the urge to touch her, Hunt took a step back. "I'm looking forward to it."

"See you in a couple of hours." She flashed him another warm look before she sat back down.

Hunt kept his head down as he strode down the

hall and headed to the back door. By the time he reached the parking lot across the street from the front of Doc's office, Hunt knew that he was already gone for her.

She was special to him, and he was falling in love with her. It didn't make a lot of sense and wasn't what he'd planned on, but that couldn't be helped. This relationship of theirs felt like it was in the hands of a higher power.

He was getting pulled along, and there wasn't anything he could do about it.

Instead, he was going to accept that she was the woman for him and move on. He was going to continue to get better, both physically and mentally. He was going to appreciate Kinsey's sweet and irreverent nature.

He was going to stop fighting and accept that she would be on his mind all the time. Here, he'd just said goodbye to her and he was already anticipating the next time he was by her side.

He wanted to protect her from Dillon, and from the rest of the world, too. He didn't want to just make sure that she felt safe and secure, he wanted to make sure she had a reason to smile.

Maybe they could grab some dinner together before she went home and he headed back to finally paint the walls in Doc's office.

Focused on restaurant choices, Hunt almost ran into Wayne and Jamison on their way to Jamison's vehicle.

"Hunt, just the person we wanted to see!" Wayne called out as they switched directions and headed toward him. "What are you doing right now?"

"I was about to go to a job. Why?"

"We need a hand," Jamison said. "A woman came into Loaves of Love this morning in tears. Long story short, she lost everything in a fire, she's in some kind of temporary space with her two kids, but neither she nor the kids have beds to sleep on."

"What do you need?"

"I was able to get a queen and a twin bed for them, and Chloe ordered a bunch of bedding that's going to be delivered to the gal's apartment in a couple of hours," Jamison said, "but we need some help delivering them."

"And you have a truck," Wayne said. "Plus, I think I might be able to find them a bedside table and a dinette set at the resale shop."

"Let me guess, those items need to be delivered too?"

"Yeah." Looking a little sheepish, Wayne added, "I know it's late notice, but is there any chance you could give us a couple of hours of your time?"

Once again Hunt was glad that the banker was on vacation and that he hadn't had a problem with Hunt working at his house a little bit at a time.

Mentally pushing their porch lights off for another day, he nodded. "I'll help you in any way that

I can, but you guys know I can't move anything too heavy, right? Not with my knee."

"Your knee isn't a problem. A buddy of mine can meet us at the apartment to help carry stuff in," Jamison said.

"Also… I need to be back by five thirty."

Wayne looked at his watch. "If everything works like clockwork, we might get back in two hours. It'll be tight, though. What do you think, J?"

"I don't know. Maybe you could help us with the first round? I'll get on my phone and try to get my buddy Adam to help."

Hunt knew Jamison's buddy was a lawyer. It was doubtful that a guy with a job like that was going to be able to take off at a moment's notice. Plus, he wasn't born yesterday. He knew how this mission was going to go. Anything that everyone thought would take one or two hours would probably take double that.

In addition, if Edna was spearheading this, then she probably had another team of folks gathering clothes, toys, and toiletries. Finally, there was the likelihood that something was going to go wrong, because something always did.

These guys needed help, and the woman they were helping needed a place to sleep. Which meant that he wouldn't be able to walk Kinsey to her vehicle. Or have dinner with her.

But how could he say no? This poor mom was trying to house her children. He couldn't ignore that. "I think I can rearrange something and help you guys out."

"I know we're putting you on the spot," Wayne said as he clasped his hand. "I appreciate it."

"No thanks are needed. I'm happy to help. What should we do first?"

"Can you take your truck to Loaves of Love? One of the volunteers there ran to a clothing closet and got a couple of things," Wayne replied. "Plus, Edna said she wanted to give the kids a couple sets of muffins."

"Give me a minute to shoot off a text."

Still standing next to his truck, he pulled out his phone and texted Kinsey his change in plans.

She replied almost immediately. No worries. I'll be fine.

He still didn't feel good about it, though. She'd just forgiven him for running off after that kiss. I really am sorry.

I understand. I'm not upset.

Okay. Don't forget to ask Doc to walk you out.

Okay, but I'll be fine.

Even in a text, he could tell when Kinsey was only saying what he needed to hear. Kinsey, ask him.

I'll be fine, Hunt. Stop worrying.

He didn't feel great about that, but he didn't want to harp on her. Plus, he had been the one to change plans. If he'd felt like she was in danger, he would've never agreed to help Jamison and Wayne.

So he settled on giving her the benefit of the doubt. At least promise me that you'll be careful. Scan the parking lot before you go out. And text me.

Hunt!

I know. But humor me. Text me when you get home.

If I do, will you stop by later?

He grinned. Yep.

I'll cook us dinner!

Dinner? Hunt had no idea that Kinsey knew how to cook. He didn't care if she could or she couldn't, though. All he wanted was to see her again. Smiling, he typed out another quick response. Can't wait. See you then. But be careful.

"You ready to go, Hunt?" Wayne called out. "We really do need to get on our way."

He clicked the key fob in his pocket and unlocked his truck. "I'm ready. Let's go."

CHAPTER THIRTY-SIX

DR. MARTIN HAD felt so sorry for Kinsey having to deal with his cranky patients that he'd handed her a hundred-dollar bill after the last patient left for the day.

"Doc, what's this for?"

"It's a thank-you for your help today."

"I can't accept this. I was doing my job."

His expression serious, he nodded. "You were doing your job, but you also went above and beyond today. Thank of it as hazard pay." He patted her hand. "Order a pizza when you get home or something."

Having a little extra spending money sounded great, especially since she could use it to buy the ingredients for the lasagna she was going to make Hunt. But it still felt weird. "Larry, did you give everyone else a bonus for today, too?"

"Nope."

"Then why me?"

"Because we've already talked about me owing you. And, you're my daughter, silly girl. Now, stop arguing and shut down this office so you can leave."

"Yes, sir." She smiled before heading to the reception area with a handful of rags and some spray cleaner. Wiping all the tables and chairs down was going to take a while, but it would make her feel like she was earning that bonus.

After setting the reception area to rights, she organized her desk and pulled files for Tuesday morning's patients. Finally, at five thirty she locked the door, set the alarm, and headed out to the parking lot.

Maybe her mind had been on her grocery list, or it had been the crazy, long, never ending day that had made her be so oblivious to her surroundings.

Or it could be that Hunt had given her such a circle of security that she'd begun to believe it was real.

All that did matter was that she was alone in the parking lot, Dillon was in front of her, and she had no recourse but to face him.

Sure, she was scared, but she'd also come a long way from the scared little girl that she used to be. She'd even grown since meeting Hunt. She no longer felt so alone in the world. She had more confidence. It was time to stop running.

Walking toward Dillon, she looked at him directly in the eye. "Here you are. Again."

"Well, this is a big change." Dillon raised his eyebrows. "Are you finally going to talk to me?"

"I'm not sure. Are you finally going to tell me why you've been stalking me this past month?"

"*Stalking* is a pretty strong word, Mackenzie."

She felt as if she'd been slapped. No one ever used her real name. Most people weren't even aware that Kinsey was a nickname. Well, no one except Stephanie and Dr. and Mrs. Martin. And the other kids who'd been in that home.

Forcing herself to remember that she wasn't helpless, she said, "Don't call me that."

"Why? Does it still hurt to hear the name your mommy and daddy used to call you?"

Ignoring the question, she folded her arms over her chest. "Why are you here, Dillon?"

"You don't want to take a guess?"

"Not really. You act as if we know each other. Until I saw you at the sandwich shop, we hadn't seen each other in years. I don't know you and you don't know me. We're strangers."

"That's where you're wrong. You knew me pretty well when we were at the Walters' house. You used to never shy away from talking to me. Sometimes you'd even look for me." He lowered his voice. "Kinsey, you acted as if we were friends."

A lump formed in her throat as she tried to tamp down the emotion.

Dillon wasn't wrong. When she'd first gotten to the Walters' home, she had thought of him as a friend. She'd been so lost and had been so sheltered, it had never occurred to her that the other kids wouldn't be nice. Or if not nice, she'd thought they would at least be understanding of how grief-stricken she'd been.

She'd been wrong.

The four kids in that home were a ragtag mess. Kinsey went through each day in a daze. Then, there was a little girl named Pamela who was autistic and in her own world. Another kid whose name she couldn't remember had been pulled from an abusive home and lashed out at everyone. Finally, there was Dillon. He was the oldest, and the kid who'd been so bad and disruptive that his social worker had warned that he'd be placed in a group home if he received another complaint.

It was as if Dillon had known he didn't have a chance, though. Nothing was going to change at that house. The fosters didn't care and his social worker was overworked and out of ideas.

"You're right," she said at last. "Back then, I thought I could trust you. I thought you were misunderstood. Different than everyone said you were."

"Maybe I was. Maybe I was hurting just as bad as you were, Mackenzie. What if you weren't wrong?"

She inwardly recoiled at the idea. "But I wasn't. You were just as bad as everyone thought."

"The oil was an accident."

"You might not have wanted me to get burned,

but your actions caused it." It took everything she had to not rub the scar on her leg. She'd gotten the burn when some hot oil from a frying pan had flown out while the two of them were doing dishes. He'd been teasing her, she'd pushed him away, he'd lost his grip on the pan, and she'd gotten burned.

It had hurt so bad. She'd screamed and cried. Mrs. Walter had run her to the emergency room. The burn had been bad enough for her to stay overnight. When she got back, she'd learned that Dillon had already been moved.

Eventually, Stephanie took her to a different house.

No way was she going to give him the satisfaction of seeing that she still had a scar from their time together.

"We both know you pushing me caused me to fall and break my wrist," she said in a low tone. "And don't even try and twist the situation into something that it wasn't. You were chasing me!"

"I haven't forgotten."

"Neither have I."

Dillon folded his arms over his chest. Leaned back against the side of her car. It brought back memories of when he used to stand much the same way in the Walters' house. He would lean against the walls in the playroom. In the hallway outside her bedroom. Against the garage door when he watched her.

He'd looked so confident, she'd wanted to keep her distance. Avoid him at all costs. Now, though, she realized it was all an act. He'd become skilled at acting like he didn't care.

TONIGHT, IN HIS own way, Dillon was as uncomfortable as she was.

"Did you know what happened to me after that accident?"

She forced herself to not divert her eyes. "You went to the group home."

He lifted his sunglasses to the top of his head. "That place they sent me to wasn't a group home. It was a juvenile detention center, Mackenzie. I was thirteen, and they put me in a place where sixteen- and seventeen-year-olds were there for assault, stealing, battery, you name it. It was a prison."

"It wasn't a prison."

"You have no idea. There were bars on the windows. Guards everywhere. It was as bad as you can imagine. It was worse than I had ever dreamed it would be. And it was all because we had that tussle and you accidentally got burned."

No way was she going to take the blame for his bad behavior. "It was more than a tussle, and it wasn't the only thing you did." She lowered her voice. "You were mean to Pamela, too. And that's just who I know about."

"After all this time, you're still not going to take any responsibility for what happened to me?"

With anyone else, Kinsey might have felt guilt. Maybe she would have apologized even if she thought they were in the wrong. But not with him. "Is that why you wrote me a note? Is that why you're here? Because you needed closure?"

"I wrote you that note so you'd take me seriously."

"Oh, I did."

Dillon studied her expression. Tilted his head. "I can't change the past, Kinsey. Isn't it time you forgave me?"

"I'd forgive you if I thought you actually felt remorse. But I find that hard to believe. We both know you did a dozen things a day to keep me on edge. You teased me. Taunted me. Pushed me. Lied." Swallowing hard, she added, "And yeah, you might not have meant to burn me, but you did. You kept threatening me with that oil. I totally thought you were going to hurt me." She waved a hand. "And when that hot oil hurt my leg, you lied to Mr. and Mrs. Walters. The other kids were too afraid of you to say a word, and you took advantage of that."

"You're making me sound worse than I was."

"I'm making you sound as bad as you were," she corrected. Kinsey felt as if every emotion that had been bottled up inside her had finally come tumbling out. She wasn't sure if she could stop herself even if she wanted to. "Dillon, there were a lot of things you might not have wanted to happen, but you absolutely wanted me to be afraid of you. You liked that I was afraid of you. Don't ever deny that."

Dillon looked away. She wasn't sure if that was because he was embarrassed or because he didn't like her answer. She supposed it didn't matter.

Looking at him, seeing how he was struggling, still attempting to hurt her. Still refusing to take any blame for his actions...she realized that she only felt pity.

Her months at the Walters' house was years ago. A different lifetime. Back then, she'd been scared, in shock, and helpless. She'd felt as if she was completely alone in the world.

But that wasn't who she was any more. She'd built herself a family. She'd found people to love and who loved her.

Why was Dillon still fixated on something that had happened so many years ago?

"What is wrong with you, Dillon?" she whispered.

Maybe it was her tone that caught him off guard, or maybe it was the question. Whatever the reason, some of the anger that had emanated from him dissipated. He stared at her for a full second. "Nothing."

"Are you sure? Because what happened between you and me was a long time ago. More importantly, we were just kids. I wasn't even a teenager yet. Why can't you let it go?"

"You don't understand. You ruined me. Going to the detention center changed my life."

Kinsey felt for him, she really did. But it sure didn't give him a pass. "Dillon, don't you get it? You deserved to get sent there. If not for everything that happened to me, for everything you did to Pamela."

"I didn't deserve that."

"Okay, let's say you're right. Do you think you're the only person who had something bad happen to them? Something so bad that it changed their life, too? You really ought to get some help. Following me around, stalking me, and making me uncomfortable isn't going to make your life better."

"Is yours all that different?"

"Yes." There was not a bit of doubt in her mind about that. She had a job. She had found people to care about and who cared about her just as much. The pastor at the church she went to called them God family. People that weren't related to her by blood but became part of one's life.

"I'm in a good place, Dillon."

Confusion shadowed his eyes before he blinked. "I doubt it," he said. "There aren't 'good places' for people like you and me."

"You're wrong." Softening her voice, she continued. "Dillon, I don't know what happened to you when you were a little boy, but I do know that it wasn't something you deserved. I don't know what happened to you in that detention center and I'm sorry if what did happen there was something just as bad."

"You have no idea what it was like."

The pain in his eyes was heartbreaking to see. She ached for the boy he'd been. Truly wished that his childhood had been different. But that wasn't possible.

All that was possible was to move forward each day…and following her around and placing blame on her shoulders wasn't okay.

Forcing herself to remain calm, she said, "You're right. I don't. But what happened in the kitchen that day wasn't my fault." Taking a fortifying breath, she added, "I don't want to call the police, but I will. You have to leave me alone." Her pulse was racing. She didn't want to back him into a corner but she was done allowing him to control her movements.

"You're not going to do anything, Kinsey. You always hide behind someone stronger. But your guy isn't here now. It's just us. And you're too weak to do anything for yourself. You always were."

His words were painful to hear. Even if there was a grain of truth in them, he wasn't completely right. It was time to stand up for herself. Her insides were quaking as she pulled out her phone.

Just as she cleared the screen and typed *9*, he reached for it. "No, Kinsey."

Jerking out of his grasp, she cried out. Her phone landed on the ground.

A woman walking by stared at what was happening, but instead of offering to help, she rushed away.

"No," he said again, this time grabbing Kinsey's wrist. The same wrist that had been broken so long ago.

He squeezed it so tight, she feared he was cutting off her blood flow. When she pulled away, he squeezed tighter. She could feel the edges of his nails dig into her skin.

"Someone help me!" she called out. "Please!"

"Shut up," he said.

"No." She glared at him as she yelled again.

And then, just like she'd conjured him up, she heard Hunt call her name.

"Hunt?" she yelled.

"Right here, Kinsey!"

She turned to look for him. There, on the edge of the parking lot, were Hunt, Jamison, and Sean Copeland. They were running toward her.

Dillon jerked her again, but this time Kinsey barely noticed. All she could see was that Hunt was just steps away, and several of her friends were right behind him.

Next thing she knew, Hunt and Jamison had

Dillon against the wall and Edna was calling the police.

As the tears fell, Wayne wrapped an arm around her. "You're okay," he said.

Her heart still beating a mile a minute, she stared at everyone in wonder. "Where did you all come from?"

"We've been helping a woman get settled into her apartment," Edna said. "We came back to the parking lot to drop everyone off and heard your call for help." She pressed a hand to her heart. "I couldn't believe it."

"Of course we rushed over right then and there," Wayne said. "I'm glad we got here in time."

"I'm glad, too," she replied.

He patted her on the back before returning to Edna's side. When Kinsey was alone again, a delayed reaction kicked in and she started shivering.

Cope noticed. "Is your wrist hurting real bad?"

"My wrist?" She looked down at her arm. There were red marks from Dillon's nails. He'd broken the skin in a few places. Drops of blood were forming. It seemed swollen, too. "I had forgotten about it."

"Maybe the paramedics can look at it or something."

"I'll be all right."

As sirens rang in the distance, she shared a look with Hunt.

He was barely glancing at Dillon. Instead, his

focus seemed to be entirely on her. *It's almost over*, he mouthed.

She nodded. The problem with Dillon was almost over. But now that she was no longer in danger, she hoped that Hunt wouldn't back away again. She didn't think her heart could take that.

CHAPTER THIRTY-SEVEN

HUNT HAD DONE two tours of Afghanistan. He'd gone without showers or food for days at a time, parachuted out of helicopters, been lost in the wilderness, and just about had his leg blown off. All of it had shaken him up. None of it had come close to the way he'd felt when he heard Kinsey cry out for help.

For as long as he lived, he'd remember that moment in detail. The way her voice had squeaked, as if she was just seconds away from breaking into tears. And then there was the way she was trembling.

"Cope, come over here," he called out. When the teenager approached, Hunt said in a low voice, "Stand here with Jamison, okay?"

"Yeah. Sure."

Hunt knew Cope wouldn't have to do a thing. Jamison could handle anything on his own. Besides, it was obvious that all the fight had gone out of Dillon and he was now worried about the consequences of his actions.

Two police cruisers pulled into the parking lot.

Two officers, one man and one woman, got out. As they paused, taking in the scene, Hunt strode to Kinsey's side.

"Hunt," she said.

It was obvious that she was barely hanging on.

But the thing was she didn't need to do that anymore. She could let down her guard, and he would take on her battles. He gently pulled her into his arms. "I've got you now."

It was as if Kinsey's entire body had been waiting for those words. She leaned against him, wrapping her good arm around his middle while keeping her bruised wrist tucked safely in front of her stomach.

There was so much about this entire situation that angered him, but he pushed those thoughts away. He was going to have to deal with them later, after Kinsey was relaxed and happy again. "It's over."

"I was so scared." She sniffed.

"I know." He pressed his lips to the top of her head. When she started crying, he ran a hand up and down her spine. "I'm so sorry, sweet girl," he whispered.

She hugged him harder, keeping her face averted. Hunt didn't know if she was too distraught to realize what was happening or if she simply didn't want to see Dillon again.

He supposed it didn't matter. He was watching everything for her.

As one of the officers took hold of Dillon and the other spoke to Edna and Wayne, Hunt divided his focus between the officers and Kinsey.

Her tears didn't abate. They soaked through his T-shirt, breaking his heart and triggering his anger. If the police hadn't been right there, Hunt would've been tempted to hit the guy, or tried to shake some sense into him at the very least.

But of course, he wasn't doing nothing. He was taking care of Kinsey. She needed him. He continued to rub her back, murmuring all sorts of promises and endearments. Anything to get her to relax.

Every so often Edna or one of the guys would look his way. So did the officers. Hunt returned their glances, silently signaling for everyone to give Kinsey a few more minutes. Yes, the tears were hard for him to see, but he realized that Kinsey needed the release as much as she needed him to hold her.

At last, she looked up. "I… I don't know what's wrong with me."

"Adrenaline rush," he said. "It kicks in when you're scared and eases when the crisis is over." He swiped a thumb across her cheek, catching yet another stray tear. "It doesn't feel good when it happens, though."

"You're right. It doesn't."

"When you're done talking to these guys I'll take you home. We'll have a Coke or something. That'll help."

Kinsey nodded, though her expression was doubtful.

"Excuse me, Miss Zaleski?" one of the officers called out.

She stepped out of his arms. "Yes, that's me. I'm Kinsey."

The officer, who looked like he was in his early sixties, had kind eyes. "We need to ask you some questions about what happened."

"All right."

When she glanced his way, obviously looking for help, Hunt held out his hand and introduced himself. "Hey. I'm Hunt Vargo. Do you mind if I stand with her?"

"Are you her boyfriend?"

"I am."

The cop shrugged. "That's fine."

Hunt reached for Kinsey's hand and linked his fingers through hers. When she started to talk, slowly recapping everything that had happened that afternoon, and in all the weeks before, Hunt stayed quiet.

Every so often, the officer would ask a question or request she expand on something she said. It was obvious that he was trying to organize his notes.

Kinsey answered each question carefully and thoughtfully. She was doing well, and he was so proud of her.

Finally, she added, "Is he going to be all right?"

The officer blinked. "Are you asking about Dillon?"

"Yeah. I know it sounds strange, but I don't want anything bad to happen to him. He had a rougher time than I did growing up. I just want him to leave me alone."

The officer glanced at Hunt.

He shrugged. Her ability to give Dillon grace after everything that he'd put her through seemed incredible to him.

The officer said, "I understand, miss, but I'm afraid that we're still going to need to visit with him a spell. Now, you said he took ahold of your wrist?"

"Yes." She lifted her arm.

It looked even worse than it had ten minutes ago. A muscle jumped in her cheek, revealing that she was in a lot more pain than she'd been letting on.

The officer frowned. "Hey, Benedict?"

A paramedic, who had been standing next to the ambulance that had pulled in while Kinsey was being questioned, strode over.

"Kinsey here has something that we need to check out. Her wrist is swollen."

"I don't think it's broken or anything," she blurted.

"Yes, miss," Benedict said. "You're probably right, but we need to make sure. Come have a seat and we'll get a better look at it."

When she glanced Hunt's way, he nodded. "I'll be right here, Kinsey."

The officer turned to Hunt. "We're going to need that documented."

"I hope so."

"Now, if I could ask you a few questions…?"

"Of course. Whatever you need."

For the next ten minutes, the police officer asked him about his relationship with Kinsey, what he saw when he and their friends had first spied Kinsey and Dillon, and then he wrote down all of Hunt's contact information.

Thirty minutes later, Dillon was escorted away in the back of the police cruiser and the paramedic, after pronouncing her wrist to be badly bruised but otherwise okay, released Kinsey to go home.

After hugging Edna goodbye and thanking the others, Hunt ushered Kinsey to his truck. Cope had volunteered to drop off her car at her house with his girlfriend within a couple of hours.

After helping her get settled in his passenger seat and buckled up, Hunt got in his side and turned on the ignition. Beside him, Kinsey looked pale but otherwise okay.

"You have a couple of choices about where to go now," he said. "We can go to Claudia and Larry's house. I texted them after the officer interviewed me. You can go into your old bedroom. I know both of those guys will love nothing better than to fuss over you."

"What are my other options?"

"We can go to my house. We can sit in the living room, order something in, and I'll take care of you as best as I can." Claudia and Doc would also be able to come over and check on her.

Kinsey raised an eyebrow. "Or?"

He smiled. "Or I can take you back to your loft."

"Will you come up with me?"

"I'll do whatever you want me to do," he said softly. He meant every word. All that he cared about was putting her somewhere she could rest.

"I love Claudia and Larry, but I don't want to see them right now. All I want to do is take some ibuprofen, drink that Coke you mentioned, and veg out on the couch."

"That's what we'll do, then." He pulled out of the parking lot, making a mental note to give the Martins a call as soon as Kinsey was settled.

"That's it?"

He glanced her way, realizing that she was smiling at him in a bemused way. "Yeah. Why?"

"Oh, I don't know. It's that I never expected you to be so easygoing or agreeable when I first met you."

Hunt couldn't help but laugh. "I never expected to be this way either. I guess wonders never cease, huh?"

When she chuckled softly, Hunt's entire body relaxed. She was going to be just fine, and they were, too.

CHAPTER THIRTY-EIGHT

One week later

"WHAT ARE YOU still doing here?"

Kinsey turned around to see Hunt striding toward her. He was frowning, and it was obvious he was about to give her a piece of his mind. Turning around in her swivel chair, she folded her arms across her chest and took a moment to admire how he looked.

Hunt might've been getting ready to give her a lecture, but at least he was going to look good while he did it. He had on a snug light blue T-shirt, faded jeans, work boots, a tool belt, and scruff on his cheeks. Honestly, he kind of looked like a construction worker in an old commercial. The type of guy who made women stop and stare when he walked by.

"Kinsey, you didn't answer me."

"I know." When he raised one eyebrow, she fought back a smile. "I think you know why I'm still here."

His expression darkened. "I can't believe this.

Doc told me that he wasn't going to overwhelm you this week."

"Settle down. I'm fine."

"Kins, it's only been a week since the incident in the parking lot."

That was how Hunt liked to describe it. *The incident.* He took such care of her. He was always so conscientious about her feelings. It was sweet.

But it was also unnecessary. She'd recovered almost completely after a good night's sleep. When she'd awoken the next morning, she'd discovered that Hunt had not only cleaned her kitchen after she'd fallen asleep but filled her coffee pot—and somehow had gotten someone to bring over six chocolate chip–banana muffins from Loaves of Love.

She'd spent the morning sipping coffee, eating muffins, and thinking about how blessed she was to have so many friends who cared about her.

Returning to the present, Kinsey lifted her chin. "I know how long it's been since Dillon cornered me. But I'm all recovered. I'm fine."

"Still..."

It was obvious that her little game with Hunt had lasted long enough. "I didn't stay late to do work, Hunt."

"You didn't?"

She shook her head. "I stayed to see you, silly."

And...there went all of Hunt's bluster. As he walked closer, she could see something new shining in his eyes. Amusement, maybe. Or was it relief? Or…something more.

Tossing his tool belt onto the floor, he closed the gap between them, then knelt down in front of her. He was so close that she could smell the detergent on his clothes and the faint scent of rosemary and mint. He reached for her hand and linked his fingers with hers.

"What am I going to do with you?" he said. "Ever since we got to know each other, you've spun me up in circles. Half the time I barely know which way is up."

Kinsey was pretty sure there was a compliment in there, but maybe not? "I don't mean to make you feel that way."

"I sure hope not." Lifting one of her hands, he pressed his lips to her knuckles. "I'll take it, though. I'll take you any way I can have you, Kinsey." Still staring down at their linked hands, he lifted her bruised wrist. "I hate that he did this to you."

She didn't want to talk about Dillon or her wrist. "It's fine. The bruises are fading."

"They shouldn't have been there in the first place."

"Hunter." She paused until he lifted his head. Until their eyes met. "Stop worrying about me. I'm good. I'm sleeping well and can now walk all over town without worrying that I'm going to run into Dillon. The drama is over. Now, stand up so you don't hurt your knee."

Hunt looked like he was going to argue but then complied. Letting go of her hands, he used both of his to push himself off the ground. His sharp inhale was the only indication that the movement pained him.

"You should be more careful."

"Is this what you're always going to be like?" he asked.

She stood up. "I don't know what you're talking about."

"Bossy."

Kinsey opened her mouth to defend herself but then closed it just as quickly. Because he did have a point. She sure did have a good time telling Hunt Vargo what to do. "Probably." She felt a little embarrassed. "But on a positive note, I seem to only be that way with you."

"Only with me?"

"Yes. With everyone else I'm very easygoing." Actually, she was kind of a pushover with everyone else. She'd lived most of her life avoiding conflict.

"Hmm."

"I'll try to be better."

"Don't." He wrapped his hands around her waist. "Don't change a thing about yourself. I want you to stay the same as you are."

Kinsey had a feeling that it was a good time to

say something witty and cute right back athim, but she currently had no words in her brain. She felt kind of speechless.

And so she did something better. She looped her hands around his neck, lifted herself up onto her toes, and kissed him. As she hoped, Hunt took control over the kiss. Hugged her closer. Made her feel as if she was precious and special.

When he lifted his head, he said, "I think it's time we made our relationship real."

"It already is. We gave up pretending about a week ago, remember?"

"I remember, but I'm talking about making things something more permanent." While she stared at him, trying to figure out what he meant, he reached into his pocket and pulled out a ring.

A ring! With a diamond in it!

"Hunter?"

"I was going to do this when I was on my knees in front of you. I had it all worked out…until you decided I needed to stand up."

"Wait a minute. Don't blame—"

"Stop. Don't argue. Just say yes. Kinsey Zaleski, I need you in my life. I need you to look out for my knee when I don't, to make me smile when I'm frowning, to bring light into my life when it feels too dark. But more importantly, I want to do those things for you. I want to be the person who you lean on. Who you don't have to make promises to or be on your best behavior with. I want to be the guy who sees you with no makeup on and messy hair. Who you watch movies with and walk dogs beside." He lowered his voice. "I want to be the man who loves you." Reaching up, he swiped a tear she hadn't even realized was falling down her cheek. "Kinsey, would you marry me?"

She stared at him. Stared at the goodness that was Hunter Vargo.

Kinsey nodded. Because for maybe the first time in her life…she had no words. The moment was too special, and the things he'd said were too dear.

Hunt smiled, lifted the hand he was holding, and slipped that beautiful, simple solitaire diamond on her ring finger. Pressed his lips over it and then enfolded her in his arms.

And then kissed her again. Right there in the reception area of a dentist office. Long after everyone who was anyone had gone home.

In a place where they'd both found love and acceptance and friendship and family.

A place where they had found everything that had been missing in their lives. Where they found everything that mattered.

EPILOGUE

"MY FEET ARE killing me," Wayne announced as he plopped down onto the new sofa in Edna's office at Loaves of Love. "Whose idea was it to get hitched on a Friday night? Things like that should be outlawed."

Edna felt like rolling her eyes. Her husband had danced all night in his spiffy leather tennis shoes. She, on the other hand, had been in heels. And support hose! He had no idea how confining those felt.

Of course, no one had made her kick up her heels either. But boy, had it been fun! "As much as my own feet would agree with you, I think outlawing weddings on Friday night sounds a bit harsh, dear. And as far as whose idea it was to get married on a Friday night…well, I'm pretty certain it was either Kinsey or Hunt," she replied. "It's common for the bride and groom to decidc when and where they want to say their vows."

"Yeah, yeah." He stretched his neck from left to right. As if such a move would get all the kinks out. "I'm just saying I wouldn't have minded sleeping in today. These old bones don't recover like they used to."

"I'm sore all over, too." Sitting down beside him, she rubbed her hip. "I can't believe that Larry and Claudia started a conga line after Kinsey and Hunt had their first bite of cake." She chuckled. "Or that we jumped right in."

Wayne wrapped an arm around her shoulders. "We sure had a good time, didn't we?"

"We sure did."

Closing her eyes for a second, Edna let her mind drift back to the festivities. Kinsey and Hunt's wedding had truly been a lot of fun. They'd had the service in a small chapel in the country, then the reception was in both the Martins' and Vargos' backyards. One of the yards had a large tent with tables, chairs, and a dance floor, while the other yard had a firepit, a band, and plenty of outdoor seating under the hundreds of white twinkling lights that had been strung in all the trees. For some reason, there had even been all the fixings for s'mores, though Edna wasn't sure why anyone would want to eat s'mores at a wedding reception.

But just around midnight, there were Hunt, Kinsey, and both sets of parents roasting marshmallows!

Edna would never have imagined that such a wedding would work, but it did. There was a huge crowd, the music was fifties and sixties rock and roll, and the bride and groom seemed almost oblivious to everything but each other.

Hunter had worn his uniform, resplendent with his many medals, and Kinsey's fluffy, long, white wedding gown was covered in lace. Then there were their dogs Bonnie and Clyde. Bonnie had worn a wreath of roses around her neck, and Clyde had donned a jaunty black bow tie. When they'd followed Kinsey down the aisle, the entire congregation had chuckled.

Then, later, when Hunt had held Kinsey in his arms for the first dance while the dogs sat with Stewart and Joanne, Edna was pretty sure the entire guest list had sighed in appreciation.

Now the bride and groom were on their honeymoon. They'd found a secluded inn in southern Kentucky. Their parents were likely going to spend the next five days cleaning everything up.

Speaking of which… "You know, we should probably stop by the Martins' house to see if they need a hand."

"We will. When we're done here."

"Oh, we don't have to stay long. Like I told you this morning, all Valerie needed was for us to unlock the building and get everything in the kitchen ready. She's in charge of Loaves of Love today."

"That's great news," Wayne said as he stood up. "We can get out of here, stop by Larry and Claudia's to see if they need a hand, and then go out to lunch. We'll be home and watching the Guardians play by two or three." He beamed.

"Look at you! You suddenly have a new spring in your step."

"Eh, I'm not that old. I just needed a couple of minutes to regroup." Wrapping an arm around her shoulders, Wayne ushered her out the door.

As they walked down the hall, Edna thought about all the couples she'd helped over the last couple of years. All were special, though none had touched her heart as much as Kayla and Sean Copeland.

She still remembered the first time she met Kayla. She'd been scared and so sweet. And hungry. If Edna dwelled on that too much, tears would still fill her eyes. Boy, she hated to see someone go hungry.

"Hey, you all right?" Wayne asked.

"Yep. I was just thinking about something."

"I bet I know what it was." He leaned down. "You're sad that Hunt and Kinsey are married now."

Edna tried her hardest to appear affronted. "I am most certainly not!"

"I think you are. You're disappointed that you can't meddle in their lives anymore."

"I'm glad I can't. They were a lot of hard work. Convincing them to 'pretend' to date took a lot of doing." Especially since she'd known that they'd wanted to be dating each other in the first place. "I desperately need a break."

"Uh-huh."

She glanced at him sideways. Perhaps adding that *desperately* had been a bit much. "I am very much looking forward to stopping by the Martins' house, lending them a helping hand, and then doing nothing for the rest of the day." Realizing that sounded awfully boring, Edna blurted, "I'm excited to watch that baseball game. It will be so fun."

"You've said you'd rather watch paint dry than sit through another nine innings."

"I was exaggerating. I'd rather watch baseball than do that."

"Let's get on our way, then. What do you think about tacos for lunch?"

Just as Edna was about to answer, Valerie hurried over. "I'm sorry to bother you two, but Edna, do you have an extra minute?"

"Of course. What's wrong?"

Valerie lowered her voice. "A man just came in for food."

Edna exchanged a glance with Wayne. Some of their clients could seem a little scary at the first meeting. "Are you worried about being alone with him? If so, Wayne can go with you."

He nodded. "I'll be happy to do that."

"Oh, no. It's nothing like that." Valerie took a deep breath. "The problem is that the man has three little boys with him." Her eyes widened. "They're triplets."

"He has triplets?"

"Oh, yes. They're nine years old. They seem like good boys but restless. And to make matters worse, their poor dad is a widower. He looks exhausted."

"I bet he is," Wayne said.

Valerie continued. "I can give him food, of course, but I really think maybe the two of you might be able to do something more than that for him? I think he needs some reassurance." She smiled softly. "And maybe a five-minute break from his life. I know I would."

"We'll be right there, Valerie," Wayne said.

Looking completely relieved, she smiled. "Thanks. I told the dad that I needed to get the key to the food bank. I better go let them in."

"We'll be right behind you," Edna said. When Valerie was halfway down the hall, she steeled herself to apologize to Wayne. As much as she was eager to help this man and his boys, her husband deserved a day off from this place. "Honey, you can go back and sit in my office. I'll try to be quick."

But he was already tapping out something on his phone. "I'm not going anywhere, Edna."

When he returned to his phone's screen, she said, "What are you doing?"

"I'm texting Madison and Cope to see if either

of them could stop by. And Courtney over at the dog shelter."

"Because?"

"Because she told me that someone just brought in a spaniel with eight six-week-old puppies." He grinned as he looked up from his phone. "Talk about perfect timing! Maddie said they just pulled into the parking lot to bake muffins. They're going to like this job a lot better."

"I'm still confused about why you mentioned the pups."

"I mentioned them because if there's anything that goes well with nine-year-old boys, it's eight puppies to entertain. Courtney said she'd come right over to assure the dad that everything was safe, then Cope and Maddie can walk them across the street and help her get everything set up with the dogs."

"That will give that dad those five needed minutes. Maybe even ten." She did love the way Wayne's mind worked.

Wayne grinned. "Yep."

As they got closer to the food pantry's entrance, Edna could've sworn she heard a man's deep voice murmur. It was followed by Courtney giggling. Giggling!

Courtney was usually serious. It was a big deal when she cracked a smile. Hmmm.

"Wayne, do you happen to know if Courtney is seeing anyone?"

His lips twitched. “No, but I have a feeling she might be seeing someone very soon.”

“One can only hope.” Edna smiled as she realized that she wasn’t going to have to clean up a backyard or watch baseball that afternoon. She had a man to help, three little boys to introduce to a batch of puppies, and a certain auburn-haired animal shelter worker to quiz about her love life.

It was turning out to be a great day.

* * * * *